SECRET

BOOK 2

THE
DRAGON
PATH

SECRETS OF THE TOMBS

BOOK 2

THE
DRAGON
PATH

Helen Moss

Orion
Children's Books

First published in Great Britain in 2015
by Orion Children's Books
An imprint of Hachette Children's Group
and published by Hodder and Stoughton Ltd
Orion House
5 Upper St Martin's Lane
London WC2H 9EA
An Hachette UK company

1 3 5 7 9 10 8 6 4 2

Text © Helen Moss 2015
Interior illustration © Leo Hartas 2015

The paper and board used in this paperback are natural and
recyclable products made from wood grown in sustainable forests.
The manufacturing processes conform to the environmental regulations
of the country of origin.

A catalogue record for this book is
available from the British Library.

ISBN 978 1 4440 1041 1

Typeset by Input Data Services Ltd, Bridgwater, Somerset

Printed in Great Britain by Clays Ltd, St Ives plc

www.orionchildrensbooks.co.uk

SECRET

RYAN FLINT JUMPED down onto the platform and hurried towards the ticket barrier, scanning the crowds for Cleo.

It was six months since their adventures in Egypt, and life back home in Manchester had seemed a little dull compared with searching the tombs of pharaohs for the long-lost Benben Stone. Double maths and football practice just hadn't been the same since.

There was still no sign of Cleo. Ryan glanced at the text messages on his phone.

She said she'd be arriving at the station half an hour ago. Perhaps she's been kidnapped! But we're not in the Valley of the Kings now, he reminded himself. *Things like that don't happen in London on a rainy September afternoon . . .*

Still, he couldn't help feeling relieved when he spotted her talking to a guard at the other end of the concourse. There was no mistaking that long black plait, and who else but Cleo would go out in a baggy yellow-and-black striped jumper that must have been donated to a charity shop by a giant bumblebee? At least she'd ditched her favourite hiking trousers with the zip-off legs for an ancient pair of skinny jeans.

The guard was explaining something. Cleo was nodding. Then she headed off, weaving through a chicane of luggage trolleys, in a purposeful but totally random direction. *Yep,* Ryan thought, *that's definitely Cleo.* She might be an expert in everything from astrophysics to zoology, a mathematical mastermind and fluent in languages that most people hadn't even heard of, but she had absolutely no sense of direction. He elbowed his way through the tide of commuters until he was directly behind Cleo, who was now peering up at the departures board.

'This is a customer announcement,' he blared in his best computerized voice. 'Would Miss Cleopatra Calliope McNeil report to the lost property office immediately?'

Cleo whipped round at the sound of her name.

She wasn't the only one turning to stare. Ryan would've liked to think it was the comic genius of his spoof announcement that was attracting attention, but it was Cleo everyone was looking at. She had the kind of impossibly perfect face you usually only saw in paintings or statues. You stopped noticing it after a while, but at first sight it was like those cartoon chase scenes when someone steps on a rake and the handle flips up and smacks them right between the eyes.

2

'I wasn't *lost*!' Cleo protested. 'I was just . . . er . . . going to get you a snack on the way. I thought you might be hungry.' She glanced around, her eyes lighting on the pizza stand behind them. 'Yes, that's it, I was going to get you some pizza . . .'

Ryan pretended to believe her. After all, it *was* lunchtime. He breathed in the scent of hot pepperoni.

'Brilliant idea,' he said, turning to join the queue. 'I'm starving.'

He would never admit it, but he'd been slightly nervous about meeting Cleo again. Should he greet her with a handshake, a bear hug or that air-kissing thing people did? If so, was the appropriate number of pecks one or two, or even three? But he needn't have worried. Cleo wasn't interested in greetings. She was already pulling him by the sleeve of his hoodie. 'There's no time to eat now. We're going to see my grandmother.'

'Your *grandmother*?' Ryan echoed. 'But we're flying to China today, in case you'd forgotten!'

Cleo frowned at him. 'Of course I haven't *forgotten*. We'll only be half an hour at Grandma's. That still gives us plenty of time to get back to the hotel, meet up with my parents and get to the airport by four o'clock. If we get moving, that is. I've got a cereal bar you can have on the way.'

'Yum,' Ryan muttered, hurrying after her. 'Who could possibly want a delicious pizza dripping with melted cheese when they could have a slab of dried-up oaty stuff?'

'Exactly. Oats are much more nutritious,' Cleo agreed. 'Slow energy release . . . Hang on, where's your mum?' she interrupted herself. 'She's not here!'

'Ten out of ten for observation!' Ryan laughed. 'Mum had

3

a last-minute meeting with her editor at the newspaper, so she's coming on the next train. She'll get a taxi straight to the airport.'

Cleo nodded and looked round.

'Now, where has the Underground station gone?'

Ten minutes later, they were jammed together in a crowded Tube train. Soggy scarves and raincoats steamed in the heat. Ryan tried to ignore the double buggy that was rammed against his knees.

'Dad can't wait to start investigating those unexplained deaths.' Cleo's voice came from somewhere near Ryan's left armpit. 'There are over a hundred bodies all jumbled together. It could be some form of ritual killing . . .' she went on, unaware that the entire carriage was straining their ears to catch her every word. 'The Chinese team suspect poisonings . . .'

There was now total silence apart from a faint jangle from someone's headphones. The lady with the double buggy craned in so close that she almost fell in on top of her twins. Ryan grinned. Their fellow passengers clearly thought that Cleo's dad was some kind of CSI detective on the case of a ruthless serial killer. Little did they know that the victims had been dead for over two thousand years! Cleo's dad was, in fact, an archaeologist. Both her parents were. But Dr Pete McNeil specialized in *paleopathology* – ancient death and disease – which was why he'd been invited to study the grisly findings near Xi'an. A pulse of excitement scooted up Ryan's spine. *This time tomorrow we'll be in China!*

4

'Next stop,' Cleo said. 'It's only a few minutes' walk to Grandma's.'

There were disappointed sighs as the passengers all went back to their Kindles and newspapers. Grandparents were a big let-down after serial killers.

'Why this sudden urge to see her now?' Ryan asked.

'She just phoned this morning and said that she needed to see me before we left. She was very mysterious about it.' Cleo puffed out a breath, ruffling the fringe off her forehead. 'When Grandma tells you to do something, you don't ask why, you just jump to it. I suppose you don't get to be the first black woman to receive the Lifetime Achievement in Archaeology Medal without being a bit fierce,' she added with a touch of pride. 'Her name's Eveline May Bell.'

'Of course! The Lady of the Trowel,' Ryan said, remembering seeing the initials *E.M.B.* engraved on the handle of the old archaeologist's trowel Cleo had always carried in Egypt.

Cleo nodded. 'Grandma gave it to me for my ninth birthday. She used it on some of her most important digs.'

Ryan glanced down at the empty belt loops on Cleo's jeans.

'Where *is* your trusty bum bag, by the way?'

'It's *not* a bum bag!' Cleo shoved him in the ribs with her elbow. 'It's a tool belt. As you know perfectly well!' She gave him another shove for good measure. 'I'm hardly going to carry it around London. The trowel's sharp. It would count as a concealed weapon. That's an arrestable offence.'

Ryan couldn't help laughing at the thought of Cleo being carted off to the police station by the Serious Trowel Crime Unit, but then a memory flashed into his mind. That trowel really *was* sharp. He'd used it to hack through the ropes

5

that had tied them both to a table leg in a concrete hut in Egypt . . .

'Your grandmother's trowel probably saved our lives,' he said. 'We'd have been dumped in the desert as an all-you-can-eat buffet for the vultures without it.'

The other passengers all perked up again at this exciting turn in the conversation. But the train was already slowing down.

'Russell Square!' Cleo announced. 'This is our stop.'

It was still drizzling as Ryan and Cleo emerged from the Underground. Red buses and black taxis swished past, spray flying from their tyres.

'Do you need to get a gift for your grandmother?' Ryan asked, reaching out and catching Cleo's arm just in time to stop her stepping in a lake-sized puddle.

'A *gift?*' she asked, as if this were the outlandish custom of a lost Amazonian tribe. 'Why?'

'Haven't you read *Little Red Riding Hood?*'

Cleo frowned. 'Of course! It's a European folk tale traditionally told to warn children not to stray into the forest. What's your point?'

Ryan rolled his eyes. Cleo could be so literal sometimes!

'She's visiting her granny *with a basket of food*. The *point* is that people usually take flowers or chocolates or something.' *Normal people, that is,* he added to himself. 'I always take my gran pear drops . . .'

'She's not exactly the flowers-and-chocolates sort of grandmother,' Cleo said, jabbing at the button on the pedestrian crossing. 'And, anyway, it didn't do Red Riding Hood much good, did it?' She paused. 'Although she does quite often talk about liquorice, I suppose . . .'

Ryan ran into the nearest newsagent's shop and bought a box of Liquorice Allsorts. When he caught up with Cleo and pushed the box into her hands, she was already turning into a side street lined with elegant houses of chocolate-brown brick picked out with cream paintwork. She stopped in front of a dark blue door, climbed the steps and rapped the knocker – a gleaming brass lion with a ring in its mouth. *The Gracemont Home for Retired Archaeologists*, Ryan read on the plaque above it.

A young woman with a vacuum cleaner ushered them into a high-ceilinged hallway. Black and white photographs and old maps covered the walls. Newspapers were fanned out on a mahogany table, and the earthy scent from a vase of rust-coloured chrysanthemums mingled with fresh coffee and dusty radiators.

It's more like a cross between a museum and a grand hotel than an old people's home, Ryan thought. The only giveaway was the stair lift.

Moments later they were pushing open a door on the second floor. The curtains were closed, and as Ryan's eyes adjusted to the gloom he made out walls lined with shelves of ancient bronze pots and figures. A row of masks stared down at him with vacant eyes and mocking grins. A sudden movement from deep within a velvet armchair made him jump, his heart hammering.

Cleo switched on the light.

'Hello, Grandma! It's me.'

The old lady who peered out from the cushions was

encased in thick tweedy trousers, men's leather shoes and a startlingly orange polo-neck jumper. Her dark brown skin was freckled with age spots, her white hair as fluffy as a dandelion clock. She greeted Cleo with a jab of her walking stick.

'And who's this?' she demanded, looking Ryan up and down as if he might have wandered in off the street, her eyes magnified behind her glasses. 'Tall, lanky fellow? Is he with you?'

Now I know how Little Red Riding Hood felt, Ryan thought. Although he suspected *this* granny could eat him alive without any help from a passing wolf.

'Looks like he's off on an expedition,' Eveline Bell added, poking at Ryan's huge backpack with her stick.

Ryan let the pack drop with a thud. It was crammed so full of art materials there'd hardly been room for anything else. He was planning to spend a lot of time painting mountains and pagodas and other typically Chinese scenes. He was secretly hoping he might even get a chance to draw a giant panda.

'I'm Ryan Flint,' he said, stooping to shake the old lady's knobbly hand. 'Pleased to meet you.'

'Aha! So you're the young man who led my granddaughter into all manner of trouble in Egypt.'

Ryan was about to protest that Cleo had proved perfectly capable of leading *herself* into trouble, when Eveline Bell threw back her head and howled with laughter. She had the same wide gap between her front teeth as Cleo.

'Good for you!' she spluttered.

'Ryan and his mother are coming to China with us,' Cleo said, perching on the arm of her grandmother's chair. 'Julie

Flint is a journalist. She's going to write some articles about the dig.'

'What's that you've got?' Eveline Bell cut in, pointing at the box on Cleo's lap.

Cleo looked embarrassed. 'We ... erm ... brought you a present.'

'Whatever for?' Eveline grumbled. 'It's not my birthday.'

'It was Ryan's idea, actually,' Cleo said, shooting him a *told-you-so* look.

Ryan almost burst out laughing. Cleo and her grandmother were like clones! Had they really never heard of the whole visitors-bring-gifts concept?

But when the old lady saw the Liquorice Allsorts her eyes lit up.

'Ah, yes,' she murmured, stuffing a handful into her mouth. 'This takes me back to my travels in the Gobi Desert. Boiled liquorice root was laid out to dry on the roofs of the mud huts ...' Her voice trailed off and she closed her eyes and chewed noisily, seeming to forget all about her visitors.

'You wanted to tell me something, Grandma?' Cleo prompted after several minutes. 'Before I leave for Xi'an ...'

Eveline Bell's eyes snapped open and she stared straight ahead.

'Yes!' she murmured, slowly turning to face Cleo. 'That's right. I have a secret to tell you ...' There was a long pause. 'A secret that I have kept for many years,' she continued at last. Her teeth were black with liquorice. 'A dark, dangerous secret.'

Ryan shivered as if an icy wind had sliced through the stuffy room.

2

JADE

A DARK, DANGEROUS *secret?* Cleo had her doubts.

'This isn't about Hector again, is it, Grandma?' she asked. Hector Pink was Grandma's ninety-one-year-old next-door neighbour in the Gracemont Home for Retired Archaeologists. They'd been engaged in a bitter feud about the discovery of a cache of Shang Dynasty oracle bones since 1967. The last *dark secret* Grandma had confided was that she'd caught Hector sneaking into her room to steal her notes for the book she was writing. Cleo glanced across at the desk under the window. It did look unusually empty.

'Has he been up to his old tricks again?'

Grandma made a harrumphing noise. 'Of course not!

I've had no more trouble from Pink since I put my security measures in place.'

'Security measures?' Cleo asked.

'Mousetraps hidden among my papers.' Grandma shook with laughter. 'That'll teach him to keep his sticky fingers to himself! And anyway,' she added, 'I don't have to worry about that snooping little weasel any more. I've finished my memoirs and I've donated all my notes to the History of Archaeology Museum.'

I hope you took the mousetraps out first, Cleo thought. 'So what is this secret?' she asked.

Grandma closed her eyes and leaned back against her cushions. 'Something far more important than Hector Pink.' Suddenly she clutched at her chest. 'It's an ache right here . . .'

Cleo jumped up and began to check her pulse. Grandma had suffered several minor strokes in the past, but she wasn't showing any symptoms: no droop at one side of her face, no slurring her speech. Cleo patted her hand.

'It's probably indigestion from all the liquorice. I'll fetch your anti-acid pills . . .'

Grandma snapped open her eyes. 'What on earth are you talking about, Cleopatra?'

'I think your grandmother means a *metaphorical* ache,' Ryan whispered. 'You know, like a broken heart sort of thing.'

No way, Cleo thought. Eveline Bell wasn't the type to have metaphorical aches.

But Grandma was smiling at Ryan. 'That's right. Although it's not a *broken* heart, but a *troubled* one.' Her hearing, at least, was as sharp as ever. 'It happened in Xi'an. It was 1936.' Her voice had become slow and mechanical, as if reading from an

11

invisible script. 'My parents were with the diplomatic service and they were far too busy to be bothered with an eight-year-old daughter. I ran wild with the local children. When a pair of British archaeologists turned up to excavate some new sites out near the tomb of the First Emperor, I started to tag along. They let me help sort through the small pieces of pottery . . .'

Cleo couldn't hide her disappointment. Grandma had told her this story many times. She always said that was how she first became interested in archaeology.

'But what about the *secret*?' she pressed.

'I'm coming to that.' Grandma's voice dropped to a whisper. Cleo had to lean in to catch her words. 'It was a stifling hot day at the end of summer. The men could hardly contain their excitement when they found the hidden entrance. They were slapping each other on the back. "We hold the key to a discovery of immense historical significance," they said. "We'll be the great heroes of Chinese archaeology."' Grandma paused and shuddered. 'But then everything went wrong. They should never have set foot inside that terrible place . . .' She flopped back against the cushions. 'There were dragons down there,' she murmured. '*Fire-breathing* dragons . . .'

Cleo and Ryan looked at each other.

'*Fire-breathing dragons?*' Ryan mouthed.

Cleo shook her head and shrugged. She'd never heard this part of the story before. She stared at her grandmother, whose eyes were flickering behind closed eyelids as if she were watching a hidden scene unfold.

'There was a cameraman with them,' she said. 'A Frenchman. He filmed it all . . . they didn't know I'd followed them, that I'd seen it too . . . I ran away . . . as fast and as far as I could.' Grandma opened her eyes, grabbed her walking stick and pointed it at one of the bronze pots on the shelf.

'Hand me that one!' she commanded, her voice suddenly back to full strength.

Ryan took it down.

It looked to Cleo like a standard Shang Dynasty wine vessel with a lid in the shape of a pig. It was a replica, of course. All the originals from Grandma's excavations were in museums in China.

Grandma took the pot and gazed at it for a long moment. Then she eased off the pig lid and placed it on her lap. Cleo noticed that Ryan had shuffled closer, his eyes wide and fixed on the pot as if an evil genie might burst forth. He touched the St Christopher pendant and the Egyptian scarab amulet that he wore around his neck. Cleo had never met anyone as hopelessly superstitious. But as Grandma reached into the pot and took out a small silver key, she couldn't help holding her breath too.

'What does it open?' she asked.

'The box, of course!' Grandma said.

Suddenly Cleo understood. 'You left a box in Xi'an when you were a child. You want us to find it and open it.'

Grandma sighed. 'Don't be ridiculous, dear!'

Cleo was about to argue that, while her theory might have been wrong it had been entirely logical, when Grandma cut her off.

'The box is right here!' She banged her walking stick on the ground between her feet. 'It's under my chair.'

Cleo and Ryan both dived to their knees so fast they bumped heads.

Ryan reached under the velvet frill around the bottom of the armchair and pulled out the empty Liquorice Allsorts box.

'I don't think Grandma meant *that*!' Cleo said. She felt under the chair and slid out a flat rectangular wooden box that looked as if it might contain an antique chess set. She leaned down and blew away the dust.

Ryan sneezed.

Cleo ran her hand over the lid of the box. The smooth burled rosewood had been inlaid with tiny sections of other kinds of wood – walnut, ebony and mulberry – along with ivory and mother-of-pearl to form a Chinese mountain scene, complete with pagodas, waterfalls and bridges.

Grandma held out the key.

'Well, don't just goggle at it. Open it!'

Cleo's fingers fumbled with excitement as she inserted the tiny key into the lock and turned it. Was the dark and dangerous secret lurking inside? She eased the lid up with her thumbs and it fell back, held in place by two ornate gold hinges. Inside was a faded sepia photograph of her grandmother as a young woman, looking like a 1940s film star in a wide-shouldered jacket with nipped-in waist. *And was that a wedding veil?* The handsome Chinese man next to her was standing to attention.

'Is that my *grandfather*?' Cleo murmured. All she knew about her mother's father was that he'd died when Mum was a teenager.

'Not *that*!' Grandma snatched the photograph from Cleo's hand. 'Look underneath.'

All that was left in the box was a small red silk pouch. Cleo pulled open the drawstrings and slid a ring of bright green jade onto her palm. It was smooth and warm to the touch. As she held it up, she noticed six lines in a cross-hatch pattern worked in gold on the inner surface.

'A bracelet?' Ryan asked.

Cleo showed it to her grandmother. 'Is the secret about this, Grandma?'

Grandma shrank back in her chair as if Cleo had thrust a venomous snake at her.

'Yes, that's it.'

She reached out and folded Cleo's hand around the ring of jade. 'Take it back to Xi'an.'

'Of course,' Cleo said. 'But where . . .'

Grandma didn't seem to hear. 'I'm not going to be around much longer,' she said. 'I'm ready for death. But I don't like unfinished business.' She gripped Cleo's hand so hard the jade bracelet dug into her palm. 'I could never go back to that terrible place. Which is why I'm asking you to do this for me. Return it to the Dragon Path.'

Cleo was so surprised she could only nod.

'Can you narrow it down for us a bit?' Ryan asked. 'Where is this path?'

But Grandma didn't answer. Instead she patted Ryan's hand. 'Keep Cleo safe from harm for me, young man.'

Ryan grinned. 'I'll do my best. But exactly what kind of dragons are we talking about here?'

Grandma patted his hand again. 'She's my favourite granddaughter . . .'

'I'm your *only* granddaughter!' Cleo protested.

Grandma smiled and closed her eyes. She seemed to be drifting off to sleep. Cleo had a hundred questions for her but, before she could ask them, a nurse bustled in with a tray of pills and a cup of tea. She felt Grandma's forehead and put a blanket over her knees.

'I think you two have worn her out. She needs to rest now.'

3

FILM

HALFWAY DOWN THE steps to the street, Ryan looked back at the dark blue door as it thudded shut behind him.

'Wow!' he whistled. 'Did that really just happen?'

Cleo stopped on the next step down. 'I know! I can't believe that Grandma has known about a highly significant archaeological site all this time and didn't think to mention it to anyone.'

Ryan stared at her. Out of all the incredible stuff that Eveline Bell had told them, *that* was what Cleo had picked out as the take-home message?

'What about the fire-breathing dragons?' he laughed, jumping the last few steps to the pavement in one. 'And the dark, dangerous secret and the mysterious jade bracelet? It's like something out of *The Lord of the Rings*.' Ryan put on his rumbling movie trailer voice. 'In a world of danger, the brave young hobbit must complete a perilous quest and return the treasure to the dragon . . .'

Cleo frowned. 'I'm not a hobbit.'

Yet again, Ryan thought, *my sparkling wit is wasted!* Cleo obviously had no idea what he was talking about. As they began to walk back towards the main road he noticed she'd slipped the bracelet onto her wrist. Deep sea-green with lighter swirls of sage and flashes of emerald, it seemed to glow against her caramel skin. It was, he realized, a perfect match for her ridiculously green eyes.

'Jade's meant to be really lucky, isn't it?' he asked.

'It's believed to bring good fortune and protect the wearer. Not that that's why I've put it on, of course,' Cleo added hastily, pushing the bracelet up under the sleeve of her jumper. 'It's just for safekeeping.'

'Of course,' Ryan laughed. Suddenly he thought of something. 'No offence, but how come your gran entrusted *you* with this whole dragon-hunting mission? Why didn't she ask your mum? She's the professor of archaeology, after all.'

'Grandma and Mum don't get on.' Cleo stopped to press the button on the pedestrian crossing. 'I don't know why, but they fell out when Mum was about my age. In fact,' she added, 'there aren't many people that Grandma *does* get on with.' She frowned and prodded the button again. 'She seemed to like you, though.'

Ryan laughed. 'My natural charm is irresistible.'

Cleo looked unconvinced. She began to march across the

road without waiting for the lights to change. Ryan dodged the traffic to catch her up.

'Hurry up!' she shouted over the roar of a double-decker bus. 'We've got a discovery of *immense historical significance* to track down!'

We? Ryan thought. *No one asked me!* Then he remembered that they had, sort of! He'd promised Cleo's gran he'd look after her. There was a screech of brakes as Cleo stepped out in front of a pizza delivery bike. Did Eveline Bell have any idea what a tall order she'd given him? But as he pulled Cleo to safety, Ryan couldn't help sharing her excitement. *We made a good team searching for the Benben Stone in Egypt*, he reflected. It would be fun to have a new treasure hunt to work on in China – and this time they wouldn't have a bunch of ruthless maniacs like the Ancient Order of the Eternal Sun on their tails! Of course, they had to *get* to China first. He checked the time on his phone. They needed to get a move on.

But when Ryan looked up, Cleo was nowhere to be seen! He squinted into the sunlight – the rain had stopped and the wet pavements were glittering like liquid gold – and saw her in silhouette, hurrying off in the wrong direction.

'Hey!' he called. 'The Tube station's *this* way!'

Cleo turned and jogged backwards. 'There's somewhere else we need to go first!' She waved for Ryan to follow. 'And it's *this* way . . .'

'Three little words!' Ryan panted as he drew level with her. 'Planes. Don't. Wait.'

'That's four words, actually.' Cleo didn't break her stride. '*Don't* is a contraction for *do not*. That's why there's an apostrophe.'

Ryan knew better than to argue grammar with Cleo.

'Where are we going?' he asked.

'The History of Archaeology Museum,' Cleo said in a matter-of-fact tone. 'It's not far.'

'You want to go to a museum?' Ryan groaned in disbelief. 'Why?'

'I told you! We've got a mysterious historical site to uncover.' Cleo slowed a little as they ploughed through a group of tourists. 'Which obviously means finding the Dragon Path – whatever it is – and following it. Grandma said that there was a cameraman filming the archaeologists when this terrible thing happened with the dragons. He'll be dead by now, but there's a good chance that he left his records to the History of Archaeology Museum. Lots of archaeologists do. It's renowned for keeping an archive of letters and journals and old films. '

Ryan could see she had a point. 'Yeah, your grandmother said she'd given the museum all her notes for her memoirs.'

'Exactly! That's what gave me the idea.' Cleo stopped to consult a map on a sign at the corner of a small square. 'If we can see that film, we should be able to figure out where it was taken and where we need to look for the hidden entrance to the Dragon Path . . .'

'Great theory,' Ryan interrupted. 'It's a shame we have precisely zero minutes and zilch seconds to do anything about it.'

'Actually,' Cleo said, glancing at her oversized digital watch – the kind that is millisecond-accurate, even if you happen to be in outer space or at the bottom of the ocean – 'It's two minutes past two now. If we're in and out of the museum in twenty minutes, that still leaves us thirty-eight minutes to get to the hotel at three – which is when my parents are planning to leave for the airport.' She jutted out her chin. 'But if you don't want to come, that's fine. I'll go on my own.'

Ryan sighed. He was starting to regret his promise to Eveline Bell already! He glanced across the square and spotted the History of Archaeology Museum on the opposite corner. *If we're quick*, he thought, *we can just about make it.*

'Come on!' he said, grabbing Cleo's sleeve and taking a short cut through the private garden in the middle of the square, pretending not to see the *Keep off the grass* signs.

The History of Archaeology Museum had been built by knocking all the townhouses along one side of the square together to form a huge gallery. Glass cases contained artfully arranged black and white photographs, notebooks and journals full of spidery brown handwriting, and old tools. There was even a display dedicated entirely to trowels.

'I love this place,' Cleo sighed, stopping to breathe in the smell, the way other people might do in a cake shop. Then she marched up to a desk at the far end of the gallery, her trainers squeaking on the polished wooden floor.

'We're looking for any films that were taken in the area of Xi'an, China, dating from 1936,' she announced.

The young man behind the desk peered at Cleo over his horn-rimmed glasses, head to one side, as if straining to hear a very faint noise. He was sporting a grey pinstriped suit teamed with a red silk waistcoat, bow tie, and a pocket watch on a gold chain. *Was it some kind of wear-fancy-dress-to-work-for-charity day?* Ryan wondered.

'Do you have anything that matches that description in the archive?' Cleo asked in a louder, distinctly impatient voice.

'No need to shout!' Bow Tie Man – who, according to the badge pinned to his lapel, was Anthony Chetwynd, senior

21

archivist – slowly swivelled his chair towards his computer. 'Name of archaeologist?'

'We don't know,' Cleo said.

'Name of site?'

'We don't know.'

Chetwynd tutted. 'Name of cameraman?'

Cleo shook her head.

This could go on for hours, Ryan thought. 'Could you just do a search on *Xi'an* and *1930s*, please?' he asked.

With a deep sigh, Chetwynd entered the search terms into his computer database, circling his finger in the air before jabbing accusingly at each letter on the keyboard. *Was he trying to beat the World Slow-Motion Typing Record?* Ryan wondered.

'No matches,' Chetwynd said at last.

At least we'll be out of here in well under twenty minutes, Ryan thought.

'Never mind,' he told Cleo as they headed for the exit. 'It was always a long shot. Anything could have happened to that film. Perhaps the cameraman donated it to a museum in Paris or somewhere, since he was French.'

'No, wait!' Cleo suddenly turned and headed back to Chetwynd's desk. 'Try looking for *Hsian*, not *Xi'an*. They were still using the old Wade–Giles spelling system for Chinese names in the 1930s.'

Ryan had no idea what Cleo was talking about, but it seemed to mean something to Chetwynd. The senior archivist blinked slowly and did some more snail-paced typing. 'Well, there is *one* item here . . .'

'What?' Ryan and Cleo shouted in unison.

'*Harold A. Stubbs and Dr Cedric P. B. Lymington,*'

22

Chetwynd read out. *'Various sites near Hsian, 1936. Film donated anonymously, 1953.'* He muttered under his breath. *'Hsian* really should have been cross-referenced with *Xi'an.* I'll just correct that now.'

'No-o-o!' Ryan shouted before Chetwynd could spend another hour or two pecking at the keyboard.

'Do you have that film on computer?' Cleo asked.

Chetwynd straightened his bow tie. 'Almost certainly. We have a rolling programme of making digital copies of all archive materials.'

Cleo flashed Ryan a victorious smile.

'Can we see it?' she asked Chetwynd.

The archivist nodded. 'You'll need to submit a written request, of course.' He took a form from a drawer and slid it across the desk. 'We'll let you know within three working days whether you have permission to view it.'

'But we have a plane to catch!' Cleo protested.

'Your poor time management is hardly my concern.' Chetwynd smoothed down his silk waistcoat. 'Now, I must get on . . .'

Suddenly Ryan had an idea.

'Let's pop round and see Sir Charles,' he said to Cleo. 'I'm sure he can sort this out for us.'

Chetwynd looked up from the computer screen. 'You *know* Sir Charles Peacocke?'

Ryan smiled. 'Oh, yeah, we're close personal friends.'

Cleo's eyebrows shot up. *OK,* Ryan thought. *'Personal friends' might be stretching the truth just a little.* But the director of the Department for Museums and Culture was Cleo's mum's boss, and Ryan had met him in Egypt once. *That makes us practically best buddies!*

'I'll see what I can do.' Chetwynd gestured towards a door. 'Go into the viewing room and I'll send the file to Computer Station One.' He narrowed his eyes at Ryan. 'You'll have to leave your bag in a locker, though.'

Two minutes later, Ryan and Cleo were installed in front of the computer. At last an icon in the shape of a movie camera popped up on the screen.

Cleo's hand shot to the mouse. 'Here goes!' she murmured.

Ryan was just as excited to see the film as Cleo, but he hoped it would be short.

Their twenty minutes were almost up.

4

MISSING

CLEO HELD HER breath as she clicked the mouse. Grandma said that the terrible Dragon Path incident had all been captured on film. *If this is the right one,* she thought, *we could be about to see something extraordinary.*

A black and white image appeared on the screen. Two men in white shirts and old-fashioned baggy trousers stood posing for the camera. The taller of the two, his face shaded by a panama hat, was leaning on the handle of his spade, smoking a pipe. The shorter man sported a dashing moustache and a wave of fair hair that flopped across his forehead, just as Ryan's did. He held up a board with the words *SEPTEMBER 1936, TOMB OF UNKNOWN*

HAN DYNASTY GENERAL, NEAR HSIAN on it.

Wondering which was Cedric Lymington and which was Harold Stubbs, Cleo clicked on *Play*. The grainy silent film flickered into life. The two men began a tour around a dig site, the tall man pointing out trenches and walkways with his pipe, the other talking and laughing with some local workmen who were hauling out rubble.

The action stopped abruptly. White specks and squiggles zipped about the screen like bacteria under a microscope, and then the men were back, holding up another sign. It was a more professional-looking black-painted clapperboard this time, with the words *NEW SITE, SOUTH-EAST OF LINTONG VILLAGE* chalked in capitals. The two archaeologists were now marking out a plot in a wheatfield with wooden pegs and string. The next scene was more of the same. Cleo leaned closer, peering at the grey pixels.

'I can't see anything special,' she sighed. 'These just look like routine minor digs . . .'

'Yeah,' Ryan agreed. 'Where are the dark secrets? Where are the fire-breathing dragons? I've seen more exciting gardening programmes!'

Cleo sank her head into her hands. The display at the bottom of the screen showed that the film had little more than a minute left to run. Lymington and Stubbs were still in the wheatfield showing some fragments of pottery to an audience of curious villagers. She was starting to wonder whether these were the archaeologists Grandma had been talking about after all, when Ryan suddenly grabbed the mouse. He paused the film, zoomed in and jabbed at the screen. The camera had panned to a group of local children sitting in a circle playing a game with stones. One girl was glancing up. She was dressed in a quilted jacket and trousers like the others, but her skin was darker and her hair, fastened at one side with a ribbon, was thick and curly. Her smile revealed a gap between her front teeth.

'It's Grandma!' Cleo murmured.

'Yep, I'd recognize that face anywhere,' Ryan said with a grin. 'She looks a lot like you. At least it proves we've got the right guys.'

There's still a minute to go, Cleo thought, as she re-started the film. Something *had* to happen before the end. The clapperboard, marked *CAVE AT FOOT OF MOUNT LI*, came up, heralding the next scene. It got off to a promising start, with the two men abseiling down a cliff to the mouth of a cave – the tall one with his pipe still clamped between his teeth. *This is it,* Cleo thought, as they disappeared into the cave. *This must be the hidden entrance to the Dragon Path. Any second now . . .*

Ryan leaned closer, gripping the sides of the desk.

'And cue dragons,' he murmured, '. . . when you're ready, guys . . . any time now would be good . . . '

When the two men finally emerged from the cave mouth, brushing dust from their trousers, the taller one seemed to be squinting down at something in the palm of his hand, but the image was far too fuzzy to make out what it was. The man with the moustache grinned and patted him on the back. Then the film went blank.

'What?' Ryan grumbled. 'Not even a wisp of dragon smoke!'

Cleo shook her head miserably. Lymington and Stubbs looked rather pleased with themselves. But they definitely weren't acting as if they'd just discovered something that would turn them into great heroes of Chinese archaeology.

The film had already skipped to the final scene: a board with the words *BREAKING CAMP* on it was followed by the fair-haired man stomping around a tent, throwing equipment into crates. After a few seconds he looked up, a strange, haunted expression on his face, held up his hand and shouted at the cameraman to stop filming.

Cleo couldn't believe it.

'We must have missed something,' she muttered, scrolling frantically back and forth through the film. 'Where is it? *Where is it?*'

Ryan reached over and clicked on *Pause*. 'Sorry, but we really have to get going.'

Cleo knew he was right, but she couldn't drag her eyes away from the screen. The film had stopped at the frame with the last clapperboard, the words *BREAKING CAMP* staring back at her, frozen in time. That's when she noticed the symbol in the top left corner of the board. She pointed at the screen. 'That's weird . . .'

Ryan was already halfway to the door. He turned back and looked over Cleo's shoulder. 'What is? You mean that squiggle like a little stick man running along?'

Cleo frowned up at him. 'It's *liù*, the Chinese character for six. I thought you were going to do that online Mandarin Chinese course I told you about?'

'I didn't quite get to the bit on numbers . . .'

Cleo shook her head. Numbers were in the first lesson. But she let it go.

'They've marked each clapperboard with the number of the scene it introduces . . .'

'And?' Ryan prompted.

'This is Scene *Six*.'

Ryan rolled his eyes. 'Yeah, I got that.'

'I only counted five scenes.' Cleo went back to the start and fast-forwarded through the film to check. There was the first signboard, marked with a single horizontal line, the Chinese character for one. Next came two and three, and then four – the scene with the men abseiling into the cave. Then the final scene, six, *BREAKING CAMP*.

'I knew it,' Cleo breathed. 'Scene Five is missing!' She chewed the end of the pen. 'If it were Scene *Four* that was missing, I'd assume it was just a case of tetraphobia, of course . . .'

Ryan gave her a blank look. 'Tetraphobia?'

'Fear of the number four,' Cleo explained. 'It's seen as bad luck in China.'

'Like thirteen, you mean?'

Cleo nodded. 'The words for *four* and *death* sound almost the same. But five is a lucky number. There's no reason to leave it out.'

'Maybe they just lost count?'

'No one loses count up to *six*!' Cleo snorted. And, anyway, she had a very different theory. 'Each of these scenes would originally have been recorded on a different reel of film. They only lasted a few minutes in those days. The reel that contains the fifth scene must have been *removed*.'

Ryan shrugged. 'It might just have just fallen down the back of a sofa at some point in the past eighty years.'

But Cleo was deadly serious. Whatever was on that film, *someone* didn't want it to be seen. 'It all makes sense,' she said. 'That missing reel of film must show something going terribly wrong. No wonder the fair-haired man is in such a hurry to pack up and leave. Something has frightened him.'

Ryan gulped. 'You might be right. What's happened to Pipe Guy?' he asked in a whisper. 'He's not in the final scene!'

'Exactly!' Cleo jumped up and banged her palms down on the desk. 'Scene Five obviously shows the dangerous secret Grandma was talking about. It's the logical explanation.'

She stared at the screen in silence for a long moment.

Who had taken the missing film? she wondered. *And where was it now?*

Ryan could see Cleo's point.

There *was* something creepy about that film going missing. It was the way that Moustache Man – who had been joking around in all the other scenes – looked as if he'd seen a ghost in the last one. *In fact,* Ryan thought, as he hurried across the gallery to fetch his backpack from the lockers, *he looked exactly the way you'd expect a man to look who'd just witnessed his teammate being torched by fire-breathing dragons.*

Ryan was so deep in thought that he almost jumped out of his skin when a thin woman in a black wool dress barrelled straight into him. The tower of leaflets she was carrying slipped from her arms and skidded off across the floor.

Chetwynd wheeled round in his chair.

'Miss Gupta, for goodness' sake!' he shouted. 'You're like a bull in a china shop. Some of us are trying to work!'

Miss Gupta's chin wobbled as she took a tissue from her sleeve and blew her long, thin nose.

'Sorry! That was my fault,' Ryan called to Chetwynd. 'I bumped into her.'

30

'Thank you,' Miss Gupta whispered, as Ryan crouched to help pick up the leaflets. 'I'm new here, and if Mr Chetwynd writes any more negative comments on my report I'll be out of a job. He can be a bit of a . . . well, you know . . .'

'. . . pompous bully?' Ryan suggested.

Miss Gupta – Louisa, according to her name badge – clapped a hand over her mouth to stifle a giggle. 'I couldn't help overhearing you ask about the missing film, by the way.' She glanced across at her boss, but Chetwynd was hunched over his computer again. 'It's just possible that the film you want *is* down in the archive. It could have been missed when the others in the series were brought up to the editing suite to make the digital copies. It happens sometimes.' She glanced at Chetwynd again to make sure he wasn't listening. 'We can check against the old card index, if you like.'

'Thanks, but I'm afraid we haven't got ti—' Ryan began.

'Yes please! That would be great!' Cleo agreed enthusiastically. Ryan leaped round with a start. He'd thought Cleo was waiting for him by the entrance, not lurking behind his left ear.

Before Ryan knew what was happening, Louisa was showing them through a door off the main gallery.

'This is the Index Room,' she said, heading for a bank of wooden cabinets that ran down the middle, each containing hundreds of tiny drawers. '1936, was it?' She pulled open a drawer and flicked through the filing cards so fast that her fingers were a blur. 'Bingo!' she said, whipping out a faded yellow card. '*Harold A. Stubbs and Dr Cedric P. B. Lymington.*'

'Yes! I knew it!' Cleo almost snatched the card out of Louisa's hand. 'It says here that *six* rolls of film were donated

31

to the museum in 1953. That means Reel Five *was* there originally . . .'

Louisa nodded. 'As I said, it's probably found its way onto the wrong shelf and got left behind when the others were collected for digitizing.'

'Could we go down to the archive and have a look?' Cleo asked.

'Sorry. I'd let you if I could, but Mr Chetwynd is in charge . . .'

'Don't tell me,' Ryan groaned. 'We have to submit a form.'

Louisa smiled. 'Two, actually.'

Cleo turned on her heel and made for the door. 'I'm going to have a word with Chetwynd and *demand* that he lets us . . . Oomph!'

Ryan cringed as Cleo walked right into Anthony Chetwynd – who had chosen that precise moment to enter the room. Her nose bumped up against his red bow tie.

Chetwynd made a big deal of staggering backwards. 'We're closing now,' he announced, tapping his gold pocket watch for emphasis. 'All visitors must vacate the premises.'

'No way!' Cleo burst out. 'You can't . . .'

Chetwynd pulled a walkie-talkie from his jacket pocket. 'As you are refusing to leave and are using threatening language to a staff member, I have no option but to call Security.'

'Don't worry, we're going!' Ryan muttered.

But Chetwynd was already barking orders into his radio. 'Urgent assistance required in the Index Room. Over. Member of the public causing a disturbance. Over . . .'

Ryan could hardly believe his ears. Cleo McNeil – the

genius daughter of two of the top archaeologists in the country – was being thrown out of a museum!

'Let's get out of here,' he said, steering Cleo firmly by the arm, 'before you assault someone.'

They were almost at the main exit when a security guard burst out from a door near the trowel display and sprinted across the gallery towards the Index Room – obviously in response to Chetwynd's call for back-up. It was when Ryan noticed the sign on the door from which the guard had emerged that an idea popped into his head. He knew he should push it straight back *out* of his head and carry on walking.

But he also knew how much the Dragon Quest meant to Cleo.

He glanced at the clock at the end of the gallery. Two thirty-five. *We'll have to take a taxi to make it to the hotel in time now anyway,* he thought. *Even if it does mean using up half my spending money for the entire trip before we even leave London!*

As long as we're only ten more minutes . . .

ARCHIVE

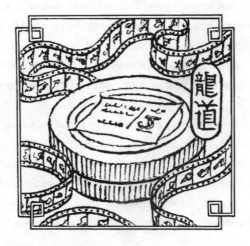

CLEO SEETHED WITH rage as she stormed towards the exit of the History of Archaeology Museum.

The missing reel of film was almost certainly sitting on a shelf in the archive only a few metres below her feet and Anthony Chetwynd was stopping her from seeing it. *Causing a disturbance,* indeed! How dare he? That film could have captured a major archaeological discovery. A senior archivist, of all people, should recognize the importance of finding it immediately . . .

'All right, I'm coming!' she snapped at Ryan, who was dragging her along so fast he was almost pulling her arm off.

Cleo felt something dig into her wrist. The jade bracelet!

She'd almost forgotten about it. *But Ryan's right*, she thought, as she felt the smooth jade pressing into her skin. *This isn't only about finding a lost archaeological site. I made a pledge to Grandma. She trusted me with her secret and I can't let her down. I have to return the bracelet to the mysterious Dragon Path.*

Not that Cleo believed in fire-breathing dragons, of course. And she was quite sure her grandmother didn't either. Dragons were mythical creatures, the stuff of legend and fantasy films. No, Grandma must have been referring to a path that led to a place connected with a dragon legend – there were plenty of those in China, where dragons were symbols of good fortune and prosperity, not the scary monsters of European myths. *Even so*, Cleo thought, *Grandma had clearly seen something as a little girl that had terrified her so much she'd never spoken of it again, and had never gone back to the Dragon Path – even though she became an archaeologist and excavated other sites all over China.*

They'd reached the front door now, but instead of opening it, Ryan had stopped and was pushing her back. *He really did behave in a most illogical manner sometimes*, Cleo thought. Ever since they'd arrived at the museum he'd been hustling her to leave, and now he suddenly wanted to stay! And why was he ducking down, eyes flicking from side to side as if he were about to make a dash across enemy territory?

'Over there!' he hissed, pointing at the door marked *Film Archive*. 'It's now or never!'

Was this one of Ryan's unfathomable jokes? Cleo wondered.

'But there's a security pad,' she pointed out. 'We don't know the code.'

Ryan shook his head. 'We don't need it. That guard who just came steaming out of there was in such a hurry to stop you murdering Chetwynd he didn't shut the door properly.'

Cleo took another look. It was true. The door was ajar.

'But we can't go into the archives without permission . . .'

'It's our only chance of finding that film.'

Cleo knew it was wrong, but she couldn't stop herself. She darted across the gallery, yanked open the door and dived through. Ryan – complete with his bulky backpack – was right on her heels. In the seconds before the door clunked shut behind them Cleo heard the voices of Anthony Chetwynd, Louisa Gupta and the guard as they came out from the Index Room into the main gallery.

'A pair of teenagers?' the guard was saying. 'Yeah. I just saw them by the exit. They were on their way out.'

Ryan grinned. 'We made it! They think we've left!'

Cleo leaned back against the door and looked around. They were standing on a small landing at the top of a metal staircase lit only by the green glow of an emergency lamp high on the wall. She gripped the cold steel bannister with both hands, suddenly feeling sick. *The guard could come back at any second. I shouldn't have let Ryan talk me into this!*

'Hurry up!' Ryan hissed. 'We'll miss the plane if we're not in a taxi in ten minutes . . .'

Cleo pulled herself together. She looked at her watch. 'Eight and a half, actually.' She felt in her pocket for her keyring and switched on the tiny torch attached to it, then tiptoed down the steps. The finger of torchlight slid across row after row of floor-to-ceiling steel shelving racks crammed with thousands of flat round metal film canisters, some stacked in piles, others propped on their sides like plates on a kitchen dresser.

Cleo shivered – the basement room was clearly refrigerated to help preserve the delicate old film stock – and began to examine the labels at the end of each shelf. It appeared to be a fairly straightforward classification system. The racks were organized according to the country where the film was shot and then by year. She ran along the central aisle and quickly located the China section. Then she narrowed it down to 1936. That still left an entire shelf to look through.

She beckoned to Ryan and they worked their way along, checking each film canister. Cleo was beginning to give up hope when she spotted a pile of battered film cans at the end of the shelf.

'Yes!' she murmured as she gently picked up the top one and read the typed label stuck down with dog-eared yellow tape: L&S/1936/1.

'L and S,' Ryan whispered. 'That *has* to stand for Lymington and Stubbs.'

Cleo nodded. She could hardly breathe for excitement as she did a quick count. There were six films in the pile!

'This one says L&S/1936/2,' Ryan said, waving the next film canister at her. 'I guess that means it's Reel Two.' He grabbed another. 'Yeah, and this is Reel Three.'

Cleo looked through the rest of the pile. Reels Four and Six were there and, at the bottom, Reel Five!

'The missing film!' she breathed as she lifted it down. She wondered how the archivists had managed to overlook it. She turned the canister over in her hands. On the base was a small dent and a patch of rust that almost obscured the letters *P. S.*, scrawled directly onto the metal in white pen.

'Open it, then!' Ryan urged.

Cleo grasped the lid and twisted. To her surprise, it came

off without the slightest resistance. Inside was a tightly coiled strip of reddish-brown film.

Ryan stepped back. 'What's that horrible vinegary smell?'

'Acetic acid. It's released as the film starts to disintegrate . . .' Cleo broke off, realizing all of a sudden that their daring raid on the Film Archive had been for nothing. How were they going to view the brittle old acetate film without a special projector? Even if they *could* somehow break into the museum's laboratory to use their equipment, they didn't have time. This was torture! She had the missing film in her hands, but no way of unlocking its secret.

That's when she felt a tap on her shoulder.

Cleo's thoughts flew into a tailspin. *The security guard! I've been caught red-handed. Now Chetwynd can add burglary and criminal damage to my list of crimes. He'll call the police! We'll miss the plane!* She whisked round and began to protest her innocence.

'I wasn't going to steal it!'

'We just wanted to see if it was here!' Ryan blurted at the same time.

But it wasn't the security guard.

'Louisa!' Cleo gasped. She was so relieved her knees almost buckled beneath her.

'I saw you two slip in here when we were coming out of the gallery,' Louisa whispered, glancing back towards the staircase. 'Lucky for you, no one else noticed. What do you think you're *doing*?'

Cleo held up the canister. 'We found the missing film.'

Louisa barely glanced at it.

'You've got to get out of here! The guard's coming back and if he catches you, you'll be in no end of trouble.' She

38

plucked at the sleeves of her dress. 'And so will I. No doubt Chetwynd will make out it's all my fault for letting you look in the Index Room.'

'We're on our way.' Ryan smiled at Louisa as he picked up his backpack and swung it on to his shoulder. 'Thanks for the help.'

But Cleo stood gazing down at the film canister. She couldn't bear to walk away and leave it behind. Yet she could hardly steal it right under Louisa's nose.

'Come *on*!' Ryan groaned. 'We need to get a taxi.'

Still Cleo didn't move.

Louisa held out her hand. 'Oh, give it here!' she snapped. 'I'll make a digital copy as soon as I can get some time in the lab. Write down your email address and I'll send you the file. Anything to get you out of here!'

Cleo would have hugged her if she'd been the hugging type. Instead she thrust the film into Louisa's hands and began to rummage in her bag. But before she could find a pen and a scrap of paper, the door at the top of the stairs clanged open. Fluorescent lights flickered on and heavy footsteps clattered on the metal steps.

Cleo sprang back between the high shelves, pulling Ryan with her. As she did so, she quickly whispered her email address to Louisa. *Had Louisa heard it?* she wondered as she crouched in the shadows, the hard edge of the bottom shelf digging into her backbone.

'I know there's someone down there!' the guard bellowed. 'Show yourself!'

'It's just me, Gary!' Louisa called brightly, stepping out into the aisle. 'I came down to look for my . . . er . . . *phone*. I think I must have dropped it over here somewhere,' she said loudly, hurrying away towards the far end of the archive. 'When I was down here earlier. Could you help me look?'

Cleo inched to the end of the shelving rack and peeped out. The guard was kneeling next to Louisa, peering under a shelf in the corner.

'We'll have to make a run for it,' Ryan whispered. 'Now!' But as he straightened up, his backpack brushed against the shelf. The metal rattled. Cleo froze, her heart about to burst through her ribcage.

'What was that noise?' the guard boomed.

'What noise?' Louisa asked. 'I didn't hear anything.'

'Over there in the stacks.' The guard got to his feet and pointed to where Cleo and Ryan cowered behind the rack.

'Maybe it was a mouse!' Louisa's voice had a distinct note of panic about it now.

'A mouse?' The guard snorted. 'Chewed its way in through the concrete, did it?'

Cleo swallowed and braced herself for the worst. *We might as well be mice,* she thought. *We're caught in a trap.*

But just as the guard began to march towards them there was a crackle and a squawk. He stopped, pulled the walkie-talkie from his belt and shouted into it. 'Receiving. What's that? Speak up!'

Cleo and Ryan hurtled across the aisle and up the stairs. There was no point trying to be quiet. Their footsteps on the metal steps rang out and echoed off the bare walls. Cleo heard the guard yell, 'What the—' and then, 'Stop right there!' as he charged after them.

Tumbling out into the gallery, a strap from Ryan's backpack snagged on the door handle. As he stopped to wrench it free, Cleo looked back to see the livid face of the guard puffing

40

his way up the steps. He was almost at the top. She grabbed Ryan's arm and together they sprinted across the gallery and out of the front door.

Still running, they dodged through lanes of traffic and across the square. When Cleo finally dared to glance back, the guard was standing in the museum doorway, looking up and down the street. A bus rumbled by, blocking her view. When it had passed, she could see the guard jogging along the pavement in the other direction.

'We did it!' she gasped, sinking onto a wall at the side of a café.

Ryan slumped down next to her panting for breath. 'The mice got away!'

Cleo couldn't help laughing, but she stopped suddenly when her phone rang. Pulling it from her bag, she noticed the time at the top of the display as she answered. It was exactly three o'clock. *Oh, no,* she thought, *the plane to China . . .*

'Cleopatra!' Mum yelled. 'Where on earth are you?'

Cleo opened her mouth but before she could reply, Mum was shouting again.

'We're leaving for Heathrow *now*! You'll have to get the express train from Paddington and meet us there. We'll bring your luggage. And I hope you've got a *very* good explanation for this!'

Cleo looked at Ryan – who had just answered his phone and was having the same conversation with *his* mother – in search of inspiration. Ryan knew how to talk his way out of anything!

'We were just running an errand for Cleo's grandma,' he said.

6

POISON

RYAN LOOKED UP from his sketchbook.

He was sitting on an outcrop of rock on the northern slope of Mount Li. Watery sunlight glinted on the morning mist that lay across the plain below. The jagged peaks of the Qinling mountain range, thickly pelted with blue-black evergreens, seemed to float on cushions of cloud.

He chewed the end of his paintbrush and contemplated his landscape. *Not bad,* he thought. It was starting to look like a traditional Chinese watercolour. He quite fancied adding a dragon or two flying round the mountaintops, but dragons were something of a sore point. They'd been in China three days, and Cleo hadn't stopped talking about her grandmother's *dark, dangerous secret*. Ryan was keen to solve the mystery too, but Cleo was totally *obsessed*. She must have checked her email inbox a million times, but there was still no message from Louisa Gupta with the missing film from the archive . . .

The muffled drone and beep of traffic drifted up from the roads far below. Ryan stood up, stretched, and turned to look into the cave behind him. It seemed things hadn't always been quite so peaceful on this mountainside. Something pretty gruesome had kicked off a couple of thousand years ago. The limestone wall at the back of the cave was perforated by hundreds of holes, each containing a single human body and sealed up with wax. It was like a giant wasps' nest full of larvae in there.

The mouth of the cave – little more than a narrow fissure – had remained unnoticed until a few months ago, when workers had started digging further up the slope to put in new power lines. The outer layer of rock had tumbled away in a mini landslide to reveal the grisly human honeycomb within.

Ryan didn't venture far inside. All those dead people neatly stored in their little cubbyholes gave him the creeps. He hung back in the entrance and watched the archaeologists going about their business. Cleo was working alongside her mum, Professor Lydia McNeil, clearing rubble from one of the newly opened niches. The others were all gathered beneath a spotlight, examining a body that had been removed from its cell. Ryan glimpsed its brown leathery skin, clinging – as if shrink-wrapped – to the bones. The bodies, Cleo had told him, had been naturally mummified in the cool, dry conditions of the cave. Pete McNeil, Cleo's dad, looked up, polished his glasses, and placed them back on his freckled nose.

'This was a young man, seemingly healthy, no obvious disease process.'

The Chinese woman next to him tucked her precision-bobbed hair behind her ears and nodded. 'And there's no evidence of battle injuries.' Professor Han Suyin, the boss of the team in Xi'an, spoke English with a marked Scottish accent. Ryan had been introduced to her on the first day and heard the story of how she'd made friends with Cleo's dad when they were both archaeology students at Edinburgh University – which was why Professor Han had invited him to come and have a look at the death cave.

'I'm super-excited about the new test results we got back from the lab this morning. The stomach contents are *gorgeous*!'

Ryan grinned. There was only one person who could refer to the half-digested stomach contents of long-dead corpses as *gorgeous*! Alex Shawcross was Pete McNeil's graduate student and had been with them on their trip to Egypt. With her golden curls and posh accent, you'd think she'd be into sipping champagne and nibbling caviar sandwiches at royal garden parties, but Alex's passion in life was death – the gorier the better!

'And all those minerals in their systems,' she said. 'Gold, silver, jade . . . '

Ryan watched as his mum looked up eagerly from her notebook. Her blonde spiky hair still featured the pink streak she'd dyed in over the summer, while working on an undercover investigation for a big news story involving a rock band.

'Do you think they could have been stealing jewels by swallowing them?' Being an investigative reporter, Mum always had an eye out for a criminal angle.

Alex shook her head. 'Jewel smuggling wouldn't explain the chemical burns.' She took a pack of sweets from her pocket, offered them round, and then bit the head off a jelly baby. 'And there are *heaps* of other poisons. We've got mercury, arsenic, lead, cyanide, ricin . . .' She listed the toxins as if they were the flavours on offer in an ice-cream parlour.

'I'm thinking mass suicide?' Professor Han suggested.

'What about ritual sacrifice?' Cleo piped up.

Alex shook the bag of sweets under Ryan's nose. For once, he wasn't hungry.

'I think I'll just go outside again,' he muttered.

The sun was gaining strength. Glad to be back in the world of the living, Ryan leaned back against the warm rock and took one of his *Dragon Ball* manga books out of his Manchester United backpack. He'd only read one page when he was joined by Tian Min, the student who'd been assigned to the McNeils as their guide and general assistant. He was also a translator – although Lydia McNeil spoke fluent Mandarin, having spent her childhood travelling between archaeological sites in China with her mother, Eveline Bell.

Tian Min slouched against the rock and gazed down at Ryan's comic.

'Cool! I love *Dragon Ball*.' His smile showed large, crooked teeth.

'I brought some of my favourites with me to read while we're here,' Ryan said. 'Just to get into the zone.' He hesitated, realizing his mistake. 'Although *Dragon Ball* is Japanese, not Chinese, so maybe I've got my zones in a muddle.'

Tian Min sat down. 'No muddle! The *Dragon Ball* story has Chinese roots. It was inspired by an old book from the Ming Dynasty, *Journey to the West*. If you want to get some more Chinese comics,' he added, 'I know the best shops. I can take you tomorrow, if you like.'

Ryan held up his hand for a high five. 'Cheers!'

They sat in friendly silence looking out over the plain. The mist had cleared to reveal the busy roads and tall apartment blocks of the town of Lintong. The huge city of Xi'an, about twenty miles away, was a smudge of mustard yellow smog on the western horizon. Closer in, on the lower slopes of the mountain, the foliage of maple, birch and oak blazed red and gold and copper. Lower still, the trees gave way to the dust and bustle of a construction site for a new hotel. But the stand-out feature of the entire view was the flat-topped pyramid-shaped hill rising straight out of the plain. Huge, symmetrical and cloaked with evergreens: the tomb mound of the First Emperor of China.

Tian Min rubbed his hands over high cheekbones cratered with old acne scars.

'Seven hundred thousand men worked to build that mausoleum,' he said. 'They say there's an entire city under there. A palace full of priceless treasures. A scale model of the universe, with rivers and seas of liquid mercury!'

'Is it true that nobody has been inside?' Ryan asked, remembering the information he'd read in Mum's guidebook.

Tian Min nodded. 'There are supposed to be booby traps – like huge crossbows triggered by secret mechanisms. And it's full of poisonous mercury vapours.' He made a strangled choking sound. 'There'll be ghosts, too . . .'

'Ghosts?' Ryan echoed.

46

'All the craftsmen who worked on the mausoleum were entombed alive with the emperor's coffin.'

Ryan shuddered. In Egypt he'd come face to face with the skeletons of the servants who'd been locked in the secret burial chamber of Queen Nefertiti. What was it with ancient royals and burying their subjects alive? One thing Ryan did know: he hoped never to set eyes upon a scene like that again.

'I know it sounds like something out of *Dragon Ball*,' Tian Min laughed, 'but it's all real. Qin Shi Huangdi conquered many warring states and became the First Emperor in 221 BC. He is still one of the most famous emperors in our history. *Qin* is where the word China itself comes from . . .' He broke off and listened to a voice calling from the cave. 'Sounds like I'm needed back on duty.' He started to get up. 'Alex Shawcross is very pretty, isn't she?' he whispered. 'Before my mother died last year, she told me her one wish was that I should find a nice girl and get married. Do you think Alex would be interested if I asked her to go for coffee with me?'

'Go for it, mate!' Ryan laughed, although he was pretty sure that Alex Shawcross was not at all the kind of girl Tian Min's mother had in mind. She'd be happier dissecting a chicken than cooking it for her husband's dinner!

'What was that all about?' Cleo asked, coming out of the cave just as Tian Min went in.

'Oh, just sorting out Tian Min's love life with some of my world-famous romantic advice.'

Cleo looked decidedly uninterested in romance. She slid her trowel into her tool belt and wiped her dusty hands on her white cotton scarf.

'We've named the cave the Tomb of a Thousand Poisons,' she announced, settling down next to Ryan. He tried to hide

47

the *Dragon Ball* comic, but it was too late. The word *dragon* had set her off again.

'I'm starting to wonder whether Louisa's ever going to send us the Lymington and Stubbs film . . .'

'Haven't you got enough of a mystery to keep you going with the crime of the century in there?' Ryan asked, nodding towards the cave.

'You mean, crime of the *bimillennium*,' Cleo corrected him. 'Carbon dating shows that the bodies are just over two thousand years old.'

Bimillennium? Ryan repeated to himself. Only Cleo could throw a word like that into casual conversation. But two could play at that game!

'Ah, yes,' he said in his most knowledgeable voice. 'That'd be around the time of Emperor Qin Shi Huangdi, First Emperor of China in 221 BC, if I remember correctly.'

Cleo looked impressed. 'You've been doing your homework!'

'Yeah, I've done *masses* of research.' Ryan's *research* had, of course, consisted entirely of his conversation with Tian Min, but he didn't feel the need to share that with Cleo. His eyes drifted back to the emperor's tomb far below. It really was enormous – larger even than the mightiest Egyptian pyramid.

'I just can't believe that nobody's got in there for a sneaky look!'

Cleo sipped from a bottle of water. 'It's true. The imperial mound has never been excavated.'

'Because of the self-firing crossbows and toxic gases?'

'It's not only because of booby traps,' Cleo explained. 'The Chinese authorities are worried the contents might be damaged if they're exposed to the air. They want to wait until there's better technology for preserving everything. Until then, they're working on digs in the area all *around* the tomb – like the famous Terracotta Army.'

Ryan nodded. He'd read about the thousands of life-sized clay warriors that had been buried to protect the First Emperor in the afterlife.

'It's so frustrating,' Cleo sighed. 'Whatever Lymington and Stubbs were on to, it might be even bigger than the Terracotta Army. If we could just find this secret Dragon Path that Grandma told us about . . .'

'We'd be the great heroes of Chinese archaeology!' Ryan finished her sentence, remembering the words that Cleo's grandmother had used. 'Isn't that what Lymington and Stubbs thought, too?'

'I'm not interested in personal glory!' Cleo snapped. 'It's about contributing to our understanding of ancient civilizations.'

Ryan wasn't *entirely* convinced, but he didn't push it. 'Yeah, personal glory's totally overrated.'

Cleo gazed down at the jade bangle, which she still wore on her wrist, and began to twist it round and round. 'And anyway, I promised to return this for Grandma.' She shuffled round to face Ryan, hugging her knees to her chest. 'We need to start following a second line of investigation.'

'What do you mean?' Ryan asked.

'We may never see the missing film,' Cleo explained. 'Maybe Louisa didn't hear my email address, or the film was too badly damaged to make a digital copy. So, we need to look for other clues.'

'Like dragon footprints?' Ryan joked.

Cleo ignored him. 'I think we should try to find the cave that Lymington and Stubbs abseiled into in Scene Four. That's the last place we see them before Scene Six, when one of the men has vanished and the other is packing up camp in a panic. There has to be a connection.'

Ryan cast his mind back to the film; the two men coming out of the cave, smiling and patting each other on the back.

'There's no way they'd just fought off an army of fire-breathing dragons,' he pointed out. 'Moustache Man's hair wasn't even out of place.'

Cleo nodded. 'No, but they did look pleased with themselves – as if they'd found *something* interesting. I've been thinking: perhaps they did find the entrance to the Dragon Path in that cave and they were just playing it cool.'

'You mean, stiff upper lip and all that?' Ryan asked, imitating an old-fashioned BBC English accent. 'No one could play it *that* cool if they'd seen a dragon – even in the 1930s!' But then he pictured the scene again. 'Pipe Guy had found something, though. He kept looking at it in his hand.' Ryan held up his own hand and frowned at it, as if examining a small object. 'Perhaps he'd picked up a bit of really amazing pottery . . .' he added as a guess.

To his surprise, Cleo didn't tell him off for making out that archaeologists were all obsessed with pottery. Instead, she grabbed his hand, as if to take a closer look at the imaginary object he held.

'Of course!' she cried. 'Grandma said the men talked about having the *key* to the big discovery.' She jabbed at Ryan's palm. 'I bet *that's* what they found in that cave. Not the entrance to the Dragon Path itself, but a key or clue that led them to find it somewhere else . . .' Cleo suddenly dropped Ryan's hand and thumped her knees with her fists. 'If only we knew where that cave was, we could have a look around and try to figure out what clue they found.' She gazed down the slope. 'It must be round here somewhere. The clapperboard on the film said *AT FOOT OF MOUNT LI*.'

'Well, it's a big mountain,' Ryan sighed. They were surrounded by miles of wooded slopes and rocky cliffs – and this was only one side. The cave on the film had been above a sort of ledge on a bare cliff. That didn't help much. There were cliffs like that everywhere you looked.

'It must have been so different in the 1930s,' Cleo murmured. 'No big roads or high-rise blocks. It was just fields and orchards and small villages then.'

But Ryan had stopped listening. He jumped to his feet. There might be hundreds of cliffs, but there was only one rock that looked exactly like a . . .

'Meerkat!' he exclaimed.

7

PUPPIES

'MEERKAT?' **CLEO ECHOED.** She wondered whether Ryan had been sitting in the sun too long. Or was he teasing her? Now he was pulling her to her feet and waving his arms around. He seemed to be pointing at something further down the mountain.

'Meerkat!' he cried again.

Cleo shaded her eyes against the sun and followed his eye line. Ryan was staring intently at a spur of rock that jutted up from the cliff above the hotel building site.

'You mean that stack-shaped limestone formation?'

Ryan nodded. 'That rock was on the film. Right above the cave in Scene Four. Don't you remember?'

Cleo looked at the rock. It looked like all the other rocks. 'Are you sure?'

'Of course I'm sure. It's exactly like a meerkat on lookout duty.'

Cleo took Ryan's word for it. She had to admit he had a much better visual memory than she did, which seemed unfair, as she'd studied advanced neuroscience courses, while Ryan probably didn't even know his optic nerve from his visual cortex.

'Come on!' she said, bundling Ryan's art things into his backpack for him. 'Let's go and find that cave . . .'

At that moment, a delighted squeal came from the Tomb of a Thousand Poisons behind them.

'Ooh, look at this!' Alex cried. 'There are some *super* skin ulcers on this corpse.'

'Anything to get away from this place,' Ryan laughed.

They skidded down the steep mountain trail. Further to the east the mountainside was zigzagged with wide paved paths. There were viewpoints and cafés and signboards describing points of historical interest, and even a cable car to the summit. But here, further west, the mountain was wilder, with only a barely trodden dirt-and-dried-leaf trail that wound down through the trees until it met the top of a gravel track where the team's jeeps were parked.

'We can cut across here,' Ryan said at last, pointing to an almost invisible fork in the path. Cleo followed, sticking close to Ryan, unsure of her bearings on the short cut. But, sure enough, the terrain gradually began to level out and they left the trees behind to enter a maze of backstreets.

As they wove past a small hardware store with cables and ceiling fans and plastic buckets spilling out onto the pavement, a fruit stall and a restaurant with tanks of live fish outside, the rumble and thud of heavy machinery grew louder. The air became thick with grit and dust, which caught in Cleo's throat and stung her eyes. They turned a corner and found themselves facing a high wire-mesh fence. Giant photographs on wooden hoardings advertised the new resort hotel that would soon spring up: palm-fringed swimming pools with glamorous women lounging around in fluffy white robes. *Grand Imperial Hotel and Spa*, the signs announced. *Where Heavenly Dreams Come True on Earth* . . .

'Well, it's not making *my* heavenly dreams come true!' Cleo grumbled, peeping through a gap between the boards. She could see the cliff at the far side of the building site. Beneath it, a huge digger was scooping up clods of red earth as it gouged out trenches for the hotel's foundations. 'I'd much rather get a look at that cave than sit around a pool in my dressing gown any day!' But the site entrance was protected by a barrier and guards were checking the delivery trucks that rattled in and out. Cleo kicked a pebble against the hoarding. 'Well, that's it, then. There's no way they're going to let us in to have a scout around.'

'We *could* try the back way,' Ryan shouted over the clang of a crane dropping steel girders into place.

Cleo looked around. *What back way?*

Ryan was pointing at something near the base of the fence. For a moment Cleo was baffled. All she could see was a black-and-tan dog of indeterminate breed. Then she saw what he meant. The dog was scrabbling with its paws and squeezing through a hole in the fence.

Cleo shook her head. If they were caught sneaking onto the building site without permission, there would be serious trouble. And, anyway, building sites were dangerous places.

'We don't even have hard hats . . .' she murmured.

'They've sheared off a whole section of that cliff below Meerkat Rock to make room for the hotel buildings,' Ryan said, looking over her shoulder through the gap in the hoarding. 'It looks as if they're preparing to bring down some more of it . . .'

It was true. Bulldozers and cranes were gathering ominously around the base of the cliff. *If the key to finding Grandma's dangerous secret is somewhere in there, it will be lost forever,* Cleo thought. She glanced back to the dog's feathery tail disappearing under the fence. She looked at the cliff, then at the bulldozers and then at Ryan.

'Maybe we *could* go in just for a very quick check,' she said. 'If we find anything interesting we'll tell my parents and Professor Han and see if they can get the construction work stopped while a proper search takes place.'

As they wriggled under the fence it seemed that they were in luck. Most of the builders were on a break and were gathered around a plastic table at the other end of the site, drinking tea from flasks and slurping on slices of watermelon. Dodging concrete mixers and piles of scaffolding poles, Cleo and Ryan scurried across the site to the foot of the cliff.

Ryan stopped and pointed. 'Look! There's the cave, about five metres up.'

Cleo scanned the cliff until she saw a recess, like a single dark eye staring back at her. 'Yes, I can see it. Just below Sitting Monkey Rock.'

'*Sitting Monkey Rock?*' Ryan repeated.

'Names should always be appropriate to their local environments,' Cleo explained. 'Meerkats are only found in southern Africa. Monkeys are native to China, so it's much more suitable.'

Ryan laughed. 'Except that rock doesn't look anything like a monkey!'

Cleo glanced back at the builders. Their break wouldn't last much longer.

'We can't waste time arguing about it now,' she said.

She looked up at the cave. It wouldn't be a difficult climb. It wasn't very high and there were boulders banked up against the foot of the cliff to scramble up – which was odd, now she thought about it. 'If that's the cave that Lymington and Stubbs found,' she said, 'why didn't they just climb up to it? Why did they go to all the trouble of abseiling down?'

'Because there was a massive overhang just beneath the cave back then,' Ryan said. 'You could see it on the old film. They'd have needed to be Spiderman and crawl upside down to get round it from below. Like I said, part of this cliff has been cut away recently; the overhang's not there any more.'

Cleo stepped forward for a better view, wondering yet again how Ryan could remember the film in such detail, when a hot, powerful hand gripped her shoulder. Her heart almost burst with shock.

'What do you think you're up to?' a man's voice yelled in Mandarin.

Cleo opened her mouth but no words came out. It seemed to have ceased all communication with her brain.

The man spat out a volley of shiny black watermelon seeds. Cleo stared down, watching the seeds hit the ground around her feet like bullets, sending up little puffs of dust. Out of the corner of her eye she could see that a second man had grabbed Ryan's arm and twisted it behind his back.

'Tell them we were worried about the dog,' Ryan hissed. He nodded his head towards a corrugated iron storage shed nearby. The dog they'd followed through the fence was curled up in a corner with a litter of puppies. 'Tell him we just wanted to rescue the little puppies.'

Cleo agreed that the shed didn't look like a very suitable home for puppies, although she couldn't believe that Ryan thought this was a good moment to raise the issue. She wondered whether there was a Chinese equivalent of the RSPCA ...

'Er, do you know of any animal charities near here?' Cleo asked the builder politely, glad that Mum had taught her Mandarin Chinese from an early age.

'Ouch!' she gasped as the man gave her shoulder a rough shake. And then 'Owww!' as she felt another jolt of pain. This time it was Ryan kicking her on the ankle.

'Look *upset*, for goodness' sake!' he hissed. 'Cry or something!'

Suddenly Cleo figured out what Ryan was getting at. 'We saw the poor mummy dog come in to her puppies,' she said in the most pitiful voice she could muster, turning her 'owww' of pain into a sob. 'We were worried she might have an infection after the birth. There's always a risk of ...' She faltered, realizing she didn't know the Mandarin words for *mastitis* or *metritis,* so she changed tack. 'We thought the puppies might run out in front of the machines ...' She deliberately sniffed in a lungful of dust that made her sneeze and her eyes water. She rubbed them a bit to encourage the flow of tears. *'Poor* little puppies.'

Several other builders had now joined their two colleagues, who began to recount Cleo's feeble tale. There were snorts of disbelief and then howls of laughter. She made an apologetic face at Ryan. She'd tried her best.

But suddenly the man took his hand from her shoulder. 'Don't worry,' he said. 'Those puppies are fine. The mother had been chased out of the pack and we found her wandering in the traffic. They're safe in the shed.'

The other man let go of Ryan. 'Bao Bao is our lucky mascot,' he said. 'Now, get out before the foreman catches you.'

8

NOODLES

RYAN RUBBED HIS arm as they hurried away from the building site along a twisting side street. When tantalizing smells of red pepper, garlic and ginger wafted out from a small restaurant, he insisted they stop for an early lunch. As they entered, he had to duck beneath a pair of red paper lanterns hanging over the door.

'They're meant to bring prosperity and good luck,' Cleo said, taking a seat at a small table. 'Red is the most auspicious colour in China.'

Ryan flexed his sore arm. 'I *need* some good luck after that encounter.'

Cleo sighed. 'I know. How are we ever going to get

back onto the building site to check out that cave now?'

Thanks for the sympathy, Ryan thought. But then he remembered Cleo's Oscar-winning performance at the building site and grinned. 'I don't think that act will work a second time.' He ground his knuckles in his eyes and pretended to sob. *'Those poor little puppy-wuppies* . . . In fact,' he added, 'I still can't believe it worked the *first* time. Those builders must be seriously soft in the head!'

'It was *your* idea,' Cleo laughed.

'Well, you must have melted their hearts with your beauty and charm.'

Cleo snorted so hard she made herself cough.

OK, Ryan thought, *maybe just the beauty. Scratch the charm!*

A girl with a short elfin-style haircut wearing a lime-green tracksuit bounced in from the kitchen, a tray of glasses on one arm and a pile of menus on the other. The excitable elf effect was heightened by the fact that she made her way to their table with a hop and a skip and, when she turned to set down the glasses, it was with a graceful twirl.

'Ni hao!' she said. 'Hello!'

At first Ryan had thought the girl was only ten or so, but as she greeted them, he realized she was probably fourteen or fifteen – the same age as he and Cleo.

'Ni hao,' he replied. He took a menu and thanked her with a mumbled *'xie xie'*. He had now used up his entire armoury of Chinese phrases.

'Let's have the *biang biang* noodles,' Cleo said. 'They're a local speciality.'

Ryan nodded wisely, as if he'd been about to pick that dish himself – even though he couldn't read a word of the menu. *You couldn't go wrong with noodles.*

As soon as the waitress had skipped away with the order, Cleo returned to business. 'Our only option is to ask Professor Han to request that the building work is halted for an archaeological survey. But even if we can persuade her to put in a request, it could take weeks to arrange . . .'

Ryan nodded but he was only half listening. The waitress was back already, placing two enormous bowls on the table.

The noodles smelled delicious, in a thick broth full of meat and vegetables and spices. Ryan tore his chopsticks from their paper packet and dug in. For a moment he thought something must have accidentally fallen into his bowl – like a leather belt or a pet anaconda. Then he realized that it was actually a giant noodle. He tried to lift it out with his chopsticks. It slithered back into the bowl, splashing sauce all over the table. He tried again. This time the mutant noodle fell off and landed in his lap.

Cleo, of course, was wielding her chopsticks like a grand master. She looked up from nibbling on a noodle and smiled. '*Biang biang* noodles are the traditional wide noodles of Shaanxi Province. Legend has it that they were created for the First Emperor.'

'That figures,' Ryan muttered. 'Tian Min said the emperor had seven hundred thousand men working on his tomb, and he probably had another few thousand making all those clay soldiers for his Terracotta Army. There can't have been anyone left in the kitchen to cut the noodles into a sensible size!'

The waitress, who was hovering nearby, bouncing up and down on tiptoes, burst out laughing.

Ryan was impressed. Not only had she understood his joke, she'd laughed at it too.

'Your English must be brilliant,' he said.

She blushed and straightened her apron. 'I work hard at school.' Then she smiled. 'You are very funny.'

Ryan thought he saw Cleo roll her eyes.

The girl held out her hand. 'My name is Wu Meilin. You can call me Meilin. I live here with Aunty Ting when my parents are away working in Shanghai.'

'I'm Ryan Flint,' Ryan said. 'And this is Cleo McNeil.'

Ryan flinched as a blast of noise exploded from the kitchen. It sounded like a street fight, but just one tiny old lady, her face as wrinkled as a walnut shell, came hobbling into the café, brandishing a ladle at Meilin. Chinese was a noisy language, Ryan had noticed. Ordinary conversations sounded like stand-up rows. But Chinese shouting took *loud* to a whole new level. He raised his eyebrows at Cleo.

'What's going on?'

'It sounds like Meilin was meant to have made a batch of noodles this morning, but she went to gymnastics practice instead.'

The yelling got even louder.

'Why's the old lady pointing at me like it's somehow my fault?' Ryan asked.

Cleo grinned. 'She's asking Meilin why she's wasting time flirting with a goofy-looking Western boy . . .'

'*Goofy-looking?*' Ryan spluttered. 'I bet you made that bit up!'

The door slammed and the old lady stomped out.

'She's going to the fish market,' Cleo told Ryan. 'She says Meilin had better have those noodles made before she gets back, or else!'

'We'll help you make the noodles,' Ryan offered when

Meilin returned to their table. 'Won't we?' he added, turning to Cleo.

Cleo stared at him. 'But I've no idea how to make noodles.'

Ryan made a shocked face. 'You mean you haven't done a degree course in Noodleology?'

Cleo jabbed him with a chopstick. 'There's no such thing as Noodleology!'

Meilin smiled. 'Don't worry. I can do it later. Aunty Ting will be a long time at the fish market. She always stops to talk to the other old ladies.' She darted away to the fridge and returned with two bottles of a fizzy drink the same luminous green as her tracksuit.

'Free,' she said, handing them straws.

Ryan slurped the green drink. It tasted like melon, only a hundred times sweeter.

'So why do you want to get into the building site?' Meilin asked. 'I heard you talking about it just now.'

Ryan was about to explain about the jade bracelet and the dragons and the fact that that there was a cave on that building site that might just hold the key to the biggest archaeological discovery of all time, but then he noticed Cleo shooting him a look that told him that was all classified information.

'Oh, we were just trying to rescue some puppies,' he said.

Meilin smiled. 'Is that the real reason? You were talking about a cave. Did you mean the little round one in the cliff?'

Cleo nearly swallowed her straw. 'That's right! The one beneath Sitting Monkey Rock.'

What happened to classified information? Ryan wondered.

Wu Meilin made a puzzled face. 'Sitting Monkey Rock?'

'She means the rock that looks like a meerkat,' Ryan explained.

'Meer-kat?' Meilin asked. 'I don't know that word.'

Cleo looked smug. 'I *told* you they don't have meerkats in China.'

Ryan took no notice. Instead he did his best impression of a meerkat on lookout duty.

'Ah, yes! I've seen them on TV.' Meilin stood up straight and peered around with her hands tucked up under her chin, joining him in the meerkat mime.

Cleo rolled her eyes so far they almost disappeared into her head.

'The cave?' she prompted. 'Do you know something about it?'

Meilin nodded. 'Yes, I've heard—'

'What?' Cleo's eyes glittered with excitement. 'Is there a local legend about a dragon in there or something?'

Meilin laughed. 'No, nothing like that! I just heard some of the men from the site talking about it. They come here to eat most days. The guy operating the crane with the . . .er, what do you call it . . . the breaking machine?' Meilin paused and swung her arm like a pendulum.

'The wrecking ball?' Ryan suggested.

Meilin nodded. 'Yes. That's it. He said he saw some ancient Chinese characters carved into the stone when he started knocking down the cliff near the cave. He told the foreman about it, but he told him to just carry on with the demolition.'

'How dare he?' Cleo fumed. 'That cave could be a highly significant site!'

Meilin looked worried. 'But the men said that they had been given the all-clear to blow up the rest of that cliff!'

'Blow it up?' Cleo and Ryan echoed in unison.

Meilin nodded. 'You know. *Bang!* With dynamite.'

'When?' Cleo demanded.

'Soon. Maybe today.'

Cleo jumped up so fast she knocked over her melon juice. 'We have to go back and see what's in there before the whole cave's destroyed.'

Ryan wished it were that easy. 'We can't just walk in and say, *Sorry guys, it's us again, the puppy patrol. Would you mind not blowing us up while we take a look around that cave up there?*'

'I can help . . .' Meilin said, dashing to the kitchen at the back of the restaurant.

Ryan stared at the pint-sized girl in her lime-green tracksuit. Unless she had secret *Dragon Ball*-style superpowers, how was Meilin planning to ward off an irate gang of burly builders?

Meilin stood in the kitchen doorway beckoning for them to follow. '. . . with noodles.'

CAVE

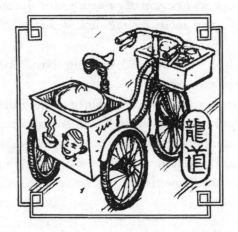

NOODLES? CLEO WONDERED as she followed Meilin and Ryan into the tiny kitchen crammed full of pots and pans and festooned with strings of red peppers and garlic and bunches of herbs. How could noodles possibly help them get inside the cave to see what Lymington and Stubbs had found there?

Cleo eyed Ryan and Meilin suspiciously. Were they ganging up and playing a joke on her? But, as Meilin ran out of the back door, Ryan's face showed that he had no idea what she was up to either. They watched in bemusement as Meilin crossed a cluttered yard, opened a shed and wheeled out a large three-wheeled bike with square metal containers attached to front and back. Meilin went back into the shed.

This time she returned with a blackboard and chalks. She knelt down on the back step and started to write out a sign.

'*Today only!*' Cleo read out loud. '*Half-price noodles from Aunty Ting's restaurant!*'

Meilin smiled up at her. 'The builders will stop for lunch very soon. Aunty Ting is famous for the best noodles in Lintong. They will be so busy queuing for the special offer they won't see you enter the building site.'

'Genius!' Ryan declared.

Meilin raced back into the kitchen. 'Now, we just need some noodles!'

Genius? Cleo wondered, as Meilin removed the tea towel from a stainless steel bowl and wrestled a gigantic ball of dough out onto a wooden board. Cleo wasn't so sure. It was, in fact, one of the most ridiculous plans she'd ever heard. But she had the distinct feeling that if Meilin had suggested jumping over the fence on tame kangaroos Ryan would've hailed it as stroke of sheer brilliance. He was already washing his hands and copying Meilin's every move as she divided the dough into lumps and patted them down into rectangular slabs.

Meilin picked up one end of a rectangle in each hand and began waving it up and down, stretching the dough into a longer and longer strip.

'See?' Ryan told Cleo. 'Nothing to it.' He grabbed a slab of dough by the ends and flung it up in a sort of Mexican wave action.

Cleo hung back. She wasn't going to be side-tracked by this ludicrous scheme. What they needed was a *sensible* plan for getting into that cave. One that didn't involve noodles.

But then Ryan's aerial dough strip broke apart in the

middle. One end slapped him sharply round the ear, the other shot upwards and stuck to the ceiling. Slowly it peeled away and dropped onto his head.

Meilin doubled over with laughter. Cleo couldn't help joining in.

'Come on, Cleo!' Ryan said, grinning as he shook the dough out of his hair. 'You can't be any worse at this than I am!'

On the other hand, Cleo thought, *I don't actually have a sensible plan. And this could be our only chance to look inside the cave before it's dynamited out of existence.*

She washed her hands. 'It's simply a matter of lining up the gluten protein molecules,' she said as she grabbed a lump of dough and began to fold and stretch.

Half an hour later the bamboo racks suspended from the ceiling were all draped with long wide noodles. Meilin wiped her hands down her apron. 'That is enough! You load the noodles on the bike while I put the broth in containers.'

'To the noodle-mobile!' Ryan cried.

To Cleo's astonishment, the noodle plan worked perfectly.

She and Ryan hid behind a parked van and watched as Meilin rode the tricycle up to the site entrance. She was obviously well known to all the guards and they waved her in through the gate. There was a lot of laughter and shouting and pointing at the special-offer sign, and then, just as Meilin had predicted, a rowdy queue of builders began to gather.

'Go, go, go!' Ryan hissed.

They ran along the fence, crawled through the hole and

darted across the building site. The tools and machines were still and silent, like giant toys left behind in a sandpit. The only movement came from Bao Bao, who looked up from her puppies as they passed the shed and acknowledged them with a soft yip.

They stopped at the foot of the cliff, panting for breath, and surveyed the approach to the cave below Sitting Monkey Rock. The hunks and chunks of rock that had broken away when the builders demolished the overhang had piled up on the ground, forming a craggy heap that almost reached the bottom of the cave.

Ryan pulled himself up onto a boulder. 'Easy! It's practically a staircase!'

A staircase without anything holding it together, Cleo thought. The loosely stacked rocks could shift at any moment. She'd sprained her ankle in Egypt and this looked like the perfect way to do it again, but she gritted her teeth and began to scramble up behind him.

At the top of the rock pile, Ryan reached across a metre-wide gap and swung himself up onto the narrow ledge that was all that was left of the overhang beneath the cave. Cleo stretched to do the same, but she was much shorter. She could barely curl her fingers over the rim of rock. She braced herself to jump, but only succeeded in kicking a small avalanche of stones away from under her feet. She began to slip back down the bank.

Suddenly she felt Ryan grab her wrists from above. He began to pull her up, but he'd caught hold of the jade bracelet and it slipped off in his hand. For a long, petrifying moment Cleo dangled by one arm in the breach between the rock pile and the cliff face. Then, spurred by equal measures of adrenaline and desperation, she lunged upwards with her other hand. Ryan snatched hold and hauled her up, until at last she was able to scrabble her way onto the ledge.

Cleo lay on her stomach, catching her breath and looking out over the building site. Everything was just as before. There were no hordes of enraged guards and builders running in their direction. She was so relieved, she laughed out loud. 'We did it!'

Ryan handed her the bracelet. 'I thought you said jade was meant to protect the wearer? This piece nearly killed you. Maybe it's cursed?' He lowered his voice to a Hallowe'en cackle. '*Beware the Dragon's Curse!*' He grinned. 'It's just lucky that I was here to stop you falling into a hole – yet again.'

Cleo didn't need reminding that Ryan had rescued her on more than one occasion in Egypt. 'It's nothing to do with luck or curses,' she pointed out. 'It was a simple accident. It's a little loose on my wrist.' But instead of putting the bracelet back on, she slid it into her jeans pocket. 'I don't want to lose it,' she said, in case Ryan thought she'd suddenly developed a superstitious streak. 'Thanks for pulling me up, by the way,' she added.

But Ryan was already crawling along the ledge towards a huge limestone slab that had fallen on its side, blocking the bottom half of the mouth of the cave like a giant stable door.

'You didn't think Meilin's noodle plan would work, did you?' he said over his shoulder.

'I never said that!' Cleo protested, shuffling after him.

'You didn't have to! Your face was doing the talking.' Ryan knitted his brows, pursed his mouth and flared his nostrils.

'I have never made that face in my life!' Cleo was about

70

to add her own observations about Ryan's soppy expression when he was watching Meilin, when suddenly she forgot all about their argument. There was writing carved into the stone near the bottom of the slab! This must be what the builders had seen. Still on her knees, she twisted her neck to read the characters. 'Wow! It's in small seal script. This is *amazing*!'

'Er, *small seals*?' Ryan asked, sitting up and doing a vague flipper-clapping action.

Cleo couldn't help laughing. 'Not the marine mammals! A seal is for stamping your name or other information.' She sat up on her heels. 'This small seal script is really old. It dates from the Qin Dynasty.'

'The time of the First Emperor?' Ryan whistled. 'That's a whole *bimillennium* old? Can you read it?'

Cleo shook her head. 'No. We'd need my mum for that. She can read everything from bronze script to large seal to clerical . . .'

She broke off. Ryan wasn't listening. He was already climbing over the limestone slab.

Cleo scrambled up after him.

She couldn't wait to see what lay inside the cave.

Immense historical significance . . . the words repeated over and over in her head, beating in time with her racing heart. Lymington and Stubbs must have climbed over this very stone almost eighty years ago. Was this where they'd discovered the key that led them to their momentous archaeological discovery? Or could it even be the entrance to the Dragon Path itself?

As she slid down the other side of the slab, Cleo felt the jade bracelet in her pocket pressing against her hipbone.

She clutched Ryan's arms as he reached up to steady her landing.

Was Grandma's dark and dangerous secret about to be revealed?

10

IMMORTALITY

'**I WISH I'D** brought my dragon-proof vest,' Ryan joked.

He was ninety-nine-and-a-half per cent sure that they weren't actually going to meet any fire-breathing dragons in the cave, but his remaining half per cent was terrified and it needed a few wisecracks to keep up its courage. He could tell, from the way that her fingernails were digging into the flesh of his arm, that Cleo was feeling the same way. She was covering it up with extreme bossiness.

'Just a quick look round,' she said briskly. 'We don't have much time. Obviously we can't go too far inside in case of rock falls. And don't touch *anything*!'

Ryan saluted. 'Yes, ma'am!' he muttered.

Cleo took her torch from her tool belt and flicked it on.

After a moment of dazzled blinking, Ryan began to take in the scene. The cave was bigger than he'd expected, extending back into the mountain until it dissolved into impenetrable shadow. It was littered with hundreds of beautifully decorated bronze pots and jars and trays of every shape and size. Some still stood on wooden chests and tables. Others had fallen to the ground, their spilled contents visible as dark splashes on the stone. Implements of every kind – ladles, scoops, tongs, knives and others he couldn't identify – hung from hooks on the walls alongside bundles of dried herbs and spices, just as in Aunty Ting's kitchen. A ring of blackened charcoal marked the site of a fire pit. Next to it stood a huge iron pestle and mortar.

Ryan ducked and took a few steps inside. The air felt cold and smelled of chalk and wet pavements. He headed for a table strewn with animal bones, feathers, seed cases, something black and wizened that might have been a dried toadstool, and the remains of legions of beetles. Glancing round to check that Cleo wasn't watching, he reached out and touched a sprig of spiky leaves. They crumbled to dust.

Cleo looked up from examining some cow-bell-shaped metal objects on the other end of the table. 'These were weights,' she said. 'They must have been for measuring out ingredients.'

Ingredients? Ryan thought. *Was this where the celebrity chefs of the day cooked up the latest delicacies for the emperor?* He couldn't help feeling deflated. He might not really have expected dragons, but he'd hoped they were on to something a bit more edgy than a two-thousand-year-old kitchen.

Cleo began feeling inside a cauldron-shaped pot to check

out the contents. Ryan was about to remind her of the *no touching* rule when she held up her hand. Her fingertips glittered in the torchlight.

'Is that *gold dust*?' he spluttered. Maybe they were in edgier territory than he'd thought.

Cleo nodded. She dipped her finger into an iron pot. This time the residue was emerald-green. 'Powdered jade,' she murmured.

Ryan picked up a measuring scoop. 'The stuff in here is bright red . . .'

Cleo snatched his hand away. 'Don't touch it!'

Ryan couldn't believe it! 'Er, *you're* the one with gold and jade all over your mitts!'

'I think it's cinnabar.'

Ryan quickly put the scoop down on the table. *Cinnabar* sounded harmless enough, like *cinnamon,* but the way Cleo was eyeing the bowl he had a feeling this wasn't something you sprinkled into apple pies. 'Is it toxic?'

Cleo nodded. 'It's mercury sulphide.'

'What about this one?' Ryan asked, moving on to a bowl of bright orange-yellow powder.

'It looks like orpiment. That's—'

'Arsenic sulphide,' Ryan cut in. He'd read about orpiment for a project on art history. Artists used to use it as a pigment. It was called King's Yellow or Chinese Yellow. Great colour – the only problem was, it was highly poisonous. He stepped away from the table and glanced around the cave. 'This wasn't an ordinary kitchen, was it?'

Cleo's eyes were brighter than the ground jade that coated her fingers, and she wore a faraway smile. Ryan knew that expression.

'You've got a theory coming on, haven't you?'

Cleo opened her mouth to protest and then closed it again. 'All right, I *have* got a theory. Cinnabar, gold, herbs . . . it all adds up. I think this place was used by *fangshi*.'

'*Fang Shi?*" Ryan echoed. 'He sounds like an evil magician in a comic book . . .'

'It's not a *name*.' Cleo was now pinballing about the cave, picking up pots and putting them down, wrinkling her nose as she sniffed at bunches of desiccated fungus. '*Fangshi* is a profession. It's hard to translate, but the closest I can get is *recipe gentlemen*.'

'Recipes? So it *was* a kitchen?'

'The recipes weren't for food.' Cleo looked up from a pile of white feathers and shone the torch at Ryan. '*Fangshi* were more like alchemists. They were attempting to discover the elixir of immortality.'

Ryan stared into the light. He almost burst out laughing. She had to be joking! Then again, Cleo wasn't much of a joker, especially when it came to ancient history.

'You're telling me they thought they could live forever by eating arsenic and toadstools?'

'I know it sounds weird. But the First Emperor was obsessed with immortality. He had his recipe men working day and night to try to find the elixir for him. They thought mercury had magical properties because it was a beautiful silver liquid. And gold . . .' Cleo looked down at her sparkling fingers, '. . . was thought to have life-giving powers because it didn't tarnish like other metals. There were legends about different plants and fungi of immortality too . . .'

It's like something out of Harry Potter's potions class, Ryan thought.

'See how everything is laid out in fives?' Cleo added, gesturing at the pots and weights. 'Five was a mystical number to the *fangshi*.' Before Ryan could reply, she was heading towards the back of the cave. 'Let's see what else is in here.'

'What about not going far inside?' Ryan called after her. 'And about not being long? Meilin won't be able to keep the builders away forever.' But Cleo was already disappearing into the shadows, her torch beam dancing up and down over the rocky walls. Ryan sighed and followed. When Cleo had a theory, all bets were off!

As they ventured deeper, the ceiling became lower and the cave narrower. *In fact,* Ryan thought, at the point when he was doubled over and could touch both walls with his arms outstretched, *I now declare this cave officially a tunnel.*

Suddenly Cleo stopped in front of him and shone her torch into an alcove to one side. 'There's something in here!'

She dropped to her knees, took her trowel from her tool belt and used the side of the blade to sweep away fallen rubble. Soon they were looking at a mighty coffer, or chest, fashioned from age-blackened metal. Cleo wiped the top with her scarf. Ornate scenes featuring cranes and tortoises, deer and tigers, peach trees and pine forests, all worked in blood-red lacquer, gradually emerged from the dust.

'These are all symbols of immortality and long life,' Cleo murmured. 'More evidence of the *fangshi*.' She twisted round to face Ryan. 'This cave *could* be the *terrible place* Grandma was talking about, I suppose. It might be sinister enough to have frightened a child. But it's not *that* terrible. And I can't see anything to do with dragons.'

Ryan crouched down next to her. 'This *definitely* wasn't the place.'

'How can you be so sure?'

Ryan felt a little smug at having figured out something that Cleo had missed. It had occurred to him as they were scrambling up the rock pile.

'Your gran told us that she saw the terrible things happening when she *followed* the men inside the dangerous place, but in those days you couldn't climb up to this cave because of the overhang. I know your gran's a tough cookie, but do you really think an eight-year-old girl could have abseiled down the cliff on her own without anyone noticing?'

Cleo pummelled her temples with the heels of her hands. 'You're right! I can't believe I didn't think of that!' But then she brightened and looked up. 'So, if this wasn't where Grandma saw the dragons, that leaves our other theory about what happened. Lymington and Stubbs must have found some sort of key or clue in here that helped them to find the "terrible place" somewhere else . . .' She ran her fingers over the intricate branches of a pine tree on the coffer and sighed. 'The problem is that it could be anything. There are so many magical *fangshi* symbols and objects in this cave, it's hard to know where to start looking . . .'

'Yeah, it makes me wonder why Lymington and Stubbs didn't look more excited when they came out of the cave,' Ryan murmured. '*If* they'd just seen all this stuff.'

'That's it!' Cleo said suddenly. 'They *didn't* see all of this.'

'Well, unless they wandered round with their eyes closed . . .' Ryan began.

Cleo ignored him. 'That slab of limestone in the entrance.

78

I noticed it when I was looking at the small seal writing, but I didn't notice that I'd noticed, if you see what I mean.'

Ryan nodded and then said, 'I have absolutely no idea what you're talking about.'

'The upper surface of the slab is darker than the rest,' Cleo explained, 'and it's not coated with dust or lichen . . .'

Now Ryan saw what she was getting at.

'You think it only broke away from the cliff quite recently? Oh yeah,' he added, answering his own question. 'I bet it fell when the builders started knocking this part of the cliff face down.'

Cleo stood up. 'If that rock was standing upright when Lymington and Stubbs came here in 1936, then it would have totally blocked the mouth of this cave. Whatever they found, it must have been near the entrance because they couldn't have got any further.' She tugged at Ryan's arm. 'Come on. Let's go back and look.'

But at that moment, something made Ryan jump so violently that he cracked his head on the rocks.

Voices! Other people were in the cave. And they were getting nearer.

Cleo spun round, her face blanched pale in the torchlight. She'd heard it too!

'The builders . . . they're coming to find us . . . we're in big trouble . . .'

Ryan closed his eyes and felt his stomach dissolve into ice water. This could be way worse than *trouble*.

'What if they're *not* coming to find us?' he said. 'What if they don't even know we're here? They could be setting the explosive charges to blow up the cliff.'

'Dynamite?' Cleo breathed.

Ryan closed his fingers around the St Christopher medal and the scarab amulet that hung around his neck.

And I promised Cleo's grandmother I'd keep her safe from harm . . .

I'm quite sure, Cleo told herself as she hurried towards the cave mouth, *that as soon as the builders realize we've saved them from destroying the* fangshi *cave – a priceless archaeological site – they won't stay angry for long. And they certainly won't blow us up!*

Somehow she wasn't finding herself very convincing.

And now the peculiar acoustic properties of rock and tunnel and cave were playing tricks on her ears; it almost sounded as if the voices were coming from *behind* her, deeper inside the mountain, rather than from the cave or cliff face, and they didn't sound like Chinese builders.

Suddenly she realized that it wasn't an illusion; the voices really *were* coming from inside the mountain. They were faint and distorted but, oddest of all, they were speaking in English!

Ryan caught her up and they listened in disbelief.

'Golly! What a *super* cranial deformity . . .'

There was only one person who could sound that thrilled about a misshapen skull.

'That's Alex!' Ryan murmured.

'And that's Dad whistling!' Cleo added in amazement. The mournful warble of Amy Winehouse's 'Back to Black' was drifting down the tunnel. Dad always whistled sad songs when he was happy. He saved the cheerful tunes for a crisis.

Ryan rubbed his head. 'Tell me I'm not just hearing things. Those voices are coming from the Tomb of a Thousand Poisons, aren't they?'

Cleo nodded and ran back into the tunnel as fast as she could, past Ryan, past the coffer where they'd stopped before, and on and on, climbing steeply upwards, shouting as she went.

'Dad! Mum! Can you hear me?'

'Cleopatra?' Dad's reply reverberated around the tunnel. 'Where the dickens are you?'

'Down here!' she called back. 'We're coming up to you.'

'How do you know we can even get up this way?' Ryan shouted from behind her.

'I don't exactly *know*,' Cleo admitted, 'but I've got a theory. I'm sure this tunnel connected the Tomb of a Thousand Poisons to the *fangshi* cave for a very good reason, because—'

'You can give me the explanation later,' Ryan puffed as he hurried after her. 'Let's save our breath for getting out of here before we're blown to smithereens.'

It was a long, steep climb. When, at last, Cleo's torch beam showed a solid wall of rock up ahead, she slumped against it, tears welling in her eyes. They were trapped!

'I'm sorry,' she mumbled, 'I really thought it would lead . . .'

But as she spoke, the wall gave way. She fell through it to land flat on her face.

'Amazing,' Ryan said, holding out a hand to pull her up. 'A secret entrance!'

As Cleo scrambled shakily to her feet, she realized that Ryan was right. The wall had just been a thin screen of dried mud fashioned to look like solid rock. And now she saw that they'd come out at the back of the Tomb of a Thousand Poisons in a rubbly area, where several of the honeycomb cells had collapsed together in a scatter of stone and shattered bones. She also saw the faces of her parents, Alex, Professor Han, Tian Min and Ryan's mum, Julie, all staring at her, eyes wide and mouths hanging open.

'Hi there!' Cleo said.

No one spoke.

Cleo took a step forward. 'Mum? Dad? Is something wrong? Has there been an accident?'

'I think *we're* the something wrong,' Ryan said. 'We *have* just appeared out of solid rock inside a mass tomb. That might just come across as a bit creepy. And have you seen yourself?'

Cleo looked down and noticed that they were both covered from head to foot in a shroud of dust.

Ryan grinned. 'We even *look* like the Living Dead!'

11

FRIENDS

'**IT CERTAINLY LOOKS** as if Cleo's theory is right,' Pete McNeil said as he munched on a steamed dumpling. 'Those men buried in the Tomb of a Thousand Poisons had been experimented on by the *fangshi*. The First Emperor's recipe gentlemen used them as "guinea pigs" to test out their immortality elixirs.'

Alex Shawcross nodded, her golden curls bobbing up and down. 'When the poor chaps died – which happened rather a lot, since the *fangshi*'s potions were often dreadfully dangerous – they were carted up that tunnel and conveniently disposed of in the Tomb of a Thousand Poisons. It's all terribly fascinating.'

Not to mention a massive stroke of luck, Ryan thought as he reached into the bamboo steamer and speared a crescent-shaped dumpling with his chopstick. *Not so much for the poor guinea pigs, of course – there was nothing lucky about it for them – but for Cleo and me!* He almost burst out laughing every time he remembered the team's faces when the two of them had staggered into the tomb like something out of a zombie film.

It was now three days later. Ryan and his mum had been invited for breakfast with the McNeils, who were staying two doors away from their own rooms in the university guest accommodation block. They'd made a detour on the way to pick up the delicious *jiaozi* dumplings, stuffed with minced pork and spring onions, from one of the many street vendors around the campus.

Cleo's mum poured boiling water into the teapot from the giant thermos flask that was left outside their door by Mrs Long, the caretaker, every morning. Lydia McNeil's hair was a wild tangle, pinned off her face with a spare pair of chopsticks, and she was wearing a baggy shirt that looked suspiciously like a pyjama top.

'I think I need this,' she said, gulping her tea and yawning. 'I stayed up far too late translating more of the writings from the Kitchen of Eternal Life.' She smiled at Ryan. 'That's what the *fangshi* called that cave, according to the inscription on the big limestone slab.'

'Eternal Life?' Ryan laughed. 'It was more like Dr Death's Laboratory of Doom!'

The bronze and lacquer coffer had turned out to contain hundreds of bamboo strips, on which were written the recipes for various elixirs, as well as details of the men they were tested on, the precise doses they had been given, and their gruesome symptoms.

Lydia McNeil reached for a pile of notes. 'Yes, they certainly used some unsavoury ingredients. Last night I came across instructions for making a special tea from fungi, including death caps and destroying angels . . .'

Ryan grimaced. 'With names like that, I'm guessing they shouldn't be part of your five-a-day.'

'Highly toxic,' Alex said happily. 'As were many of their other ingredients. Castor-oil seeds, apricot and peach kernels, rhubarb leaves, chrysanthemum, mistletoe, lichen, wormwood . . . Do you mind if I take the last of these scrummy dumplings?' she asked nobody in particular. She loaded the dumpling with flame-red chilli sauce and transferred it to her mouth without spilling a single drop down her fluffy white angora jumper. 'Where's Tian Min, by the way? I thought he was joining us for breakfast.'

'How did your coffee date go the other day?' Ryan asked.

Alex blushed. 'How did you know about that?'

'Ryan's quite an expert on affairs of the heart,' Cleo said with a knowing smile.

Ryan tried to kick Cleo under the table, but caught his mum's ankle instead, making her spill her coffee. Cleo had got this mad idea that he was *romantically interested* – as she called it – in Meilin, just because he'd taken her a box of chocolates as a thank-you for helping with the cave mission.

'If you must know,' Alex said. 'Tian Min took me to McDonald's because he thought I might like some Western food. He's a total sweetie!' She was interrupted by a knock at the door. 'Oh! That's probably him now.'

But it wasn't Tian Min. It was Professor Han, wrapped

up against the morning chill in a bright yellow puffer jacket. With her was a young man whose outstanding feature was a gravity-defying quiff. He was clearly very proud of it, smoothing it back every few seconds with the side of his hand.

Folding chairs were brought in from the bedroom and squeezed around the table, and cups of green tea were poured.

'Isn't Tian Min coming?' Alex asked.

Professor Han sipped her tea. 'I'm afraid Tian Min won't be available to work with the team any more. His mother was taken ill last night. He's had to rush back home to Shanghai to be with her.' She smiled in the direction of Quiff Guy. 'That's why I've brought Joey along. He's a new student here. He'll take over as your assistant.'

Quiff Guy stood up, tugging the front of his black leather bomber jacket into place and shook hands all round. 'Hey there, guys. I'm Joey Zhou.'

Cleo's mum looked up from setting a platter of fruit on the table. 'You go by an English name?'

'Oh, yes. I picked it from *Friends,* you know. It's my favourite programme.' He ran his hand over his quiff. 'Hey, how *you* doing?' he drawled in a cheesy American accent, firing the question at Alex and then at Cleo.

'Er, fine, thank you,' Cleo replied.

Ryan gaped at her. How had she reached the age of fourteen without ever seeing an episode of *Friends*? 'There's this character called Joey,' he explained. '*How you doing?* is his catchphrase.'

Cleo shrugged. 'That's basically just a greeting. How can it be a catchphrase?'

'Anyone like some fruit?' Lydia asked, offering the plate

around. 'There's pomegranate, lychee, dragon fruit."

Dragon fruit? Ryan exchanged a look with Cleo. Now that they'd ruled out the Kitchen of Eternal Life cave as being the location of Cleo's grandmother's dark and dangerous secret, they were still on the hunt for any possible dragon-related clues that could lead them to the Dragon Path.

The trouble was, you could hardly move for dragons in China. There was dragon tea, the dragon dance, Dragon Airlines . . .

And now there was dragon *fruit*! *Could this be the key*, Ryan wondered, *that would help them complete the quest of returning the jade bracelet?* Not to mention finding the archaeological site that Lymington and Stubbs had been looking for – which Cleo was sure would be bigger than Tutankhamun's tomb, Pompeii and the Terracotta Army put together. He frowned at the fuchsia-pink fruit with lime-green spines. It looked like a cross between a pineapple and a tropical fish. He glanced at Cleo. They both shook their heads. Dragon fruit was about as *dark and dangerous* as a sponge finger.

Cleo's eyes slid towards her shoulder bag, which was hanging on the back of the door. Ryan knew her laptop was in there. She was itching to check her email account, which would mean going to the main university building to get an internet connection. Ryan had pretty much given up on Louisa Gupta ever sending through the missing film from the History of Archaeology Museum. But Cleo was still clinging to the faint hope that the film would arrive and solve the mystery.

Professor Han replaced her teacup on its saucer. 'I've managed to smooth things over with the owners of the Grand Imperial Hotel. They've admitted that their security was very lax, so they won't be making a complaint about Cleo and Ryan trespassing on the construction site. They've also agreed to delay work on the cliff until we've finished exploring the Kitchen of Eternal Life and have removed all the artefacts to the Department of Archaeology here at the university.'

Pete McNeil smiled. 'All's well that ends well.'

Lydia McNeil frowned and nudged his elbow so hard he almost swallowed a lychee stone. 'Ah, yes, yes,' he mumbled. He removed his glasses, pinched the bridge of his freckled nose and directed a stern look at Cleo. 'Your mother and I wanted to have a word with you about that escapade. Sneaking onto that building site was very dangerous.'

'That goes for you too, Ryan!' His mum said sternly, wagging the teaspoon that she'd been using to stir sugar into her third cup of coffee. 'Don't do anything like that again.'

'We won't,' Ryan and Cleo said as one.

Cleo's dad hooked his glasses back over his ears and beamed at them. 'Good. I'm glad that's all cleared up then.'

Lydia McNeil rolled her eyes. She looked as if she had rather a lot more to say on the subject, but at that moment her mobile phone rang in her shirt pocket.

'Saved by the bell,' Ryan whispered.

Cleo's mum glanced at the caller ID on the screen. 'It's Sir Charles Peacocke,' she muttered. 'I wonder what he wants.' She switched into a professional speaking-to-the-boss voice as she answered the call. 'Sir Charles. How *are* you?'

She spoke for a few more minutes before hanging up. 'He says he's going to call by to see us on Friday for a tour of the Kitchen of Eternal Life. He's in this part of the world anyway for a conference in Hong Kong . . .' She looked at

Cleo and Ryan. 'And,' she added through slightly gritted teeth, 'he asked me to pass on his congratulations to you two on the discovery.'

Ryan did his best to arrange his face into a gloat-free expression. *In fact,* he thought, *this is probably our cue to leave before Cleo's mum remembers that she was about to launch into a health and safety lecture.* He got up from the table. 'Let's go,' he told Cleo. 'We've got *loads* of studying to get through this morning.'

Cleo looked puzzled. Ryan wasn't usually big on studying.

'*You know,*' he persisted. 'That really interesting *history topic* we started.' He turned to his mum. 'We're just going to the computer room in the main building for a while.'

At last Cleo got the message. She jumped up and grabbed her bag. 'Oh, yes, that's right!' she said in an over-enthusiastic voice. 'Because we need to use the internet to do some research, you know, on educational websites about the history of . . . er, historical things . . .'

Cleo was still throwing out random bits of information as Ryan bundled her out of the flat. She might have a brain the size of the First Emperor's mausoleum, but she was clueless when it came to a good cover story. Ryan had tried telling her before: stick to the truth, but keep it vague.

They hurried through the campus, across a wide paved plaza and along an avenue of tall trees that had turned bright yellow for autumn. *King's Yellow,* Ryan thought, remembering the toxic arsenic sulphate from the Kitchen of Eternal Life. He couldn't resist kicking up the puddles of leaves that had already fallen, to watch them tumble back to earth in golden showers.

They came to an imposing tower of concrete and tinted glass

that looked as if it had probably won awards for architecture, and went inside to a huge room. Students sat working at long rows of computers. The clicking of keyboards, whirring of computers and rustling of textbook pages filled the air. Ryan could almost hear brains creaking under the strain of so much learning. Just being there was giving him a headache. Cleo didn't seem to mind. She headed straight for a vacant terminal.

'There's *got* to be a message from Louisa today,' she said as she plugged her laptop into the ethernet connection.

'Touch wood.' Ryan knocked on the desk as he pulled up a stool next to her. But as they waited for the computer to fire up he wasn't really thinking about the film at all. He was replaying the conversation that had taken place in the McNeils' apartment. Someone had said something that didn't quite add up, and it'd been bugging him ever since, like a fly at a windowpane. It was something to do with *mothers*. But it wasn't about his own mum. Was it Cleo's mum? No – it was coming to him now: it was *Tian Min's* mother! Tian Min had mentioned her when they were chatting about comics outside the Tomb of a Thousand Poisons.

'Don't you think it's weird,' Ryan whispered to Cleo, 'what Professor Han said about Tian Min rushing off to see his mother?'

Cleo kept her eyes fixed on the screen. 'Why weird?' she murmured. 'I'm sure you'd go if it was *your* mum.'

'Not if she was already dead,' Ryan said.

That made Cleo look up.

'Tian Min told me his mother died last year!'

'OK, that *is* weird.' Cleo looked back at the screen and opened her email folder. 'Maybe Professor Han got mixed

up, and it was his grandmother who died, or his aunt or—
Yes!' she breathed, as a new message pinged into the inbox.
'This is it! The missing film at last.'

Ryan forgot all about Tian Min's mother, dead or alive.

12

DRAGONS

CLEO'S THUMB HOVERED over the mouse pad. Were they about to discover the secret that Grandma had kept for almost eighty years? Or would the film just contain more footage of Lymington and Stubbs hammering pegs in a field?

Ryan was balancing on the back legs of his stool. 'If I'd known we'd just be staring at a blank screen,' he said, 'I'd have brought some knitting or something.'

Cleo took a deep breath and clicked *Play*. A snowstorm of flickering cleared to reveal the now-familiar figures of Harold Stubbs and Cedric Lymington – Cleo still didn't know which was which – standing on either side of an enormous fallen tree, each with one foot up on the stump.

She thought they looked like Victorian hunters posing with a man-eating tiger they had bagged, but instead of shotguns they held a clapperboard bearing the words *TOP-SECRET LOCATION*.

'Top-secret?' Ryan tipped forward on his stool. 'Wow! Forget the knitting!'

Cleo's heart clenched with excitement as the silent film showed Lymington and Stubbs, now accompanied by three Chinese men carrying shovels and other digging equipment, climbing down a steep slope forested with pine and birch. The taller man seemed to be counting his steps, looking down every now and then at a small dark object he held in his hand. *It must be the clue he found in the entrance of the* fangshi *cave*, she thought. But however hard she peered at the grainy film, she couldn't figure out what it was.

The tall man stopped, removed his pipe from between his teeth and gave a thumbs up sign. The men all began to hack through undergrowth and rhododendron bushes with sticks and machetes until eventually the camera zoomed in on one of the Chinese diggers. He was standing near an outcrop of rock that jutted out from among the bushes, waving his machete and knife over his head like semaphore flags. And then . . . Cleo stared in dismay at the blank screen . . . there was nothing but fuzzy blackness. She turned to Ryan.

'No! It can't end there!'

Ryan grinned. 'It doesn't, look! It must just have been a damaged section of film.'

Cleo turned back to the screen. The action had suddenly started again. The men were now dropping into a tunnel through some kind of trapdoor. The cameraman must have rigged up a spotlight on his camera, because the scene was illuminated by a cone of bright white light. The tunnel was surprisingly roomy: high enough for the men to stand upright and wide enough to walk two abreast. They were all carrying cumbersome metal torches, and the multiple light sources cast intricate shadows, tiger-striping the walls as they set off down the steep tunnel.

Ryan suddenly gripped Cleo's arm. 'Are those . . . *dragons?*'

Cleo nodded. Her heart was beating so fast she couldn't speak. The tunnel was flanked by dragons, as big as lions, fashioned from a lustrous metal or marble. Arranged in pairs at regular intervals, facing each other across the tunnel, the statues reared up on their hind legs, front legs pawing the air, sabre-like claws unsheathed for attack. Their mighty heads were thrown back, jaws open, nostrils flared, spines raised along their serpentine bodies. In the criss-crossing beams of light, the dragons seemed to quiver in readiness to pounce. The men tiptoed past as if afraid to wake them.

The film stopped and started several times before the tunnel widened out into an underground room. Lymington and Stubbs rushed from place to place, examining one object after another. The Chinese men shrank into the background, exchanging nervous glances. The film jumped to a low table set with trays and pots and urns and lanterns. The tall archaeologist sniffed the contents of a bowl and a tray. The one with the moustache reached into a squat three-legged jar. Pulling out his hand, a stream of bronze discs with square holes punched out of their middles streamed through his fingers.

'They're *banliang* coins,' Cleo said. 'The currency of the Qin Dynasty.'

'Wow!' Ryan whistled. 'It's a secret underground treasure store.'

'I don't think so. It looks more like an ancestor temple. It would be part of a tomb complex.' Cleo paused the film and pointed out objects on the screen. 'All the jars and bowls probably contained food and drink that the family brought as offerings to honour their ancestor, and the lanterns would be for burning incense. Those coins could be special ghost money, offered to the dead to use in the afterlife.'

'But why have a temple underground?' Ryan asked.

'Maybe they wanted to keep it a secret so that only loyal family members knew the way?' Cleo suggested. 'One thing's for sure. It must have been for a high-ranking person, to have such an elaborate spirit path.'

'Spirit path?' Ryan asked.

'A ceremonial road leading to the tomb,' Cleo explained. 'They were always lined with pairs of statues, usually of real or mythical animals.'

'Dragons, in this case,' Ryan put in. 'So now we know why your grandmother called it the Dragon Path. It's all starting to make sense. Sort of!'

Cleo nodded without taking her eyes from the screen. She couldn't wait to see more of the tomb complex and figure out who was buried there. The signs were all pointing to an eminent Qin Dynasty nobleman or general, or even a member of the royal family. She started the film again and watched as the camera panned up to a larger-than-life-sized bronze sculpture of a man in a wide-sleeved cloak seated on a throne behind the offering table.

'I wouldn't want to get on the wrong side of *him*,' Ryan commented. 'He looks like a Chinese Henry VIII.'

Cleo could see what Ryan meant. Barrel chest, broad face, square jaw beneath a short thick beard, small eyes staring out with a look of arrogant disdain – the statue reminded her of a picture she'd seen somewhere, but before she could get a better look, the film snapped back to Cedric Lymington and Harold Stubbs. They were standing in front of a doorway behind the statue, locked in a heated argument. The shorter man with the moustache was trying to open the door, while the other was doing his best to stop him. Even without a soundtrack it was possible to lip-read his frantic cries.

'Stubbs! Come back!'

'At last we know who's who,' Ryan muttered. 'Moustache Man is Stubbs and Pipe Guy is Lymington . . .' But his words tailed away as the action on the screen suddenly took a horrifying turn.

Stubbs lunged forward and shoved open the door. There was a blur of movement as something shot across the scene. With lightning reactions, Lymington flung aside his pipe and dived at Stubbs, knocking him clear of the missile. The cameraman must have jumped back with shock; the view through the lens careened up to the ceiling. When it swung back down again, Stubbs was clambering to his feet and staggering back from the doorway. Lymington was still on the ground, head down, arms stretched, as if frozen in mid-dive. As the camera drew closer, Cleo's stomach lurched with a dreadful realization: protruding from Cedric Lymington's back, exactly midway between his shoulder blades, was the shaft of an arrow.

'What . . .' Ryan gasped.

The camera jerked upwards to show Harold Stubbs staring down at the motionless Lymington. Stubbs's eyes were dark pits of fear. His face, ghastly white, glistened with sweat. The Chinese men – one of whom, tall and gangly with sticking-out ears, appeared little more than a teenager – looked on in horror, peeping out from behind the statues of tomb guards that stood to attention on either side of the bronze throne.

Stubbs took a step towards Lymington, but then he seemed to catch sight of something. He stumbled and turned back. Looking straight into the camera, he screamed a single word.

'Did he say *cigar*?' Cleo murmured.

Ryan nodded. 'I think so. But he must have meant *pipe*.' He pointed at the screen. 'It looks like a spark from Lymington's pipe tobacco has set something alight.'

Flames were now leaping into the frame, so bright that for a few moments the film was bleached out to a white glare. But then, through the flames and smoke and light-flare, Cleo discerned the shadowy figures of Stubbs and the Chinese men running back into the tunnel to flee the inferno. There was confusion and panic as they saw that the fire was coming from the tunnel itself. Jets of flame were spurting from the dragons' mouths and nostrils, exploding into starbursts of sparks like a firework display.

Dodging the flames, the men fled for their lives. The film was still running. The cameraman was clearly hurtling along behind the others, the camera in his hands jogging up and down. Suddenly, amid the chaos, a pair of dragons slid together at high speed. The men all managed to throw themselves through the gap. But now the next pair of dragons was crashing together, and the next and the next. The camera angle pitched wildly around the tunnel – ground, wall, flame, dragon jaws, running feet – before landing on the grisly image of one of the older Chinese men, who was crushed in a deadly embrace between two dragons. The man ahead of him paused to look back, only to be blasted by a plume of flame and then he too was caught in the clutches of razor-sharp dragon claws.

At last the camera showed a lozenge of grey light up ahead. The trapdoor!

They're nearly out! Cleo thought with a surge of relief, realizing she'd been holding her breath.

And there, in the final moments of the film, they saw the small figure of a child running away down the tunnel ahead of the men. Framed against the pale patch of sky, she pulled herself up through the trapdoor and disappeared.

The film stopped. Cleo looked around, dazed, as if emerging from a deep nightmare-wracked sleep. Students were still huddled over their computers or leafing through their textbooks. She glanced over at Ryan. His eyes were fixed on the screen as if the terrible scene were still playing out on an endless loop.

'Now we know what Grandma saw,' Cleo said at last.

Ryan looked up and met her gaze. Then he reached for her hand and gave it a sympathetic squeeze.

Cleo wondered how he'd known that she had a lump in her throat.

13

GUNPOWDER

NO WONDER EIGHT-*year-old Eveline Bell was terrified by the death-by-dragon episode,* Ryan thought. *I think I need counselling and I only saw it happen on a flickering black-and-white silent movie.* He hadn't been that scared by a film since watching *The Woman in Black*. The events on the film also explained why Cedric Lymington was missing from the final scene, of course, and why Harold Stubbs had been frantically packing up to leave, with shock and horror etched all over his face.

Cleo's hand was shaking as she took the jade bracelet from her pocket and placed it on the desk between them. 'Grandma said to return this. We know what the Dragon

Path is now, but I still don't understand what it has to do with this bracelet.'

Ryan was amazed that Cleo had missed such an important detail. He clicked on *Rewind* and scrolled back to the point where the dragons started breathing fire.

'It's not a bracelet,' he explained. 'It's a piercing!' He paused the film. 'Look! All the dragons have rings through their noses. Like bulls. Or those brass lion doorknockers you can get,' he added, suddenly remembering the one he'd seen on the door of Cleo's grandmother's retirement home. He clicked on *Play*. 'Watch what happens. As each dragon starts breathing fire, the ring shoots out from its nose.'

Cleo chewed her bottom lip as she studied the film. 'Yes, I see it now.' She touched the jade ring a little gingerly, as if it might still bear traces of dragon snot. 'So Grandma must have picked this up from the floor of the tunnel.'

Ryan nodded. 'I guess the rings were something to do with the triggering mechanism.'

There must have been a pulley of some sort that propelled the dragons across the tunnel on runners, he thought, *plus a clever device for striking a spark to ignite gunpowder for the bursts of flame*. He wondered how long the dragons had been underground, waiting to leap into action. It was impressive they still worked at all, but they'd certainly been effective. 'No wonder your grandmother called it a dark, dangerous secret. Those dragons killed at least three men in that tunnel . . .'

Cleo turned to him and shook her head. She looked as shell-shocked as Stubbs had in the final scene.

'But I think it's more than that . . . something even worse.'

'How could it be *worse*—' Ryan began. But he was cut off by a 'Shush!' from the next terminal.

Cleo apologized and switched off her laptop. 'We're just going.'

Ryan couldn't leave fast enough. He needed fresh air after all that mayhem and death. As they hurried out, he spotted an unmistakeable skyscraper quiff poking up from behind a computer screen, and stopped to say hello to Joey Zhou. At first Joey didn't look too pleased to be disturbed. He was obviously engrossed in his studies. Then he grinned.

'Hey! How *you* doing?' he crooned at Cleo.

'Er, still fine, thanks,' Cleo mumbled.

'How's your project going?'

'Great, thanks!' Ryan answered, pulling Cleo away before she could attempt to explain some non-existent historical research in unconvincing detail. 'Making progress, you know. Bye!'

They headed out of the campus and walked along a busy street under a canopy of copper and gold maple boughs. A delicious smell, a cross between Bonfire Night and banana waffles, filled the air. The scent was coming from a chimney-shaped clay oven on the street corner, where an old lady was baking sweet potatoes wrapped in foil. Ryan stopped, bought two and handed one to Cleo.

They found a bench in a small park and sat down to eat. Ryan peeled back the foil to release a cloud of fragrant steam. He bit into the bright orange flesh of the potato and cursed as it scalded his tongue.

'So,' he asked, fanning his hand in front of his mouth, 'tell me how your grandmother's secret could possibly be *worse* than seeing people shot in the back and crushed, burned and impaled by dragons.'

Cleo blew on her sweet potato. 'You know I said that tunnel was a spirit path leading to an ancestor temple?'

'Yeah, you said it was part of a tomb complex,' Ryan said, just to show he'd been listening. 'Where the family could go and make offerings.'

'Well, I think I've figured out whose tomb it was. It first started to come to me when I saw the bronze statue. He looked familiar, and then I realized I'd seen his face in paintings.'

'Henry VIII's long-lost twin, you mean?' Ryan tried biting into the potato again, but it was still hotter than molten lava.

Cleo frowned down at her potato. For once she didn't seem very happy about having a new theory. 'Henry VIII didn't *have* a twin. Certainly not in China.' She looked up, saw that Ryan was joking, and gave him a shove. 'Anyway, I'm talking about someone much earlier than Tudor times.' She waited, as if expecting Ryan to guess. When he didn't, she went on, 'The style of the body armour of those guard statues was another clue. It was exactly the same as the famous terracotta warriors . . .'

Typical Cleo, Ryan thought. She'd totally missed flaming jade rings rocketing out of the noses of dragons, but she'd noticed the finer points of a clay statue's outfit.

Cleo glanced over her shoulder. 'It's the *First Emperor,* of course!' she whispered. 'Qin Shi Huangdi. He was paranoid about looters trying to break into his tomb and make off with his treasures. It makes sense that he'd have all kinds of security measures around his tomb complex – including the ancestor temple, where his descendants came to leave offerings for him in the afterlife. No doubt only the most loyal of family members would know the secret of how to get past the dragons . . .' She shook her head. 'I should have realized that was Grandma's dark secret all along. The First Emperor was known as the Dragon Emperor, after all.'

Ryan could only nod. Partly because he'd finally managed a large mouthful of very hot sweet potato, but also because he was trying to take in what Cleo was telling him. He remembered the booby traps that Tian Min had told him about. *Self-triggering crossbows!* He shuddered. That must be how Lymington had been killed: a crossbow set up over the door, primed to fell any intruders who got past the dragons and tried to penetrate further into the tomb beyond the ancestor temple.

'Poor old Pipe Guy,' he murmured. 'It seems unfair; he was only trying to stop Stubbs barging in . . .'

They ate in silence, watching a group of old men in tracksuits practising slow-motion t'ai chi exercises. In the background the shaggy bottle-green slopes of Mount Li rose up against a clear blue sky. *Was the secret tunnel hidden somewhere beneath those dark evergreens?* Ryan wondered. 'Do you think Lymington and Stubbs *knew* that the Dragon Path was going to lead to the First Emperor's tomb?' he asked.

Cleo scrunched her foil into a ball. 'I don't think so. Grandma heard them saying that their big discovery would make them great heroes of Chinese archaeology. But it was completely forbidden to enter the tomb mound then, just as it is now. They'd have been criminals, not heroes, if anyone ever found out.' She stood up to look for a rubbish bin. 'They probably thought they'd found the tomb of an important courtier or general. No wonder the Chinese diggers all looked petrified. They must have suddenly realized where they were . . .' Cleo paused as two boys ran across the path, flying long strings of tiny paper kites that swooped and darted like swallows. Ryan could tell she was deep in thought. It wasn't just the faraway expression that gave it away; Cleo had also tossed her ball of potato foil into a passing lady's shopping basket instead of a bin.

'Hang on,' she said, frowning up at the fluttering kites. 'I've just thought of something that disproves my theory. The dragon's fire . . . that must all have been done using gunpowder . . .'

Ryan got up from the bench. 'So?'

'Gunpowder wasn't developed until around the ninth century AD. That's a thousand years after the death of the First Emperor . . .'

Ryan tried to make a joke of it. 'What's a thousand years between friends?'

Cleo didn't reply. They walked across the park in silence.

Ryan looked up to see three white cranes soaring overhead, their black-tipped wings almost brushing the maples. They looked exactly like the ones on the lacquerware coffer in the Kitchen of Eternal Life.

'Watch out!' he said. 'Low-flying symbols of immortality.'

Suddenly Cleo turned and grabbed his arm. *'Immortality!* Of course! I could still be right. Historians think that gunpowder was discovered by accident by recipe gentlemen searching for the elixir of life when they were experimenting with explosive combinations of chemicals like saltpetre and sulphur mixed with carbons. What if the First Emperor's *fangshi* in the Kitchen of Eternal Life happened on it much earlier than anyone thought? It would explain the burns on some of the bodies in the Tomb of a Thousand Poisons.'

'And you think they decided to branch out and use their new invention to incinerate people with fire-breathing dragon statues?' Ryan filled in. *It gives a whole new meaning to the term 'playing with fire'*, he thought. But from what he'd learned about the First Emperor's recipe gentlemen so far, it didn't surprise him.

They'd reached the park gate and stood looking out onto the road at the stream of buses, taxis and tuk-tuks trundling by. Cleo took the jade ring from her pocket and scowled at it. 'So much for returning this to the dragon. Even if we knew how to find that tunnel, we could never enter it. We're already in enough trouble for the building-site incident. If we ventured within a mile of the First Emperor's tomb we'd be . . .' She broke off, searching for a way to express the enormity of the situation.

'Toast!' Ryan provided.

He expected Cleo to object to his choice of word, but she gave him a wobbly smile. *'Burned* toast!'

All of a sudden Ryan heard a soft crunch behind him: footsteps on fallen leaves. He stopped. The footsteps stopped. The hairs on his arms prickled. He'd had the eerie sensation that he was being watched on and off since they'd entered the park. He whipped round, but there was no one there. A swirl of crimson maple leaves fluttered up from the ground and fell back again. Had they been scuffed into the air by the feet of a stalker? *Probably just caught up in the breeze,* he told himself. *My mind's playing tricks on me. Even talking about entering the First Emperor's tomb is giving me a guilty conscience.*

14

TROUBLE

CLEO WAS STILL thinking about the Dragon Path tunnel the next morning when she settled down in her room to work through some nuclear chemistry problems. She'd travelled the world with her parents all her life and had never been to 'ordinary' school. She was used to studying on her own, but today her thoughts kept drifting away from isotopes and ions and returning to Harold Stubbs and Cedric Lymington, and the door at the back of the ancestor temple.

If I'm right, and that underground temple was part of the tomb complex of the First Emperor, what treasures would the men have discovered if they'd made it through that door?

The only written record of what might lie beneath the

tomb mound came from about a hundred years after the First Emperor's death. The Grand Historian of China, Sima Qian, told of an underground city, with palaces and pavilions and a model of the universe, with rivers and seas of flowing mercury and skies studded with constellations of gems and pearls. Although the Chinese government had decided to hold off excavations for fear of damage to the artefacts inside, probes and scans from the outside of the mound seemed to support Sima Qian's descriptions.

Cleo realized she'd been staring at the same page of *Advances in Nuclear Chemistry* for half an hour. She gave up, and began to work on one of her favourite maths projects: attempting to prove the Riemann hypothesis. She could lose herself for hours grappling with number theory.

But not today!

Cleo chewed her pencil and sighed. Her dream of being the one to locate Lymington and Stubbs's *discovery of immense historical significance* had crumbled to dust the moment she'd realized what it was. The First Emperor's tomb was a complete no-go zone. The disappointment was unbearable.

'And it's *not* just about the personal glory,' she said out loud, as if Ryan were there to hear her. 'It's about understanding the history of humankind.'

Cleo clapped her notebook shut and threw down her pencil. She took the jade ring from her jeans pocket – she could no longer think of it as a bracelet now that she knew it belonged in a dragon's nose – and turned it over in her palm.

I promised I'd return it.

Logically, Cleo knew that it would make no difference if she simply put the jade ring in a safe place and kept it – just as Grandma had for eighty years. So why did that idea make her feel so ill at ease? Now she knew what Grandma had meant when she'd said her heart was *troubled* by the dark, dangerous secret. Cleo bounced the jade ring in her palm. It only weighed a few hundred grams, but it felt as if Grandma had passed on a great burden. Ryan had joked that the ring bore the Dragon's Curse. She was almost starting to believe he might be right.

Don't be ridiculous! Cleo told herself. To snap herself out of her nonsensical imaginings, she examined the pattern of six crossed lines on the inner surface of the jade. Was it part of a larger decorative pattern that had worn away, or did it signify something? Cleo had looked it up in a dictionary of Chinese characters, but had found no matches. She copied the pattern onto a page torn from her notebook and took it through to the kitchen, where Mum was poring over photographs of the bamboo slips from the Kitchen of Eternal Life with a magnifying glass.

'Do you recognize this?' Cleo asked, holding out the paper. 'Could it be a small seal character?'

Mum frowned at the symbol for a moment and then shook her head. 'No. Why? Is it important?'

I wish I knew, Cleo thought.

Mum leaned back, rubbing her eyes. 'Do you want to help me catalogue these writings? They're in a complete muddle.'

Cleo was tempted. It was just the kind of challenge she loved. But there was something else she had to do.

'Later,' she promised. 'First I need to talk to Ryan.'

Mum looked up from the magnifying glass with a stern smile. 'You two keep out of trouble, OK?'

Cleo smiled back but she didn't answer.

Meanwhile, Ryan was studying too.

At least, he was sitting at the kitchen table with *Shakespeare for Dummies* open in front of him. He'd promised to keep up with the work he was missing at school. Right now he was meant to be exploring the dramatic presentation of love in *Romeo and Juliet*. But his brain seemed more interested in the dramatic presentation of death; it kept replaying the Dragon Path film over and over.

On the other side of the table, his mum wasn't exactly concentrating either. She'd set herself up with her laptop and a big pot of coffee, to write a piece about the mass burials in the Tomb of a Thousand Poisons. But somehow she'd heard about a recent spate of robberies of artefacts from archaeological sites and was hopelessly distracted.

'I got chatting to one of the Chinese reporters over at a looted Tang Dynasty tomb south of Xi'an,' she said. 'They think there might be a connection to the Tiger's Claw gang. Apparently they've been moving into this area lately . . .'

Ryan sighed. Why had Mum even been hanging around the crime scene in the first place? *She tells me to stay out of trouble, but she's ten times worse.* Julie Flint, investigative reporter, was attracted to criminal gangs and shady secret societies like an ant to a picnic! Over the years she'd uncovered some of the most dangerous networks on the planet. She'd nearly got herself killed in Egypt on the case of an occult group with a sideline in smuggling. She was supposed to be having a break from all that in China, just reporting on the excavation of the Tomb of a Thousand Poisons.

I should have known. Ryan thought, *that Mum would soon get bored of two-thousand-year-old misdeeds and start sniffing around for some more current villainy.*

He just wished she'd investigate something less risky. Why couldn't she be a food writer or a film critic?

'I'm going to make a few enquires,' Mum said, gulping her coffee. 'The looters might be stealing for the international black market.'

Ryan knew Mum's obsession with the underworld was all to do with Dad's disappearance. He'd gone missing in South America five and a half years ago, while tracking down a huge drug-smuggling ring that had tentacles stretching across the whole globe. She had been trying to find him ever since.

Ryan gave up on Romeo and Juliet's star-crossed romance and took out his sketchbook. He turned to a page of drawings he'd started based on the beautiful scenes that covered the coffer in the Kitchen of Eternal Life. The cranes, tigers, tortoises and peach trees were meant to be symbols of immortality, but it seemed to Ryan that they were all shadowed by death.

Tigers are almost extinct, he thought. *So are many species of crane and tortoise. And, according to Alex, even peaches have a dark side; the stones contain tiny amounts of poisonous cyanide!*

The tragic events on the film of the Dragon Path had tipped Ryan into an uncharacteristically gloomy mood. Memories of the men who'd met their deaths in that tunnel haunted his thoughts. Did their families know what had happened to them or had they waited years for them to come home? He had always believed Dad would come back one day, but suddenly he wasn't so sure. He thought about Tian

Min going to see his mother. Was she dead or alive? And then there was Cleo's grandmother, Eveline Bell.

She told us she was not much longer for this world. Returning the jade ring to the dragon might be her dying wish . . .

Ryan dropped his pencil and gazed down at his sketchbook. Somehow, he'd turned the tortoises and tigers into vampire beasts with blood dripping from their fangs. The cranes were now vultures and the half-eaten peaches were riddled with maggots.

I really *need to get out!* he thought.

'I'll go and get those batteries you wanted for your voice recorder,' he said, hurrying out of the apartment before Mum could wave *Romeo and Juliet* at him.

After an hour of aimless wandering, Ryan found himself in the narrow street he'd hurried along with Cleo to the building site only a few days earlier. He noticed the small hardware shop and remembered the batteries he'd promised to buy. Perhaps they'd have them here.

Squeezing past reels of cable, bike wheels and birdcages to the counter, Ryan found a big, lumbering boy of about his own age. He was hunched over an Xbox propped up on a cabinet containing nails, bolts and washers. He wore a black T-shirt emblazoned with an electric guitar and the words *ROCK GOD,* but his round face and gentle smile were more *overgrown-teddy bear* than rock 'n' roll.

As Ryan handed over the money for the batteries he couldn't help gazing enviously at the screen of the Xbox. Seconds later, without a word of English, the rock god had pulled up a plastic chair next to his own, and pushed a spare controller into Ryan's hands. He howled with laughter as Ryan tried to get to grips with a manic game he'd never encountered before. They were still playing *Crazy Mouse* an hour later when the rock god's grandfather came in from the workshop behind the store and chased him off to do his schoolwork.

Ryan felt a lot more cheerful as he left the shop and walked out in the late morning sunshine. Turning the corner into a small lane, he spotted a row of red lanterns and realized he was almost at Aunt Ting's noodle restaurant.

And it was almost lunchtime.

15

PROMISE

MEILIN WAS SITTING at a table outside under the red lanterns threading pieces of raw chicken onto bamboo skewers. Under her green tracksuit top she was wearing school uniform of white polo shirt and black trousers. When she saw Ryan she jumped up, smiling, and waving a kebab in each hand.

'That looks like a fun way to spend your lunch break,' he laughed, grimacing at the bowl of meat.

Meilin smiled. 'Aunt Ting is very busy.'

Ryan offered to help, even though the chicken had put him off all thoughts of lunch. He went inside to wash his hands, then pulled up a chair. As they worked she told him all about the gymnastics competition she'd taken part in the day before. She'd achieved her personal best on the beam and been placed third overall. Ryan knew nothing about gymnastics but he nodded wisely and admired the medal pinned to her collar.

Meilin paused to rearrange the kebabs on the tray.

'I always put them in groups of eight because that's the luckiest number.'

'Can I do them in sevens?' Ryan asked. 'That's *my* lucky number.'

Meilin pretended to give the matter some thought. 'Well, that's *English* luck. This is Chinese chicken, so I don't think it would work.'

They both laughed.

'Talking of luck,' Meilin said, 'what are those two charms you wear round your neck?'

Ryan showed her the St Christopher medal – a small silver disk with a picture of the patron saint of travellers carrying a child over a stream.

'My dad gave it to me not long before he disappeared.'

Then, moving on quickly before Meilin could ask any painful questions, he pointed at the scarab beetle amulet.

'Cleo gave me this one in Egypt . . .'

He broke off as Aunty Ting came hobbling out of the café, shouting so loudly that the metal kebab tray vibrated on the table.

'Have you been skipping your noodle duties again?' Ryan whispered.

Meilin cast her eyes down at the table and shook her head. 'It's about you!' she mumbled, her ears blushing as pink as the raw chicken. 'Aunty Ting is telling me not to *chase the*

114

wind by setting my sights on you because you already have a girlfriend.'

Ryan almost fell off his chair. 'She must know something I don't!'

'*Cleo,* of course!' Meilin prompted. 'She was born under a peach tree.'

Ryan was getting more confused by the second.

'It's a saying. *Born under a peach tree* means someone is very beautiful – like the blossom.'

Ryan laughed. If Cleo had spent any of her early years under a peach tree, it wouldn't have been to admire the pretty blossom. She'd have been studying photosynthesis or looking up its Latin name. As for being his girlfriend? He *had* kissed Cleo once, under a banana palm in Egypt, but it had been in the line of duty. She'd looked so horrified he'd decided against trying it again.

Aunty Ting folded her arms, glared at Meilin, tutted at Ryan and then steamed off across the street.

When she was out of sight Meilin puffed out her cheeks. 'She thinks I should get together with Gao Xin at the hardware shop.' She wagged her finger in imitation of her aunty. '*When he inherits his grandfather's business he will be a good catch for you, young lady.*' Meilin shook her head. 'Gao Xin is nice enough, but all he ever does is play computer games.'

Ryan suppressed a grin. Gao Xin was obviously the rock god he'd just been playing *Crazy Mouse* with.

'Computer games?' he said. 'Bor-*ing.*' He held up a kebab. 'You obviously need a guy who shares your interest in chicken skewering!'

Meilin giggled. 'Aunty would be even crosser with me if she knew my secret.'

'Secret?' Ryan echoed. Did Meilin lead a double life as an arms dealer or a professional wrestler?

'I'll show you.' Meilin picked up the bowl of chicken scraps and ran through the café. Ryan followed. They stopped in the kitchen to wash their hands then continued into the back yard, where Meilin moved aside a line full of washing, opened the ramshackle shed and beckoned him inside.

Behind a stack of fold-up chairs something was shifting and snuffling. Ryan's mind was conjuring up rats and giant spiders and other things that might lurk at the back of sheds when his eyes adjusted to the gloom and he made out a cardboard box in the corner. It was Bao Bao and her litter of wriggling black-and-tan puppies.

Meilin crouched down and tipped the chicken scraps onto the floor. Bao Bao gobbled them up.

'They had a security inspection at the building site after you and Cleo broke in,' she explained. 'I heard some of the builders saying that they weren't allowed to keep the puppies any more.' She bit her lip. 'If Aunty Ting finds out, I'll be for it! She doesn't believe in wasting good food on pets.' Meilin looked up at Ryan, who was stroking Bao Bao's ears. 'Why *did* you and Cleo want to look in that cave anyway?'

Ryan hesitated, uncertain how much he could give away.

'It's OK,' Meilin said. 'I'm sure you had a good reason.'

'Yes, we did. We made a promise . . . to someone . . . to do something.'

Meilin nodded seriously. 'I understand. A promise is very important. You must always keep promises.'

'Actually,' Ryan mumbled, 'we haven't done yet.'

Ryan's earlier dark mood suddenly settled over him again like a thick soggy blanket. It was the jade ring. Somehow it had become linked in his mind with the hollow ache that he'd kept so carefully locked away since Dad went missing.

As he backed out of the shed, he was sure there was only one way to put things right.

Where could Ryan have gone? Cleo wondered as she trailed down the steps out of the apartment block. She'd called at his flat twice.

Gone out for a walk, Julie had said. But he didn't even *like* walking.

She turned expectantly, hearing someone trotting down the steps behind her, but it was only Joey Zhou. Cleo pretended to be busy reading something on her phone to avoid going through that ludicrous *how you doin'* routine yet again. When she looked back out across the plaza, she saw someone approaching in the distance. Squinting into the sun, she knew straight away it was Ryan. No one else walked with that loping gait. He sort of *sailed* along. She hurried to meet him.

Ryan reached up and caught one of the huge yellow parasol-shaped leaves that were falling from the avenue of *wutong* trees.

'I've got a present for you,' he said.

Cleo frowned. 'A falling leaf? Is it meant to be lucky?'

Ryan grinned and dropped the leaf. 'Not that!' He held out a carrier bag.

Cleo took out a DVD. *'Friends, Season Five,'* she read.

'Watch and learn! Then next time Joey Zhou says *How you doin'?* you'll know what he's talking about.'

Cleo thanked him quickly, eager to move on to more important matters. 'I've been thinking,' she said. 'It's not that I believe in curses, of course, but I couldn't even focus on the Reimann hypothesis . . .'

Ryan started speaking at the same time. 'Meilin said we have to keep promises, and she's right . . .'

'What's Meilin got to do with anything?' Cleo spluttered.

'What's the Reimann hypothesis when it's at home?' Ryan asked.

There was a moment of confused silence. Then they both spoke in unison. This time their words were identical. 'We have to return the jade ring!'

Cleo nodded slowly, hardly able to believe that Ryan had been thinking the same thing. 'We owe it to Grandma.'

'And to the men who died,' Ryan added.

Cleo looked up and down the avenue to make sure nobody could overhear them. 'We won't go through that door *into* the tomb, of course.'

Ryan made a cross of his arms and reeled backwards. 'Nowhere near it! We won't even set foot in the tunnel. We'll just throw the ring inside and scarper.'

There was just one problem on Cleo's mind. 'We *did* promise we'd keep out of trouble . . .'

'Technically,' Ryan said with a grin, 'we only promised to keep out of building sites.'

Cleo cast her mind back to the conversation with their parents. Ryan was *almost* correct. 'We actually said we wouldn't do anything *like* sneaking into building sites.'

Ryan shrugged. 'From what we saw on that film, the tunnel starts in a pine forest on a mountainside. Does that sound anything *like* a building site? No! I rest my case.'

Cleo smiled, happy to let Ryan convince her. She felt as if a weight had been lifted from her shoulders, now that they had resolved to return the ring. 'But we'll have to keep this quiet from our parents. They'll only try to stop us.'

Ryan made a zipping action across his mouth. Then he made an unzipping action. 'So now we just have the minor detail of finding the top-secret tunnel entrance,' he pointed out. 'Where do we start?'

16

MEMORY

'WE START WITH some detective work,' Cleo said. 'Wait here!'

She ran back up the steps and disappeared into the apartment block.

Ryan leaned against the wall. Finding the Dragon Path was going to be a major challenge. All they had to go on so far was, (a) the tunnel led to the tomb of the First Emperor and so couldn't be too far away, and (b) from what they could see on the film, the entrance was on a slope covered with pine and rhododendron. He gazed up at the wooded flanks of Mount Li towering above the university buildings. *It must be somewhere up there*, he thought.

A plane droned over the peak on its way to Xi'an airport,

leaving a feathery contrail across the pale blue sky.

'Let's go to the computer room!'

Ryan jumped. Cleo was back, now armed with her laptop. 'What are we detecting, Sherlock?' he asked, matching her stride as they set off across the plaza.

'Harold Stubbs,' Cleo said. 'I reckon our best chance of a clue is to find out what happened to him. He obviously didn't go public about the Dragon Path – otherwise everyone in the world of archaeology would have heard about it – but he might have written *something* about it later in notes or diaries or letters . . . something that can help us locate it.'

Ryan felt a familiar buzz of excitement. This was just like old times – when they'd been investigating the disappearance of the Benben Stone together in Egypt.

'To the internet!' he declared, pushing open the double glass doors into the main building.

Ten minutes later he was feeling less upbeat. The very first result that appeared in response to Cleo's search for *HAROLD STUBBS ARCHAEOLOGIST CHINA* was an obituary, or notice of death, from the *Journal of Asian Archaeology*. Ryan stared at the screen.

'*Harold Algernon Stubbs,*' he read. '*1897–1936.*' He turned to Cleo. '1936? That can't be right. We know he made it out of the tunnel alive. We saw him breaking camp in the last scene.'

Cleo pointed to the screen, where the rest of the profile had now appeared.

'*Harold "Harry" Stubbs,*' Ryan read out in a whisper – even though they'd picked a spot well away from any of the other computer users – '*formerly of Folkestone, Kent, perished*

121

in October 1936, having become separated from his camel train during a sandstorm in the Taklamakan Desert.'

'*October* 1936,' Cleo repeated. 'Grandma said that they entered the Dragon Path at the end of summer, so Stubbs must have died just a month or so later.'

'Where's this Taklamakan place?' Ryan asked.

'The very north-west of China beyond the Gobi Desert.' Cleo looked up. 'The 1930s were a turbulent time in China. There was a civil war. Stubbs was probably trying to make his way back to England overland to escape the fighting.'

And to escape the memories of the tunnel? Ryan wondered. After surviving the crossbow and the dragons, it seemed stupendously bad luck to die in the desert a few weeks later. It sounded disturbingly like the Mummy's Curse, which was said to have afflicted Howard Carter and the other men who'd entered the tomb of Tutankhamun. Had the First Emperor wreaked revenge on Stubbs for trying to enter his tomb uninvited?

'There's nothing coming up that's remotely linked to dragons or tunnels,' Cleo muttered. 'It looks as if Stubbs took the secret to his death with him. It's so *unprofessional* not to have left any documentation . . .'

'I guess he had other things on his mind.'

Cleo closed her laptop. 'Well, that's a dead end.'

'What about the others?' Ryan suggested. 'Six men entered that tunnel.'

'We know three of them died.' Cleo counted them off on her fingers. 'Lymington and the two Chinese diggers killed by the dragons. Apart from Stubbs, that only leaves the cameraman.'

'He must have made it out alive, because the film survived,' Ryan reasoned.

'And possibly the third Chinese man,' Cleo went on. 'We don't know what happened to him. But how can we trace either of them if we don't even know their names?'

'There *was* one other person,' Ryan pointed out. 'Your grandmother. Perhaps she could help?'

'Hmm,' Cleo murmured doubtfully. 'She didn't seem to remember much.'

Ryan shrugged. 'Maybe if you told her some details that we saw on the film it might jog her memory?'

Cleo's brows scrunched together as she thought. 'You're right. Specific information could provide more efficient cues to retrieval from long-term memory.'

'Isn't that what I just said?' Ryan asked. Cleo had a knack of making the simplest idea sound complicated.

'I'm going to phone her.' Cleo pushed her chair back with a scrape that made every student in the room glare in her direction. 'Right now!'

'You do know what time it is in London?' But Ryan's question went unheard. Cleo was already bolting for the door.

Ryan followed. Cleo had elbowed through a knot of students, and was already holding her phone to her ear as she strode towards a series of ornamental ponds dotted with fountains. She stopped on a narrow curved bridge that crossed to a tiny island and spoke urgently to someone on the other end of the line.

Ryan bought a couple of pineapple kebabs from a snack cart and joined Cleo on the bridge just as she was sliding her phone back into her jeans pocket.

'How is your gran?' he asked, handing her the stick threaded with pineapple slices.

Cleo sighed. 'She seemed really confused at first. I'm worried that her cognitive function is declining.'

Ryan rested his elbows on the wooden railing and gazed down at the fat goldfish gliding among the water lilies below. 'It's three o'clock in the morning in London,' he laughed. 'No wonder she sounded *confused*. You woke her up in the middle of the night. You probably scared her half to death.'

Cleo clapped her hand over her mouth. 'Oops. I didn't think of that.' Then she smiled and nibbled a piece of pineapple. 'Actually, it might have helped. Grandma was frightened when the events in the Dragon Path took place. According to the theory of state-dependent learning, that means she should find it *easier* to remember those events when she's in the same emotional state of fear. It was in a psychology course I studied last year.'

Ryan rolled his eyes. Only on Planet Cleo could frightening the life out of old ladies be classified as *helpful*. 'So, once you'd got her quaking in terror, did she remember the name of the cameraman?'

Cleo shook her head. 'No. She just said he was French, which she told us before. Then I asked if she could remember anything about the location of the tunnel. All she could come up with was that they took the left-hand fork in the path at the rickety old bridge.'

At the word *rickety* Ryan couldn't help giving the railing a little test wobble, but this bridge seemed perfectly solid. 'Well, that's better than nothing, I suppose,' he said, trying to sound positive.

'That's not all,' Cleo said. 'Just as I was about to hang up,

124

Grandma remembered the name of one of the Chinese men.' She prodded Ryan triumphantly in the chest with her kebab stick. 'He was called Long Yi.' A piece of pineapple fell into the water. A goldfish rocketed to the surface and snapped it up. 'Which happens to be a very fitting name,' Cleo went on. '*Long* means *dragon*. Grandma said that's why it had stuck with her.'

Ryan held up a hand for a high five.

Cleo grimaced. 'Too sticky! And you haven't heard the best bit yet! Grandma said Long Yi was the youngest of the men. That's the one we *didn't* see getting killed by the dragons. Which means he might have lived to tell the tale. So, if we can just trace him . . .'

Ryan wiped his hands on his jeans. 'He'd be about three hundred years old.'

'He'd be ninety-six, actually,' Cleo fired back, 'if we assume he was about eighteen at the time of the film. But even if he's dead now, surely he would have told *someone* in his family about the Dragon Path – just like Grandma told me. So if we can track down a descendant they might know the location.'

Ryan had a sinking feeling that Cleo was about to suggest trawling through the phone book and calling everyone with the surname Long. There were nearly one and a half billion people in China! There could be thousands of Longs. His thoughts were interrupted by a trundling noise. A skinny young man in overalls was pulling a large metal trolley loaded with sheets across the paving stones. The caretaker for the guest apartments had a trolley just like that, Ryan remembered. In fact, he'd helped her with it just this morning when she'd caught the wheel on a corner of the corridor and it had capsized, sending flasks of hot water and folded towels cascading down the steps. After they'd cleared up the mess together, she'd presented him with a pack of toffees from her apron pocket and thanked him over and over in rapid-fire Mandarin. Ryan grinned. He'd thought he would never get away from Mrs . . . *Oh, that's freaky,* he thought. 'Isn't the caretaker for our building called Mrs Long?'

Cleo looked up from gazing into the pond. 'Oh, yes, you're right. But it's a fairly common name. It would be an extraordinary coincidence if she were related to the man in the film.'

'Yeah, it's a *long* shot.' Ryan waited for Cleo to laugh, but she just nodded seriously. 'A *Long* shot?' he repeated. 'Get it?'

But Cleo was already hurrying back across the bridge.

'Why do I bother?' Ryan muttered to her back.

'We have to start somewhere,' Cleo said over her shoulder. 'Come on! Let's find Mrs Long.'

Finding Mrs Long turned out to be more of a challenge than Cleo had expected. After searching half the campus, it turned out that she only worked at the university in the mornings. But just when Cleo thought they would have to wait a whole day, one of the gardeners mentioned that Mrs Long had a second job. She worked as a cleaner at the Terracotta Army Museum a couple of afternoons a week.

'Result!' Ryan said with a grin. 'Let's go.'

Cleo hesitated. 'But she might not be there today.'

But Ryan had no such doubts. 'Hey, live dangerously. We've got a fifty-fifty chance.'

'Fifty-fifty?' Cleo echoed.

'Yeah – either she's there or she's not.'

Cleo shook her head. She couldn't tell whether Ryan was joking or whether he really had no concept of basic probability theory. 'If the museum is open six days a week and Mrs Long works two afternoons,' she explained, 'the chance that she'll be there now is one in three. That's thirty-three point three recurring per cent . . .'

'Oh, well!' Ryan laughed. 'I'm feeling lucky. And anyway,' he added, 'I've been dying to see these world-famous warriors ever since we got here.'

17

QUESTIONS

THE JOURNEY TO the Terracotta Army Museum only took twenty minutes. They spilled out of the overcrowded bus, and followed the throngs of tourists past restaurants and snack bars and shops selling replica clay warriors, along with panda hats, bubble wands and balloons. There were jade stalls too, with thousands of amulets, pendants and bracelets on display. The bracelets looked just like the dragon ring in Cleo's pocket, but she suspected most were imitations, made of dyed resin or quartz.

At last they reached the entrance gate, bought their tickets and walked through the metal detector into an open paved square, landscaped with clipped bushes and flower beds, and surrounded by huge buildings constructed of pale yellow-grey stone.

'That building with the curved roof like an aircraft hangar is Pit Number One,' Cleo told Ryan. 'It's where they've found most of the warriors. There are thousands of them, and the excavation work is still in progress.'

Ryan was about to head off to join the queue, but Cleo pulled him back. Sightseeing could wait. First they had to find Mrs Long. If she was a descendant of Long Yi, the man on the film, she might just know something about the location of the Dragon Path tunnel. *And that,* Cleo thought, *would take us one step closer to returning the jade ring.*

'Let's try the museum hall first,' she said, pointing to an imposing building with a sweep of stone steps flanked by two squat square towers. 'Cleaners are more likely to be working in there at the moment. It'll be too crowded in the Pit building.'

As they walked through the black glass doors of the grand building where thousands of bronze weapons and other artefacts from the digs were on display, they were greeted by a powerful smell.

'Sodium hypochlorite,' Cleo murmured. 'Commonly known as . . .'

Ryan sniffed and pulled a face. 'Bleach.'

Cleo nodded. They followed their noses along a corridor to an area near the toilets, which had had been cordoned off with orange cones. A stout middle-aged lady in a blue nylon tabard was pushing a mop across the marble-effect floor.

'Oh, yeah,' Ryan whispered. 'That's Mrs Long. I told you I was feeling lucky!'

Luck, Cleo thought, *had nothing to do with it. It was simply*

129

a one-in-three chance. She stationed herself next to the mop bucket and cleared her throat. 'Er, excuse me . . .'

Mrs Long glanced up and down the corridor as if expecting trouble, but when she saw Ryan she broke into a radiant smile and held out her hands.

'My good friend, Ryan!' she exclaimed in Mandarin. She patted her fluffy permed curls. 'Oooh, you are a lucky girl to have such a charming young man on your arm,' she told Cleo. 'He's such a gentleman. And so tall and handsome too.' She wagged her finger. 'Don't let him get away! You will have a long and happy life together.'

Ryan smiled politely. 'What's she saying?' he asked through his teeth.

'Oh, just hello, how are you, that kind of thing.' There was no way Cleo was going to let Ryan in on Mrs Long's matchmaking nonsense. He'd never stop going on about it! But she couldn't help smiling. Ryan only knew two words of Mandarin – and he couldn't even pronounce *those* – but somehow he seemed to have befriended half of China!

Mrs Long swirled her mop in the bucket and smiled at Ryan. 'You wouldn't *believe* how far a child's sick can travel on polished stone.'

Ryan just kept grinning like crazy.

Mrs Long looked a little puzzled at his enthusiastic response to vomit distribution and turned back to Cleo. 'What can I do for you?'

Cleo fell silent. How was she going to enquire whether any member of Mrs Long's family happened to have had a narrow escape from a dragon-infested tunnel – without sounding clinically insane? Now she tried to put it into words, Cleo realized just how unlikely it was that Mrs Long had any connection to the man in the eighty-year-old film. Never mind a one-in-three chance. This was more like one in three *billion*! *But,* she told herself, *even the lowest-probability events happen sometimes. People win the lottery. Asteroids collide with Earth.*

'Mrs Long, has anyone in your family ever worked with any archaeologists?' she blurted awkwardly.

Mrs Long wiped her glasses on her apron. 'Why do you ask, dear?'

It was, Cleo realized, a perfectly reasonable question. She remembered Ryan's instructions for cover stories. *Keep it true but vague.* 'My grandmother lived near here as a child,' she said. 'We're trying to get in touch with someone she remembers.' Cleo felt rather pleased with herself. That had actually sounded quite smooth. 'He was called Long Yi,' she went on, 'and we think he worked with some archaeologists in the 1930s. We wondered if he might be an ancestor of yours.'

Mrs Long 's eyes lit up. 'Oh, yes,' she said, leaning on her mop. 'That sounds like my lot, all right. The men in my family have always worked with archaeologists. It goes back generations: diggers, guides, scouts, you name it.'

Cleo stared at Mrs Long, hardly able to believe her ears. The asteroid had landed! She beamed a triumphant grin at Ryan.

'Yes, dear,' Mrs Long continued. 'I've been tracing our family history, you see, so I know all about it. My brother helped when they were first excavating the pits here in the 1970s, you know. That's how I got this job. He put in a good word for me. And my grandfather, now he was involved with a dig up in . . .'

She paused for breath and Cleo took her chance to get a word in. 'Did any of them work with men called Lymington and Stubbs?'

Mrs Long frowned and twisted the mop in the bucket as if to help squeeze out the memory.

'English. 1930s,' Cleo prompted. She thought she might explode with suspense. She made a *this-could-be-it* face at Ryan. He grinned back and held up crossed fingers.

'Ooh, yes, dear, I do remember now. One of my uncles, Long Yi, did a lot of digging with them on all sorts of sites round this area.' Mrs Long glanced past Cleo. Her face clouded. 'Oh, no, the supervisor's coming. I'll be in trouble if he catches me chin-wagging.' She began swiping the mop at the floor at double speed. 'He's got guards with him too,' she muttered.

Cleo could see her chance slipping away. She forgot all about the cover story. 'Did your uncle tell you about any of the places they went?' she asked, raising her voice over the swish of the mop. 'Any unusual tombs or secret tunnels?'

Mrs Long didn't look up. 'You need to talk to my cousin, Long Jian,' she said. 'Uncle Long Yi was his father. He'll know more than me.'

'Where can I find him?' Cleo was almost shouting with urgency.

'He's got a pomegranate orchard. Eastern foothills of Mount Li.' Mrs Long was now on her knees, scrubbing at a stubborn mark. 'He's won prizes for his *Three Whites* pomegranates,' she added proudly.

Cleo turned to Ryan and barely stopped herself hugging him in delight.

'Success?' Ryan asked.

Cleo nodded. 'We've just won the lottery!'

She didn't say anything else because at that moment two men in military uniform grasped them both firmly by the arms and bundled them out of the building.

'What on earth did you say to her?' Ryan whispered, as they were frog-marched down the steps and across the square.

The plan had been for Cleo to strike up a casual conversation and see whether Mrs Long had heard of Lymington and Stubbs. But surely *that* wouldn't have triggered a major security alert? *Then again*, Ryan thought, *casual conversation wasn't exactly Cleo's strong point*. She'd probably just dived in and asked the cleaning lady if she knew of any good secret passages into the First Emperor's tomb.

'You didn't mention Henry VIII's twin brother, did you?' he whispered.

'Of course not!' Cleo snapped.

They were nearing a small concrete building at the side of the museum. Ryan couldn't read the sign over the door, but no doubt it said something like *SECURITY,* possibly followed by *YOU ARE NOW OFFICIALLY IN DEEP TROUBLE.*

The guard holding Cleo began shouting into a radio. Cleo listened for a moment and turned to Ryan. 'They seem to think we're journalists,' she said. 'Asking too many questions about archaeological sites. He says it must be to do with some tomb robberies that have been going on ...' She paused and listened again. 'Now he's saying we might actually be members of some violent gang that's behind all the robberies.'

She struggled against the guard's grip. 'How ridiculous! Do I *look* like a gangster?'

Suddenly Ryan understood. It must be the Tiger's Claw gang his mum had told him about. *No wonder the guards' reaction is so over the top. The museum is on red alert in case the robbers strike here.*

Cleo's guard – whose camo-patterned uniform was stretched across beefy shoulders and tree-trunk arms – hooked his radio back on his belt and pushed Cleo into the security building. Ryan felt a nudge in the back and followed. His guard was older and thinner and his uniform smelled of stale garlic.

Once inside what looked like a cross between a waiting room and an office, the younger guard took a grey plastic tray from a shelf. 'Empty your pockets!' he ordered in English.

Ryan turned out a handful of change, his bus and museum tickets and his phone from his jeans pockets and placed them in the tray.

The guard thrust his open palm towards Cleo.

Cleo's face had turned the colour of dust. One by one she passed over her phone, her purse, her ticket and . . . she glanced at Ryan, eyes wide with trepidation . . . the jade ring!

Ryan felt as if he'd just been hit in the stomach by a bowling ball. No wonder Cleo looked so worried. She had no proof that the jade ring belonged to her. This wasn't going to look good. *If we were* trying *to pass ourselves off as a pair of tomb raiders, having priceless Qin Dynasty artefacts stuffed in our pockets would be the perfect way to go about it!* he thought.

The older guard twitched his eyebrows in surprise and placed the ring in the tray with the other personal effects. Then the muscly one stabbed a finger at a row of scuffed plastic chairs along a wall plastered with posters. *Probably warnings to look out for dangerous criminals like us,* Ryan thought as he backed into a chair. Cleo slumped next to him.

Ryan ran through the situation in his mind. *If we're lucky, the guards will assume the jade ring is just a cheap bangle from one of the souvenir stands. And they'll realize we're too young to be gang members – eventually! But first there'll be hours of questions. No doubt they'll phone our parents and drag them down here before we're allowed to go. We're already on a warning for the building-site incident. We'll be grounded until the end of time!*

And if we're not lucky? The security guys will recognize the jade ring as a genuine two-thousand-year-old Qin Dynasty relic.

Would anyone believe their story that Cleo's grandmother gave it to her, having kept it a secret for over eighty years?

I've got a bad feeling about this, Ryan thought. *I wonder what the average jail term is for tomb robbing in China.*

18

WARRIORS

RYAN SCANNED THE room for escape routes. It didn't take
long. The only way out was the door through which they'd
entered and the two guards were standing in front of it. He
was running through increasingly desperate distraction plans
– shout 'Fire!', fake a heart attack, pretend an alien life form
was bursting out of his chest – when the door flew open and
a young woman stumbled into the room and collapsed into
the arms of the beefy guard.

'She's a teacher,' Cleo whispered after listening for a
moment. 'She's here with a school group. One of the kids has
gone missing . . .'

The guard was holding the hysterical teacher at arm's

length, barking at her to calm down, when she screamed a name. Suddenly the guards were yelling in panic too.

'*Chan Xiao-Ping!*' the teacher screamed again. There was more yelling and screaming. Then they all hurtled outside.

Cleo jumped to her feet. 'They think it's a kidnap. It sounds like Chan Xiao-Ping's from a VIP family. His father's a politician and his mother's a Hollywood actress.'

Grabbing their possessions from the plastic tray, Ryan ran to the door and peeped out. Cleo was right behind him. The younger guard was trying to round up the children, while the older one was calling for reinforcements.

'Now!' Ryan hissed. He eased open the door and together they bolted for the exit gate. They were halfway there when he felt Cleo tugging at his T-shirt.

'They've seen us!' she panted.

Ryan turned to see the guards sprinting after them, shouting into their radios as they ran. He looked back to the exit gate. It was swarming with guards now too. He made a split-second decision and changed direction. Pulling Cleo by the hand, he raced towards the crowd flooding into the huge Pit Number One building. They barged through a group of Japanese ladies, a Russian family and a troop of American teenagers, burrowing their way to the centre of the pack.

Swept along on the tide of tourists, they soon found themselves inside the building, on a congested walkway that led around the edge of a vast rectangular earthen pit. When Ryan finally dared to stop and look over the railing he was so stunned that he forgot they were on the run and simply gazed in awe.

In the pit, which was bigger than a football pitch, stood row upon row of life-sized soldiers, all the same sandy colour as the earth that surrounded them. Ryan had known, of course, that the Terracotta Army consisted of thousands of clay soldiers. But knowing and seeing were two very different things. There were just so many of them, staring steadfastly ahead in perfect battle formation, and they looked so real, each one individual, and all poised to fight for the First Emperor in the afterlife . . .

Suddenly remembering that they were in danger, Ryan popped his head up above the masses to look for signs of pursuit. To his dismay, there were guards moving in every direction. He swiftly ducked back down near the railing, wondering how to tell Cleo that he hadn't exactly fine-detailed the next phase of his *run-back-inside-the-building* plan yet.

That's when he realized that Cleo wasn't there.

The spot where she'd been crouching was now filled by two little girls posing for their parents' camera.

'Cleo?' he whisper-shouted, panic careening around in his chest. Had the guards somehow snatched her from his side?

'I'm here!'

The feeble cry came from below his feet. He looked over the side of the walkway. Cleo was dangling by her fingertips over the edge of the pit.

Ryan knelt and leaned down to her. 'What are you *doing?*' he hissed.

'I didn't fall down here on purpose,' Cleo hissed back. 'I lost my footing and slipped under the rail.' She groaned in pain. 'Do something. I can't hold on much longer.'

Ryan glanced around. A group of archaeologists were at work in the pit, excavating more warriors that were still half-buried in the clay like real-life soldiers lying in a muddy trench. Any moment, one of them would look up and see Cleo and raise the alarm. The guards would be on them in seconds. Ryan grabbed Cleo's wrist and yanked it upwards until she could grasp hold of the rail. Then he caught hold of her other wrist and pulled, bundling her up and over the side.

'Ouch!' she gasped, as her hip and ribs bumped over the edge of the pit and the concrete walkway.

'Sorry!' Ryan muttered. There'd been no time for style or finesse. He dragged her to her feet and merged back into the crowd.

Ryan's eyes flicked from side to side. Every time he spotted a guard, he and Cleo shrank back behind a human shield of tourists. Somehow they made it to the exit at the other end of the building. Still hidden in the heart of the crowd, they streamed out of Pit Number One and into the museum hall – where the faint hospital-like scent of bleach lingered in the air. They were passing a bank of display cabinets when Ryan spotted the reflection of two more guards in the tinted glass. He pulled Cleo back and they pressed themselves against the side of the cabinet. As they waited for the danger to pass, Ryan slid his eyes towards the display of magnificent bronze weapons – swords, halberds, crossbow bolts – wishing he could take a closer look. He read the label in English: *Qin Dynasty swordsmiths used advanced metalworking techniques. The bronze swords have stayed sharp and rust-free for thousands of years.*

Ryan peeped round the corner of the cabinet to see one of the guards staring straight at him. His heart flipped over. *This is it,* he thought. *We're cornered. Any second now, that guard's going to give chase or call on his radio, and we've had it.* But the guard didn't move. He just kept staring, his eyes like laser beams. A chill crept over Ryan's skin like the scuttle of a spider.

A voice suddenly blared out in English over the PA system.

'Everyone, please stay where you are. There has been a security incident.'

People instantly began to mill around, asking each other what was happening. Amid the chaos, guards were closing in from all sides. Ryan looked at Cleo. Cleo nodded. They were going to have to run for it. Together they darted across the hall, pushed through the nearest door and slammed it shut behind them.

They found themselves in a dark cupboard that smelled like one of Mrs Long's wet mops. Ryan cursed as he tripped over a broom.

'Agghh!' came a reply. Ryan's heart almost exploded with shock. He'd landed on top of a warm wriggling leg and it didn't belong to Cleo; she was behind him, feeling around on the wall for the light switch. The light flicked on. Ryan screwed up his eyes and saw that the leg was attached to a small bespectacled boy in school uniform.

'Chan Xiao-Ping!' Cleo exclaimed.

Of course, Ryan thought. *The missing boy.* He was huddled in the corner, with a mountain of sweet wrappers and a *Dragon Ball* comic on his lap, a torch in his hand and a terrified look on his face.

Ryan smiled at him. 'Don't worry, mate!' he said. 'We won't hurt you. What happened?'

To his surprise the little boy replied in English. 'Kang was being a bully and trying to steal all my sweets. I sneaked in here to eat them on my own, but I couldn't get out. There is no handle on the door.'

Ryan closed his eyes. Just when he'd thought things couldn't get any worse! *We're trapped. And when someone does eventually find us we'll be arrested for kidnap as well as tomb robbing.*

He turned back to Cleo. She stepped forward, then stopped short, her head yanked backwards. One end of her long white scarf had caught in the door. As she reached to tug it free, Ryan lunged and, in one move, pulled Cleo's hand away from her scarf and pushed at the door.

'What are you *doing*?' Cleo spluttered. 'Trying to strangle me?'

'*Yes!*' Ryan breathed as the door moved.

'Thanks!' Cleo muttered.

'Not *yes, I'm trying to strangle you,*' Ryan laughed. '*Yes, we can get out of here!* Look, one of the tassels has got stuck in the latch. It's stopped the door closing properly.'

Chan Xiao-Ping jumped up. When he reached the door, he turned back for a moment. 'Who are you, anyway?' he asked.

Ryan glanced at the *Dragon Ball* comic the boy was still clutching. 'We're on a top-secret mission,' he said. 'Just like Goku and Bulma.'

Chan Xiao-Ping nodded seriously. 'You can trust me. I won't give you away.'

'Good man!' Ryan held his hand up for a high five. 'Now go and tell the guards you are safe. Your teacher is very worried.'

Ryan and Cleo waited a moment and then peeped out. All the guards were gathered around the little boy. They slipped out of the door and speed-walked towards the exit without looking back.

19

POMEGRANATES

CLEO WAS RUNNING from a dragon through a dark labyrinth. She had to find the jade ring. It held the secret to immortality. A hole was opening up in the ground ahead of her. She couldn't go forward. She couldn't go back. She felt the heat of the dragon's breath on her neck and then she was falling. She could hear Ryan calling her.

'Cleo! Cleo!'

She jolted awake and lay staring at the ceiling fan, cold sweat pricking her skin.

Ryan was knocking on her bedroom door. 'Cleo! It's nearly nine o'clock,' he shouted. 'I thought we were going for a bike ride!'

Cleo jumped out of bed, catching her foot in the duvet and pitching headlong onto the rug. 'I'll be with you in a minute,' she called.

She took a deep breath and waited for the terror of the dream to subside. Cleo didn't believe that dreams had deep and complex hidden meanings, of course. They were simply the brain's way of sifting through the day's experiences to help store memories. But, however you looked at it, that dream had clearly been triggered by having to hand over the jade ring to the guards at the museum. That dreadful moment had felt like being trapped in a labyrinth and falling down a hole all at the same time.

Coming home on the bus, Ryan had joked that the jade ring had turned out to be lucky after all; it had summoned up the lost-child emergency to distract the guards. Cleo wasn't convinced. She glanced at Grandma's jade ring on her bedside table. She didn't believe in bad luck any more than good, but its silent green presence had begun to torment her somehow. She'd be glad when it was safely back with the dragons and she could forget all about it.

Cleo stood up and headed for the shower. She'd agreed with Ryan that they would set off on their bikes at nine. They weren't planning just *any* bike ride. They were bound for the famous pomegranate orchards in search of Mrs Long's cousin, Long Jian. According to Mrs Long's story at the Terracotta Army Museum, Long Jian's father had worked with Cedric Lymington and Harold Stubbs as a young man in the 1930s. He *had* to be the third Chinese digger in the Dragon Path film – the man Grandma remembered as Long Yi. As the water splashed over her, Cleo felt more and more optimistic. Long Jian was bound to have heard stories from his father about his adventures as a young man. Surely he'd know *something* about the location of the tunnel.

Cleo and Ryan were soon pedalling out of the campus on the bikes they'd hired from the university store the evening before. They took a short cut past high-rise blocks of student rooms, each with a small balcony where lines of washing hung out to dry like multi-coloured bunting, and were soon weaving through the busy Lintong traffic.

Once they'd left the suburbs, they began to climb into the eastern foothills of Mount Li, past small houses, shops and cafés. Three-wheeled motorbikes, tractors and vans buzzed up and down the winding road, their trailers laden with pomegranates, plums, peaches and pears. There were orchards everywhere. Cleo soon spotted the first pomegranate trees. The bright red fruit were as round and glossy as apples in a picture from a fairy tale, among leaves that matched the darkest shade of green in the jade ring in her pocket. She braked and hopped down from her bike. Ryan drew up alongside her.

They bought some peaches at a roadside fruit stall and asked the old lady in charge if she knew of Long Jian. She hooked a thumb towards the road and nodded. 'A little way farther up.'

Three fruit stalls – and three bags of fruit – later, Cleo and Ryan had heard the words, 'A little way farther up,' three more times. It was a sunny morning, and cycling up the steep mountain road was hot, tiring work.

'Are you sure they're not playing a joke on us?' Ryan

grumbled. He shaded his eyes and looked up at the summit of Mount Li towering above them. 'We'll reach the top and some little old lady will point to the sky and say "Just a little way farther up".'

But at their next stop – a tiny garage with a single petrol pump outside – the man in charge looked up from the engine of a motor-trike and wiped his hands down his blue overalls. 'Sure, I know old Long Jian,' he said, kicking the front tyre. 'This is his vehicle, in fact. I'm about to take it back to him. I'll give you a lift.'

Cleo and Ryan locked up their bikes and climbed gratefully into the trailer. The garage owner revved the motor, and they roared out into the road.

'Have you come to talk to Long Jian about the Pomegranate Festival next week?' he shouted, merrily beeping the horn at a donkey cart they'd missed by millimetres.

'Er, yes, that's right,' Cleo shouted back, although she'd never heard of the Pomegranate Festival. 'Is it an ancient Chinese tradition?'

Their driver laughed so hard he nearly swerved into an oncoming lorry. 'It was invented by the tourist board about twenty years ago. There's a parade. And a pretty girl plays the part of the pomegranate fairy.' He twisted round and eyed Cleo up and down. 'You'd make a *lovely* pomegranate fairy!' He took his hands off the handlebars and made a square with his fingers as if taking her photo. 'You'd have your picture in the local newspaper!'

'What's he saying?' Ryan asked.

Cleo had never been so relieved that Ryan didn't understand Mandarin. *If he knew I was being talent-spotted as a pomegranate fairy,* she thought, *he'd never stop teasing me.*

'Oh, just some jokes about pomegranates,' she said vaguely. 'They wouldn't really translate into English very well.'

They bounced along a rutted track and pulled up in the gateway to an orchard. The garage owner cut the engine. There was a sudden hush, broken only by the buzz of bees and the voices of fruit pickers teetering on ladders among the trees and packing pomegranates into baskets slung over the backs of small mountain ponies. The jammy smell of warm fruit blended with the diesel fumes from the motor-trike. Near the gate an old man was sorting pomegranates into flat boxes. He wore a shapeless black cap and, in spite of the heat, a thick black woollen jacket.

The garage owner threw the keys to the old man. 'I've brought you these two youngsters as well,' he called. With that he turned and wandered off back down the track.

'Hello, Mr Long,' Cleo said, flashing him her best smile. 'Are you busy getting ready for the festival?' She was feeling quietly confident about her new-found conversational skills after her success with Mrs Long at the museum, and was almost hopping from foot to foot with excitement. Any second now, Long Jian would be telling them all about his father's work with Lymington and Stubbs, including stories about exactly where they'd found a mysterious tunnel full of dragons . . .

Mr Long didn't look up from checking his motor-trike over.

Perhaps he's deaf, Cleo thought, glancing at the tufts of white hair protruding from the large ears sticking out from beneath his black cap. 'Can you hear me?' she bellowed.

Long Jian nodded but didn't say a word. Cleo shot Ryan a despairing look.

'Try buttering him up a bit,' he suggested. 'Say something nice about the pomegranates.'

For once Cleo's mind was a blank. She couldn't think of *anything* to say about pomegranates, nice or otherwise. Then she remembered Mrs Long's parting words, just before the guards swooped in. 'Er, we heard that you grow the best *Three Whites* pomegranates in Lintong?'

It worked! Long Jian smiled. He took a pale pink pomegranate from a basket and broke it open. The seeds and flesh were almost white. 'They are very sweet. You can try one.'

Cleo nibbled at a piece.

'I grow seventeen varieties,' the old man said proudly. 'Try this one.' He picked out several huge red pomegranates, cutting them open with his penknife and holding them out for sampling.

'Just ask him about Lymington and Stubbs,' Ryan muttered through a mouthful of pomegranate seeds. 'If I have to eat one more piece of fruit I'm going to be sick.'

Cleo couldn't resist. 'My friend says the pomegranate is really delicious,' she 'translated' to Mr Long.

The old man smiled and selected an even bigger pomegranate. 'Very good!' he exclaimed, pressing it into Ryan's hand. Ryan's face turned whiter than the flesh of a *Three Whites*. He ducked down and, for an awful moment, Cleo thought he really was going to throw up. *And then we'll never get Long Jian to tell us anything,* she thought crossly. But instead Ryan grabbed his backpack and pulled out his sketchbook.

'Tell Mr Long that this pomegranate is just too beautiful to eat,' he said. 'I'm going to draw it instead!' With that, he parked himself under a tree and started work.

'So your friend is an artist!' Long Jian looked delighted at this turn of events. 'I will ask my granddaughter to bring us tea.' He hobbled away to a ramshackle hut beyond the gate and shouted some orders. When he returned he pulled up a crate, sat next to Ryan and watched his every pen stroke.

Cleo hovered at the old man's shoulder. 'I heard that your family are famous for something else as well as excellent pomegranates,' she ventured. 'Like working with foreign archaeological teams?'

'Hmm? What's that?' Long Jian tore his eyes away from Ryan's picture and peered up at her.

'Your father?' Cleo went on. 'He worked with some English archaeologists?'

Long Jian scowled. 'No. You must have the wrong person.'

Cleo felt her stomach churn, and it wasn't just from the excess of fructose and fibre from all the plums, peaches and pomegranates she'd eaten. This *couldn't* be right. Mrs Long had sounded so sure.

'He was a digger for Cedric Lymington and Harold Stubbs?' she insisted, forgetting all about conversational skills. 'You *must* remember.'

Long Jian adjusted his cap over his oversized ears. 'Wherever did you get such an idea?'

'From your cousin, Mrs Long,' Cleo said. 'She told us that—'

The old man held up a hand to stop her. 'Long Dao-Ming!' he snorted. 'You shouldn't listen to anything that old gossip tells you. She thinks it makes her sound important to boast about her family connections.' Long Jian shook his head. 'My father had *nothing* to do with any foreign archaeologists. He died years ago.' He tapped his temple. 'He was a little crazy.' He looked up at the sound of rattling crockery. 'Ah, here comes the tea.'

Cleo turned round. Standing behind her, holding a large tray laden with teapot, cups and cakes, was a familiar figure in a lime-green tracksuit.

'But . . . how . . . what?' Cleo was so confused she couldn't even speak. Long Jian's story was completely different to the one that Mrs Long had told them at the museum. One of them had to be lying. But which one? And *why*? And, on top of that, now Wu Meilin had just strolled onto the scene!

Ryan looked up from his sketchbook. 'Hey! Meilin!' he said, smiling, as if it were perfectly normal that the girl from the noodle shop had suddenly appeared out of thin air with a tea tray.

'You've met my granddaughter?' Mr Long asked.

Cleo found her voice. 'Yes, at Aunty Ting's restaurant.'

'Long Jian is my mum's father,' Meilin said in English. 'I come up here to help Grandfather whenever I can.' She set the tea things out on a small table and offered round a plate of sticky rice cakes. Cleo almost groaned out loud. She couldn't eat another thing. She was hot and tired and queasy. And she was fed up. She'd thought they'd won the lottery when they'd found Mrs Long and her connection to Long Yi, the man in the Dragon Path tunnel. But it had all turned out to be a wild-goose chase. She knew it would be rude to leave without eating or drinking anything but she had to escape. She shot Ryan a *let's-get-out-of-here* look.

But Ryan looked in no mood to leave. He was chatting with Meilin and reaching for a cake. 'These look great. I'm starving.'

Cleo couldn't believe her eyes. Ten minutes ago Ryan was so full he was threatening to throw up! Then Meilin offered him a cake and he was suddenly starving! And now he was presenting his masterpiece – a composition of three pomegranates in a basket in traditional Chinese style – to Long Jian. 'It's for you.'

The old man slapped him on the back and pumped his arm up and down in a marathon handshake.

Well, Cleo thought, *if Ryan would rather stay here with his new friends, I'll just go without him*. She was about to get up when she felt an explosion of tingling pain all over her fingers. *Red ants!* She leaped up, flapping and slapping her hands to shake them off.

Ryan laughed.

It was the last straw.

Cleo turned on her heel and marched off down the track.

20

LIES

WHEN RYAN KNOCKED on the door of the McNeils' apartment that evening he felt a little apprehensive. If Cleo was in anything like her earlier mood she'd bite his head off. He still couldn't figure out why she'd suddenly flipped at the pomegranate orchard, but she'd stomped – and then pedalled – in stormy silence, all the way home.

He knew he shouldn't have laughed at the ant dance, but Cleo had just looked so funny jigging about as if doing a high-speed Macarena. He *had* run after her and apologized. And, anyway, this had to be about more than a few ants. Cleo wasn't the kind of girl to throw a wobbly over creepy-crawlies.

Cleo's mum, Lydia, came to the door, a bulb of garlic in one hand and a knife in the other, and ushered Ryan into the kitchen. Cleo's dad was chopping spring onions and Alex Shawcross was at the sink gutting a large carp.

'We've got Professor Han and Joey Zhou joining us for dinner,' Lydia said. 'I've just called your mum and she's coming over too. We can all eat together.'

The mention of Joey Zhou reminded Ryan of the sudden disappearance of their former guide. 'Have you heard anything from Tian Min?' he asked Alex.

Alex wiped her forehead with the back of her hand. 'No. I've tried calling him, but his phone's always switched off. It's rather a shame. He said he would take me on a tour of the city wall in Xi'an. Such a sweetie . . .'

'Yeah,' Ryan agreed. 'We were going to go to the comic book shop.'

Pete McNeil reached for some more spring onions. 'Poor lad. His mother must be very ill.'

'*Very,*' Ryan said darkly. 'Tian Min told me she was dead.'

Alex frowned down at the fish intestines in the sink. 'Now you mention it, he told me that too. He said something about visiting her grave. Goodness, that does seem a bit fishy.' She looked up from the carp and giggled. 'Sorry! That was a rather unfortunate choice of word!' Then she was serious again. 'I hope he's not in any kind of trouble.'

Lydia raised her eyebrows at Ryan. 'Talking of *trouble,* Cleo's in the living room. Have you two fallen out or something?'

Ryan shrugged. 'I wish I knew.'

Cleo was curled in a ball on the sofa hugging a cushion and scowling at the television. 'Hey, is that the *Friends* DVD I got?' Ryan asked, flopping down next to her. 'Funny or what?'

Cleo moved the cushion so that it made a barrier between them.

'How are those ant bites?'

Cleo pointed her toe at a packet of antihistamine tablets on the coffee table.

Ryan watched the DVD for a moment. Joey had a Thanksgiving turkey stuck on his head. 'Oh, come on, you can't say that's not funny!'

Cleo laughed in spite of herself. 'Oh, all right, it's a *tiny* bit funny. Although,' she added after a pause, 'there's a serious risk of salmonella poisoning.'

Ryan was baffled. 'From ant bites?'

Cleo hit him with the cushion. 'No! From putting a raw turkey on your head!'

Ryan laughed. They watched in silence for a few minutes. Then Cleo drew up her knees and rested her chin on them.

'I was so sure we were on the brink of finding the Dragon Path,' she sighed. 'Until Long Jian denied that his father had ever been *near* an archaeologist, let alone worked with Lymington and Stubbs. Mrs Long must have made the whole thing up. But why would she do that?'

Ryan shrugged. 'Maybe Mrs Long was telling the truth and old Pomegranate Man was the one telling porkies. He did have the ears.'

'Ears?' Cleo asked.

'Didn't you notice? They were like satellite dishes – just like the young guy in the film with Lymington and Stubbs. I could have sworn there was a family resemblance.' Ryan grinned. 'Meilin must have got her looks from the other side of the family.'

Cleo frowned. 'Talking of Meilin, don't you think it's weird that she turned up at the orchard today?'

Ryan wondered what Cleo was on about. 'Yeah, visiting an elderly relative,' he said sarcastically. 'That's highly suspicious behaviour.'

'On a Thursday? Why would she go in the middle of a school day?' Cleo stared at the TV screen, but Ryan could tell she wasn't really watching. 'I think someone's been following us,' she said at last. 'And,' she added, fixing Ryan with a warning glare, *'don't* tell me I'm just being paranoid after what happened in Egypt.'

Ryan threw up his hands in surrender. 'I wasn't going to! In fact, I've noticed it too, but I kept telling myself I was imagining it. I felt it when we were at the park eating sweet potatoes.'

Cleo's eyes widened. 'That's right. I felt it then too.'

'And then at the Terracotta Army Museum.'

Cleo laughed. 'Well, we *were* being followed at the museum. Every guard in the place was after us!'

'It wasn't just that!' Ryan told her about the strange incident of the guard with the laser eyes. 'But I'm sure it's nothing to do with Meilin,' he said. 'I'm starting to wonder if it might be this Tiger's Claw gang that Mum's been looking into . . .' He hesitated before putting into words the worrying possibility – the one he'd been doing his best not to think about. 'What if they've heard us talking somewhere and they know that we're looking for the Dragon Path tunnel?'

Cleo clapped her hand over her mouth. 'Of course! They think we might lead them to a secret entrance to the First Emperor's tomb, and then they can plunder it for treasure.' Then she gave a bleak sort of snort. 'Not that there's much chance of that! We're at a dead end. I'll probably end up taking Grandma's jade ring back to London with me.'

As a show of moral support, Ryan gave Cleo's knee something between a pat and a squeeze. 'We'll figure it out. But from now on we should be more careful that nobody overhears us.'

Cleo nodded. 'Leading the tomb robbers to the tunnel would be the worst catastrophe possible.'

Suddenly the door swung open. Ryan sprang back and whipped round, his heart pounding, as if he were about to be set upon by the Tiger's Claw gang then and there.

But it was only the inimitable quiff of Joey Zhou, closely followed by the rest of him. 'Cool! *Friends*!' he cried, throwing himself into an armchair. 'This is one of my favourite episodes!' When there was no reply, he picked up on the awkward silence and winked at Ryan. 'Uh-oh, I'm not *disturbing* anything, am I?'

Yes, you are, Ryan thought, *but not what you think!* 'Of course not,' he laughed. Swiftly changing the subject, he diverted Joey with an in-depth debate on the all-time best *Friends* episode until they were called to eat.

Dinner was a lively affair, as they all squashed round the kitchen table and demolished the delicious fish. Ryan forgot all about the creepy sensation of being spied upon by unknown eyes. Even Cleo cheered up and argued happily with Alex about the position of the carp's Weberian ossicles – whatever *those* were. That was until Professor Han brought up a subject that made Ryan drop his chopsticks.

'I heard they had a big security alert at the Terracotta Army Museum yesterday,' she remarked. 'Apparently there were some suspicious characters sizing the place up for a break-in.'

Ryan picked up his chopsticks again. He felt as conspicuous as a puffer fish that had suddenly ballooned to ten times its normal size. He didn't dare look at Cleo.

'Ooh, I bet that was the Tiger's Claw gang,' Mum said. 'They've definitely moved into this area. Their claw "tag" has been found at several crime scenes.'

Ryan thought they were off the hook. But then Cleo's mum pointed her chopsticks at him. 'You two were there yesterday, weren't you? Did you notice anything going on?'

'Just a scare with a missing child,' Ryan answered as breezily as he could. 'They found him hiding in a cupboard.'

'I have that problem with my socks all the time!' Joey joked.

They all laughed.

Ryan said a silent *thank you* to Joey for diverting everyone's attention.

Alex began clearing the plates. 'The university film club is showing *Raise the Red Lantern* tonight,' she said. 'Let's all go and see it.'

Ryan exchanged a glance with Cleo. *That was close,* he thought. *If our parents found out that we were the suspicious characters at the museum, we'd never be allowed out on our own again!*

'If you get bored, you could have a go at piecing this together while we're out,' Cleo's mum suggested, placing a board on the kitchen table. It was covered with what looked like the world's dullest jigsaw: scraps of white paper scrawled with smudgy faded squiggles. 'I know you two like solving puzzles.'

Ryan had detected that Cleo was in no mood to go to the film, and they'd used the excuse of working on their imaginary history project to stay behind.

'What is it?' Cleo asked.

'Fragments of a silk scroll that we found in that big coffer in the Kitchen of Eternal Life,' Lydia explained. 'These are copies, of course. The original pieces are all stored in a safe in the university. I've pieced a few bits together and translated the text where I can, but I still can't make head or tail of it.'

'Oh, yeah!' Ryan muttered as the door closed. 'My idea of a fun night in!'

'Actually,' Cleo said, fetching a lamp from the living room and placing it on the table. 'It looks quite interesting.'

Ryan wasn't sure about that. 'About as interesting as a page of algebra equations!' he joked.

Cleo held a piece up to the light. 'I know!'

The difference between us, Ryan thought, *is that Cleo is being serious.* He gazed at the board. Lydia McNeil had put together most of a wide panel covered in Chinese writing along the top of the scroll. But the bottom section was still largely empty. He began idly picking up pieces from the unused pile, shuffling them around, lining up the squiggles.

Then something caught his eye.

Maybe the silk scroll puzzle was more interesting than he'd thought.

He pointed at a small piece near the edge. 'Isn't that symbol the same as the one on the jade ring?'

MAP

RYAN HELD OUT his hand. 'Give me the jade ring a moment.'

Cleo looked up from poring over her mum's notes and translations, fished the ring from her pocket and passed it over.

Ryan studied the pattern.

He was right. It was identical to the one on the piece of paper on the board: six crossed lines, three across and three down, like a noughts and crosses grid with an extra row and column.

He slid the piece across the table.

'Oh, yes, it's an exact match,' Cleo murmured. She picked up another piece. 'There's another one here. It seems to crop up several times around the border, but it can't be part of the writing; I showed the symbol on the ring to Mum the other day. She was sure it wasn't a small seal script character.'

'So,' Ryan said, thinking aloud, 'if this symbol is all over the silk scroll from the Kitchen of Eternal Life, does it mean the recipe gentlemen had something to do with the jade rings that were in the noses of the dragons in the tunnel? I thought those *fangshi* guys were only interested in brewing up immortality potions?'

Cleo stared at the jade ring, her mouth opening and closing, as if she was having some kind of religious vision. The light from the table lamp shone on her dark hair, giving it a golden aura like a halo in a medieval painting, adding to the effect.

'Ooh!' she exclaimed, and then, 'Ooh!' again, and finally, 'Gunpowder!'

'*Gunpowder?*' Ryan repeated slowly.

Cleo nodded. 'That's the connection. Or at least part of it. The dragons' fire in the tunnel must have been sparked by gunpowder – gunpowder which was probably made by the *fangshi.*'

Now Ryan saw the link. He remembered Cleo telling him in the park that historians believed that recipe gentlemen invented gunpowder by accident when they were experimenting with their concoctions.

'And if the *fangshi* were responsible for the gunpowder,' Cleo went on, 'maybe they designed the whole set-up – the dragon booby traps, the jade rings and everything. Which means that they would have known all about the tunnel.' Her green eyes glittered as she ran her hands over the pieces. 'There must be information about the Dragon Path in this scroll. It stands to reason. Why else would the scroll and the jade ring be marked with matching symbols?'

Ryan gestured towards Lydia McNeil's notes. 'What has your mum translated so far? Perhaps we'll find some handy directions to the tunnel.'

Cleo leafed through the notes. 'Mum doesn't mention anything about dragons or tunnels,' she sighed. 'She says she thinks the scroll contained a recipe for the elixir of life. There are a lot of numbers and measurements in the text. Presumably that's giving the quantities of ingredients. Here's a line she's translated: *Take six from fifteen and leave three. For the one you seek you must find the two.*'

'It's not exactly Nigella Lawson, is it?' Ryan laughed. 'And even I know that fifteen minus six isn't three.' He rotated a piece and slotted it into a gap. While they'd been speaking, he'd almost completed a whole section of the bottom panel but, instead of writing, it was starting to look like . . .

'*A map!*' Cleo exclaimed. 'That's brilliant!'

Ryan grinned. 'Yeah, well, when you've reconstructed as many ancient silk scrolls as I have, it comes pretty naturally.'

Cleo jumped up from her chair and then sat back down again. 'Of course! It's a map of how to find the Dragon Path.'

'Not unless it's underwater!' Ryan said, pointing out the jagged coastline and the curly lines that were obviously waves.

'They could be trees,' Cleo said hopefully.

'Then how do you explain these fish?' Ryan asked. 'And this looks like an octopus. And there are even some turtles swimming around down here.'

Cleo frowned at the assembled map. She nodded once, then again, very slowly. She stared for so long that Ryan thought she might have gone into a trance. At last she spoke. 'It's fifteen *turtles*. The giant took six!'

Ryan reached out and felt her forehead. Cleo always took it hard when her theories didn't pan out, but the washout at the pomegranate orchard seemed to have tipped her over the edge. 'Are you feeling all right?'

Cleo swiped his hand away. 'It's in the legend of the Isles of Immortality. Originally there were five magical islands somewhere in the East China Sea. That's where the *lingzhi,* the fungus of immortality, was said to grow. Each island was supported on the backs of three turtles. But a giant stole six of the turtles, so two of the islands drifted away and were lost. Only three remained – Penglai, Fangzhang and Yingzhou.'

It was starting to make a weird kind of sense now, Ryan thought.

'So that's what that line of the recipe means: take six turtles from fifteen and leave three islands.'

Cleo nodded. 'But it's not a recipe. It's a *riddle*. The next line says – *For the one you seek you must find the two*. I think that means that if you want to find the *one* secret fungus of immortality, you have to find the *two* islands that drifted away.' She puffed out a breath as if she'd just run a marathon. 'If this is a map of all five Isles of Immortality, it's a *hugely* significant discovery. The First Emperor sent out expeditions of recipe gentlemen to try to find the Isles of Immortality, but they never even found the three islands that *didn't* drift off, let alone the two that did!'

Ryan studied the map. He'd pieced together outlines of three islands, but there was still a huge expanse of empty sea.

'Hang on, this might help. There's more of the riddle here,' Cleo said. '*The way to the two lies in one that brings death but is not tarnished by it. Drink the two before sands run through, for body and soul to flee from this world.'*

Cleo looked up from the notes. 'Mum's written here that she thinks these lines are part of the recipe. You have to combine two ingredients in a vessel made of gold – which doesn't tarnish – before the sand runs through some kind of timer, so that you can *flee from this world* – which was a way of saying that you would gain immortality. But if we're right, *the way to the two* means the way to find the two lost islands.'

Ryan had been thinking the same thing. *'The way to the two*. Perhaps that means there's another map somewhere. That's what could be hidden inside *one that brings death but is not tarnished by it.'*

'Yes, good idea. The map could be in some sort of gold box or case.' Cleo rested her chin in her hands and sighed. 'But how does a gold box bring death, I wonder.'

Ryan shrugged. 'Maybe it could be used as a weapon . . .' As he said the word *weapon*, he suddenly remembered the display at the museum. 'Or what about a sword?'

Cleo looked up, her eyebrows arching with interest.

'Like the ones at the Terracotta Army Museum,' Ryan explained. 'It said that there was some special process that kept the bronze swords from rusting. They looked as good as new.'

'You're right! Qin Dynasty bronze swords were coated with chromium oxide thousands of years before chrome plating was developed in the West.' Cleo pushed her fringe out of her eyes. 'But how can a map be *in* a sword?'

'I don't know, but it fits the clue better.' Ryan mimed a swashbuckling move. 'A sword brings death.'

Cleo leaned back in her chair. 'I suppose a map *could* be engraved on a sword blade ...'

Ryan got up to get a drink. 'So all we've got to do,' he said as he opened the fridge, 'is find an unknown sword with a map of the two lost islands on it, hire a boat, sail across the East China Sea – avoiding any passing ninja turtles and rogue giants, of course – collect these magic fungi, concoct a potion that isn't so toxic that it actually kills us and ...' He rubbed his hands together and cackled an evil laugh. '*Mwa-ha-ha!* We could live forever.'

Cleo laughed. 'I don't think there's much chance of that!' she said. 'We can't even find a tunnel that we know must be only a few miles away!' She sighed as she picked up the jade ring and set it down on the pieced-together scroll, so that it circled one of the mysterious symbols with six crossed lines. 'But it can't be a coincidence that this symbol is on the scroll and the ring from the dragon's nose. The *fangshi* are obviously the missing link between the two. If we could just figure out what it means ...'

Ryan was contemplating the contents of the fridge. 'Hmm, there's not much choice. Looks like pomegranate juice or pomegranate juice.' He turned to Cleo at the table. But instead of answering she was staring at him, a strange *eureka-moment* look on her face.

'*Pomegranates!*' she murmured. 'Maybe we're not at a dead end, after all.'

22

NEWSPAPER

IT WAS A *simple case of synchronicity,* Cleo thought. At the exact moment Ryan had mentioned pomegranate juice, she'd heard the distant revving of a motorbike outside. The combination had sparked a flashback memory of sitting in the trailer rattling up the rutted track to the pomegranate orchard.

Ryan placed two cartons of juice on the table. 'Go on then, spill the beans. What have I missed?'

'It was something the garage owner said when we were on the motor-trike.'

'Aha! Was it those jokes you said wouldn't translate into English?' Ryan slurped his juice. 'The way you were blushing, I thought they might be a bit on the racy side.'

'Actually, he said that I'd make a good—' Cleo stopped herself just in time. The words *pomegranate fairy* had almost slipped from her lips. 'A good . . . er . . . *ambassador* for the festival. And that I'd *be in the local paper.*' She stressed each word and then paused to see whether Ryan had got her point, but he had taken out his sketchbook. 'Are you even listening?'

'Yeah, go on, I'm just making a copy of the map on the scroll.' Ryan glanced up from what looked to Cleo like a cartoon of turtles sword-fighting with giants. 'You were saying that the garage man could get you in the papers.' He grinned. 'This could be the start of big things for you. Your chance to be an international pomegranate celebrity. You could audition for *China's Got Talent*. Can you juggle? Or tap dance?'

Cleo didn't have the slightest idea what Ryan was talking about. What did tap dancing have to do with anything? She stabbed her straw into the juice carton.

'*Local newspapers!*' she repeated. 'Think about it! If they write about pomegranate festivals, they're bound to report something major like mysterious disappearances. We know that at least two local men died in the Dragon Path tunnel. There could be a story about it in the paper. There'll be details. It might even give the location.'

Ryan added some shading to a turtle. 'I don't want to rain on your pomegranate parade,' he said, 'but who would have kept a copy of the local paper from 1936?'

'One word!' Cleo said. 'Archives!'

Ryan looked up. 'Uh-uh! Last time we went near an archive, you were almost arrested for violent assault!'

166

'I'm not suggesting we break in or anything. Newspaper archives are open to the public.' But as she said it, Cleo realized she wasn't sure that was true. And even if they were open, you probably had to apply for permission. It could take weeks. *What we need,* she thought, *is someone with connections to a local journalist who could look up the information for us.* Cleo slammed her carton down on the table so hard that pomegranate juice spurted out of the straw. *And we know just the person!*

'Julie Flint!' she cried.

Ryan snatched his sketchbook away from the spatter of purple juice drops and blinked at her.

'Your mum!' Cleo prompted.

'I do know my mum's name,' Ryan said. 'But two things. One, she doesn't have any contacts here and two, didn't we agree that we need to keep this mission well and truly under the parental radar?'

But Cleo wasn't discouraged. 'You told me yourself that Julie's been chatting to all the local journalists looking into this tomb-robbing gang. And I'm sure you can think of a way to ask her without raising any suspicions; you're really good at lying.'

Ryan sighed. 'You say the nicest things!'

Ryan knew there was no point arguing when Cleo had an idea.

He lay awake half the night trying to think of a way to ask his mum to search the local newspaper archive for stories about men being killed in a secret tunnel full of fire-breathing dragons, without giving away the fact that he and Cleo were *up to something,* like – to pick a totally random example – looking for a secret tunnel full of fire-breathing dragons! And then there was the fact that Mum would have to recruit the help of a local journalist to get access to the archive. And it was vital not to give away information that might fall into the hands of the Tiger's Claw gang.

He started the campaign at breakfast by making scrambled eggs and promising to spend the entire morning revising for the chemistry exam that was looming when he got back to school. Then, when Mum had been lulled into a positive frame of mind, he homed in with the request.

'Is there any chance you could look something up for us in the local newspaper records?'

Mum fixed him with a searching look over her coffee. 'Are you and Cleo getting mixed up in things you shouldn't be again?'

'Of course not.' Ryan picked up the plates to do the washing up, then decided against it. Being *overly* helpful would look suspicious. He piled them on the draining board instead. 'It's just something Cleo's grandmother told us. She remembered some people being killed on an archaeological dig in the mountains when she was here as a child. It seemed important to her, so we thought we'd see what we could find out about it.'

Mum poured another coffee. 'As long as it doesn't involve any more building-site raids!' She began rummaging through her bag for her phone, which was ringing somewhere. Ryan located it under a pile of toast and handed it over. After a brief conversation she smiled. 'Looks like it's your lucky day. That was a reporter I met from the *Lintong Daily News*. I'm going over to her office this morning for an update on the Tiger's Claw story. It sounds like there's been another robbery.' She grinned at Ryan as she began throwing papers and notebooks into her shoulder bag. 'I'll be back by lunch. I'll see what I can do, but I'm only handing over the info if you can show me a full morning's revision notes. Deal?'

'Deal,' Ryan muttered. *There goes my plan to do ten minutes of chemistry and then go in search of that comic shop Tian Min told me about,* he thought. *I hope Cleo appreciates the sacrifice I'm making here.*

'So what is it you want to know?' Mum asked.

By midday Ryan never wanted to see another chemical symbol in his life. When he heard Mum coming up the stairs he was thrusting a bundle of notes under her nose before she was halfway through the door.

She took the pages and looked them over. 'Are you going to remember any of this?'

Ryan made a deeply wounded face. He'd used five different highlighters, and his picture of the nitrogen cycle was miles better than the one in the textbook. *Remembering* hadn't been part of the deal. 'Come on. What did you find?'

Mum dumped her bag on the kitchen table. 'I told my reporter friend the search terms you were interested in – *unexplained death, archaeologist, Mount Li* and *1936* – and she translated them into Mandarin and looked through all the records.'

Ryan was about to burst with impatience. 'And?'

Mum sighed. 'And nothing, I'm afraid.'

Ryan waited for the fine lines round her eyes to crinkle and her top lip to twitch, signalling that she was winding him up. But there wasn't a hint of a crinkle. Not a ghost of a twitch. 'You're *serious?*'

Mum nodded. 'Nothing matched all the search terms.' She pulled a sheaf of copies of newspaper articles from her bag. 'I printed out everything that was even remotely close. You'll have to get Cleo to translate these, but there's nothing from 1936.'

Ryan flicked gloomily through the densely inked pages. He came to the last couple of sheets and noticed they were in English. 'What are these?'

'Those are from the *North China Daily News,*' Mum said, unpacking cartons from a carrier bag. 'It was an English language paper based in Shanghai. I thought it might be worth looking on their database as well, since they covered stories across the whole of north China. I've printed out a couple of reports of unusual deaths around Lintong, but again there's nothing from 1936.' Mum smiled at him. 'Perhaps Cleo's gran mixed up the dates? Never mind. I've brought some of those dumplings you like for lunch.'

But Ryan didn't reply. He was staring at the very last page. A tingle of possibility ran up his spine. He reread the headline. *FRENCH HIKER DIES IN FALL ON MOUNT LI.* He checked the date again: 1953. He scanned the first few lines of the article. The man's name was Pierre Segal.

This might just be the breakthrough we've been waiting for!

Ryan planted a quick kiss on the top of his mum's spiky blonde-and-pink hair, grabbed his backpack and charged out of the door.

Meanwhile, Cleo was helping to excavate more bodies in the Tomb of a Thousand Poisons. She was lying on her stomach inside one of the niches at the back of the cave, clearing fine rubble from a mummified corpse by the light of her head torch. She was so immersed in the delicate work that when someone tugged on her ankle she jumped. The back of her head bounced off the low rock ceiling. *This had better be good,* she thought crossly as she joined Ryan outside on the ledge.

They walked a little way down the slope and found a secluded spot under a spreading walnut tree. Ryan flopped down and leaned against the trunk. 'I feel like I've just done a triathlon,' he groaned. 'Cycling and running all the way up this hill.'

'That would be a *bi*athlon,' Cleo pointed out. 'A triathlon includes swimming as well.'

For some reason Ryan seemed annoyed. 'If you don't stop being so *literal* I won't tell you what I've found out.'

Cleo sat down, rubbing the bump on her head. It was directly above the left superior parietal lobule. She couldn't see the problem with being literal, but she couldn't wait to find out what Ryan had discovered either. 'OK,' she promised. 'I'll try my best.'

Ryan pulled a roll of paper from his backpack and handed it to her.

Cleo smoothed out the page, saw that it was a short article in English from the *North China Daily News,* and began to read.

Monsieur Pierre Segal (45) appears to have been travelling

through China alone when he fell to his death on the remote
southern face of Mt Li. Lintong Police report that his body
was found near an outcrop known locally as Sunrise Rock. The
reasons for M. Segal's visit to the mountain remain unknown.

'Your grandmother said that the cameraman was French.'
Ryan said.

Cleo couldn't hide her disappointment. Ryan had said he'd
found something important. To make matters worse, she was
starting to feel dizzy.

'Yeah, yeah, I know what you're thinking,' Ryan said.
'It's a million to one that some random dead Frenchman in
1953 is the cameraman from our Dragon Path film seventeen
years earlier . . .'

Cleo was about to point out that, given the population
of France in the 1950s was around forty million people, the
chance was considerably *less* than a million to one. But she
decided to keep the thought to herself. She suspected that it
might count as being literal.

'But it's not *just* that this guy was French,' Ryan went on.
'Don't you remember at the History of Archaeology Museum
in London? Anthony Grumpy-Trousers Chetwynd told us
that the Lymington and Stubbs films had been donated in
1953. That makes sense if it's the year that Segal died. His
family probably went through his things and gave all the
archaeological stuff to the museum.'

Cleo picked up a smooth green walnut shell from among
the golden leaves. Ryan had a point. But even with the year
1953 in common it was still a weak link.

'And,' Ryan said, 'look at the name: *Pierre Segal.* That
matches the initials that were written on the bottom of the
film case we saw in the archive: *P. S.*'

Before Ryan could even finish the sentence, Cleo was struck by the sudden realization that he was absolutely right. This *was* their Frenchman! She jumped to her feet.

'That's what Harold Stubbs yelled to the cameraman in the ancestor temple at the end of the tunnel!' Tiny starbursts sparkled in front of her eyes but she didn't care. She reached out and steadied herself on the tree trunk. 'It looked as if he was shouting "cigar", and we thought he must have meant that Lymington's *pipe* had set light to something, but—'

'Of course!' Ryan cut in. 'He was yelling "Segal" to warn the cameraman about the fire from the dragons behind him. When you're lip-reading, *cigar* and *Segal* look just the same!' He took Cleo's arm and tried to help her sit back down again, but she wrenched free. She had no time for concussion now. She was quite certain that Pierre Segal had been hiking up that lonely mountain path for one reason and one reason only: to return to the Dragon Path tunnel.

'We've got to find Sunrise Rock!'

23

MOUNTAIN

WE COULDN'T HAVE *picked a worse day to retrace Pierre Segal's footsteps to Sunrise Rock if we'd tried,* Ryan thought as he trudged up the path early the following morning.

The mountain was swathed in fog so thick and wet that one more drop of moisture would turn it to rain. Although the air was warm, the drips that slid from the overhanging branches and slithered down the back of his neck were icy-cold. He kept blinking, trying to focus, but it was like trying to make out a reflection in a steamed-up mirror: anything beyond a metre or two simply dissolved into grey-white oblivion.

Ryan had suggested waiting for a clearer day, but Cleo was

adamant there was no time to lose. They had little more than a week left in China. She'd found an old map of Mount Li in a drawer of leaflets and guide books in their apartment, and although there was no Sunrise Rock marked, there was a Sunrise *Pavilion,* high up on the south-eastern slope. Cleo was convinced the rock where Segal's body had been found must be close by.

'Suit yourself,' she'd said, when Ryan had voiced his concerns about the zero visibility. 'I'll go on my own.'

Which had meant, of course, that Ryan had no choice but to go with her. Cleo was capable of becoming hopelessly lost on a one-way street on a sunny day. Alone on a foggy mountain she wouldn't stand a chance. Not surprisingly, Mum had looked at him as if he'd lost his mind when he'd announced that they were going for a picnic on the mountain.

'I'm sure the fog will clear soon,' he'd bluffed.

It hadn't.

They'd left their bikes when the track became too steep and overgrown and had been climbing on foot for over an hour. This part of the mountain was deserted, with nothing for miles around but pine and cypress trees, rocks and streams. It was also a long way from the tomb of the First Emperor.

If the Dragon Path tunnel did start somewhere over here, Ryan thought, *it would have to run for several miles under the mountain to the other side. Then again, tunnelling through mountains was probably no big deal to an emperor who'd had an army of eight thousand life-sized terracotta soldiers and a model of the universe built in his tomb!*

The fog distorted sound as well as vision; the rasp of his own breathing and the rustle of his waterproof jacket boomed in Ryan's ears. Again and again he whisked round, thinking he'd heard something behind him. *Was that a snuffle or a grunt? The crunch of a foot on a pinecone? Or, even worse, the crunch of a huge paw?* He wished Cleo hadn't told him that brown bears and snow leopards roamed these mountain forests, even if they *were* extraordinarily rare.

He peered over his shoulder into the all-devouring fog. *There could be a leopard stalking us, or a posse of heavily armed members of the Tiger's Claw gang, and we wouldn't even know . . .*

He swung back round at the sound of Cleo's voice. She'd gone on ahead and her bright orange waterproof was the only smudge of colour in the monochrome world of fog and pine. At the same moment a commotion in the trees sent his heart ricocheting around his chest.

Only a flock of startled birds, he told himself as he jogged to Cleo's side. She'd pulled the drawstring on her hood so tight that only her eyes and nose peeked out. Drops of water clung to her eyelashes.

'Look!' she said, pointing ahead.

The fog was a brighter shade of white here, suggesting that they'd entered a clearing in the trees. Tall posts loomed out of the mist only metres away. As they drew closer Ryan saw that the posts were part of an open-sided building, supporting a roof with pagoda-style up-curled eaves. Decorative scenes of gardens and palaces adorned the ceiling. The blues and reds and greens must once have dazzled, but now the paint was peeling from the warped wood.

Cleo sank down on the low bench that ran round the inside. 'Do you think this is the Sunrise Pavilion?'

Ryan checked his compass. The pavilion was facing due east. He nodded.

'Mount Li was a favourite resort for emperors and their courts over many dynasties,' Cleo said. 'They would have come up here to admire the view and watch the sun come up.'

Ryan shivered. 'Let's start searching,' he said, trying to shake off the suffocating melancholy of the faded pavilion in its shroud of damp fog.

They walked in ever widening circles. It wasn't long before Cleo stopped with a shout. 'I've found it!'

Ryan surveyed the wide, flat boulder that jutted out from the mountainside like a natural east-facing balcony. *Yes, he thought, this must be Sunrise Rock.* He could picture the servants and ordinary folk sitting out here to watch the sunrise while the high-society crowd were living it up with champagne and canapés in the pavilion. He took his sketchbook out of his backpack and began to sketch the shadowy blue mountains and ghostly trees, which were just beginning to emerge from the fog. Meanwhile Cleo had taken a magnifying glass from her bum bag and was crawling back and forth over the rock, her nose to the ground like a bloodhound.

'What are you doing, Sherlock?' Ryan asked.

Cleo waved the magnifying glass. 'Looking for evidence of where Segal fell, of course. The newspaper article says that his body was found on this rock.'

Ryan didn't say anything but he doubted whether even Sherlock Holmes would find any clues after more than sixty years.

Cleo sat back on her heels. 'Pierre Segal must have been looking round here for the entrance to the tunnel. But *where*?'

Ryan looked up from his sketchbook. 'Well, we know one thing. If he *fell to his death* on this rock he wasn't standing

177

here at the time – unless he tripped over his shoelaces and had a very unlucky landing. You'd have to fall several metres at least to be killed.'

'Of course!' Cleo said. 'He must have been searching further up the slope when he fell.' She held out a hand. 'Come on. We need to climb higher.'

Ryan craned his neck to look up. A sheer bank of rock dotted with a few clumps of scrawny bushes disappeared into the mist. 'We'd need ropes to get up there,' he pointed out.

Cleo gestured with the magnifying glass to a stream splashing down a shallower slope to one side of the steep face. 'Not if we follow the stream.'

It was fun at first, hopping over stepping stones and helping each other up onto the larger rocks. But as they climbed, looking out for paths off to the side that Segal could have followed, the water tumbled over steeper and steeper terrain until it was no longer a stream but a frothing white waterfall.

They were crossing over a dam of large rocks above a vertical drop of water. Ryan was about to suggest turning back when his foot slipped on an algae-slimed boulder. There was a moment of limbo when, swaying and wheeling his arms, he was suspended between falling and saving himself. Then he toppled and skidded feet first down the slick rock. He clenched his teeth and braced himself for the churning, racing water and the rocks beneath.

When the impact came, it took Ryan several moments to realize that he wasn't thrashing about in the rapids, but lying on his back looking up at a band of white sky between sheer walls of rock. He turned his head to see a cascade of water that sparkled like a sequinned curtain. Spray misted his face.

He looked down and instantly wished he hadn't. He was lying on a ledge of rock barely wider than his shoulders, and there was nothing between him and the curtain of water but a bottomless black void. He tried to shrink away from the edge and cursed his backpack, which was still strapped to his shoulders. Then he changed his mind. The backpack had probably saved his life by cushioning his landing on the rock.

As his eyes adjusted to the dim light from the gap in the rocks above and the ever-moving dappled light filtering through the tumbling water, Ryan slowly figured out where he was: somehow he had dropped through a cleft in the rock and landed in a hidden cave behind the waterfall.

He clenched his fists at his sides. *This is all wrong! Cleo is the one who falls down holes.* I'm *the one who pulls her out. What's Cleo doing now?* he wondered. *Did she see me fall? Is she looking for me?* Ryan strained his ears for her voice but he could hear nothing over the pounding of his heart and the rushing of the water. *Eventually she'll have to give up looking and make her way down the mountain to fetch help.* Ryan closed his eyes. *If she loses her way in the fog, she could still be wandering through the pines as darkness falls.*

He took a deep breath and puffed it out. *I've got to get out of here before we both end up spending the night on the mountain.*

24

GHOST

Ryan opened his eyes and looked around again. The walls of rock were smooth. There was no way he could climb up. The drop below the ledge was in deep shadow. It could be five metres or fifty. He couldn't get down that way either.

He eyed the curtain of cascading water. Could he somehow climb through the waterfall? But first he'd have to cross the gap, and he couldn't risk falling.

Incy wincy spider climbed up the waterspout. The words of the nursery rhyme had turned up in his head uninvited and were refusing to leave. *Down came the rain and washed the spider* out . . . He squeezed his eyes closed, trying to force the stupid rhyme out. *Really not helping,* he told himself, but the

180

words just kept going round and round ... *Down came the rain* ... It was getting seriously annoying.

Concentrate! There was only one way out. He would have to shuffle along the ledge and hope it ran all the way to the side of the cave. The waterfall wasn't that wide, after all. Surely he'd be able to climb out onto the bank of the stream.

Very slowly he began to ease himself up to a sitting position, twisting round as he went, so that his back was against the wall of rock. The move strained his stomach muscles. He wished he'd put more effort into sit-ups in PE lessons, instead of only doing them when Mr Franklin was watching. But at last he made it. He leaned back and gulped down deep juddering breaths. Then he curled his fingers round the edge of the ledge and, taking his weight on his arms, began to shimmy along in little sideways hops.

He was making good progress when his hand brushed against something soft and damp on the ledge. At the same moment he heard a pitiful little cry. He snatched his hand back. What was *that*? A baby? *How could a baby be in the cave?* He heard the sound again. A high-pitched whimper. It must be an animal. *Incy wincy spider? No, spiders don't whimper. A rabbit, maybe, or a mouse that's fallen behind the waterfall and can't get out.* The animal was probably injured. There'd be blood, and somehow he was going to have to get past it ...

He forced himself to look down.

The object on the ledge wasn't moving. He poked at it gingerly with one finger. There was no response. In fact, it didn't feel like a living thing at all. He pulled it closer. Beneath a coating of moss and slime was a small khaki canvas satchel. It looked old-fashioned and vaguely military.

Knapsack, he thought. *That's the word for it. How did it get here?* The answer came to him before he'd finished thinking the question. *The knapsack belonged to Pierre Segal!*

The cameraman must have died in this cave.

That was his ghost I heard.

Then Ryan pulled himself together. *Don't be ridiculous. The newspaper report said the body was found on Sunrise Rock. And anyway,* he reminded himself, *there's no such thing as ghosts!* The knapsack must have slipped off Segal's shoulder as he fell down the mountain, and then rolled through the cleft in the rocks.

Very carefully, Ryan pulled free the long leather strap and looped it over his neck. *Move along,* he told himself, gearing up for the last phase of shuffling along the ledge. *Nothing to see here!* The rocky bank at the side of the cave was only a metre or so away.

Then he heard it again – that little whimpering cry. A worm of terror burrowed down his backbone. The cry obviously hadn't come from the knapsack, so what *had* it come from? He felt for his St Christopher pendant and his scarab amulet and then began to shuffle for his life.

At last he was close enough to launch himself at the rocks at the side, digging his toe into a small fissure and swinging himself up. He reached and found a handhold. *So far, so good.* He edged his lower foot up and found a little nub of rock to rest it on. He scanned the rocks for his next grip. He spotted a perfect hole just within arm's reach and was about to stretch for it when something moved.

Ryan stared in horror as an enormous face shot out of the hole. In one terrifying glimpse he took in the scabrous skin mottled with brownish shades of mud and sludge, the tiny eyes peering out from above a wide, blunt snout bisected by a grinning slash of a mouth. What kind of creature *was* it? It had the face of an eel, the skin of a toad, and it was the size of a small crocodile! Suddenly the mouth gaped open, huge and toothless and pale inside, and emitted an unearthly ghost-baby cry.

Then it lunged forward on stubby legs and hissed.

Ryan was so terrified that his feet slipped from under him. His chin bumped against the rock. He was hanging by his fingertips over the fathomless drop. He scrabbled wildly with his feet and found a toehold just as his hand lost its grip. He glanced up. That *thing* was no longer in the hole. Had it slithered back inside? Were there more of them in there? Ryan couldn't bear to think about it, but there were no other handholds within reach. He had no choice. He gritted his teeth and stretched out his arm.

At the same moment, he heard a panicky shout above him. 'Ryan! Where *are* you?'

'I'm down here,' Ryan yelled, cautiously sliding his fingertips into the hole in the rock, dreading the touch of rough, clammy skin or the bite of needle-sharp teeth. He glimpsed a flash of movement above his head.

'Grab my hand!' Cleo cried. Gratefully, he snatched his hand away from the hole and grabbed Cleo's wrist. He knew he only had a moment before his weight pulled her down too, but it was just long enough to reach for another handhold with his free hand, and with a superhuman heave he pulled himself up and over the last lip of rock onto dry land. He was at the side of the stream near the top of the waterfall.

Panting for breath, Ryan was struggling to sit up – the bones in all his limbs seemed to have been replaced by custard

183

– when Cleo half-pounced, half-fell on top of him, knocking him flat again.

'What happened?' she demanded. 'I thought you must have been kidnapped by the Tiger's Claw! I was so worried!' She stopped to draw breath and Ryan saw the horrified look in her eye as she suddenly realized she was lying on his chest in what – to the untrained eye – might appear to be a passionate embrace. She sprang back and perched on a rock. 'If it was some kind of joke to scare me,' she said crossly, 'it wasn't funny, and I'm never talking to you again.'

Ryan pushed up onto his elbows. 'It wasn't a joke. I fell through the rocks and ended up in a cave behind the waterfall.'

Cleo stared at him. *'You fell down a hole?'*

Ryan gave an apologetic grin. 'Yeah. Sorry. I know that's your department, but I thought I'd give it a go. Why should you have all the fun?'

Cleo giggled. 'As a matter of fact, I haven't fallen down a single hole since we've been in China. The one between the cave and the rock pile was a *gap*, not a hole, and at the Terracotta Army Museum it was quite clearly a *pit.*'

Ryan laughed, but then he remembered what he'd just seen. 'There's a monster down there!' he mumbled.

'Now are you joking?'

Ryan shook his head. 'Some sort of mutant toad-like thing.' He shuddered at the memory. 'It was massive.' He threw his arms wide. 'And it had eyes ... and a mouth ... and *legs* ...' He realized he wasn't exactly painting a picture for her. 'And it made this creepy sound like a baby.'

Cleo gasped. 'That sounds like a Chinese giant salamander. It's a really rare amphibian. The Chinese name for it means

184

infant fish because of its weird cry. You're so lucky to actually see one in the wild. They're a critically endangered species.'

Ryan snorted. 'Well, it critically endangered *me*. I nearly had a heart attack.'

'Did you get a photo?'

'I was dangling by one finger over a bottomless drop with an amphibian hell-beast spitting in my face. I wasn't exactly going to ask if it would like to be in a selfie with me!'

Cleo shrugged. 'That's a shame.' She passed Ryan a bottle of fizzy pomegranate juice. 'You're shaking,' she said, suddenly serious. 'And soaking wet.' She took off her jumper and handed it to him. It was the mad yellow and black giant bumblebee one, but Ryan was too cold to object. As he tried to pull it over his head, it became tangled with the old knapsack that was still hanging from his neck. What with the salamander face-off, he'd forgotten all about it.

'What's that?' Cleo asked.

Ryan took the knapsack off. 'I found it down behind the waterfall.'

Cleo pulled a face as he held out the slimy lump of canvas and leather.

'I thought it might belong to Pierre Seg—' Before Ryan could say another word, Cleo had fallen on the bundle of old leather and canvas, pulled it open and reached inside. She drew her hand out and opened her fingers.

In her palm lay a green jade ring.

They both stared at it for a long moment. It was identical to the one that Cleo's grandmother had given her except that, instead of the noughts and crosses symbol on the inside, there was a single gold line, curled at the end like a tiny party blower.

A noise in the branches overhead broke the silence. Ryan jumped. Through the melting fog, he caught a flash of lime green among the forest green of the pine needles.

Do they have parrots in China? he wondered.

The lime green creature leaped to another branch.

Or green monkeys?

'Hey! Who's hiding up there?' Cleo yelled, scrambling to her feet and stuffing the jade ring behind her back.

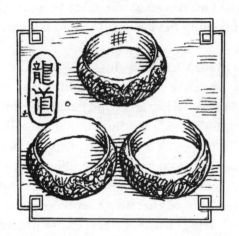

25

JOURNAL

WU MEILIN SWUNG from a low branch and dismounted with a back flip to a perfect landing. She bounced on her toes and even gave a small curtsey, as if a panel of judges were scoring her technique.

Cleo was so furious she could hardly breathe. *I was right all along! Wu Meilin has been following us around ever since we first met her at Aunty Ting's noodle restaurant.* A terrible thought suddenly struck her. *Meilin's been spying on us for the Tiger's Claw gang!*

To make matters worse, Ryan was acting as if Meilin appearing out of nowhere *for the second time in a row* was perfectly normal! He was offering her a squashed sponge cake from his backpack and asking about Bao Bao and the puppies.

Meilin smiled up at Cleo. 'I saw you looking for Ryan. I was about to come and help. Then he suddenly crawled out from the waterfall.'

Crawled out? Cleo thought indignantly. *Actually I pulled him out!* 'Well, he's fine now,' she said in a tight voice.

Ryan grinned. 'That's right. I've got Cleo to thank for rescuing me.'

That just made Cleo even crosser. Why did Ryan have to be nice just when she was in the middle of being annoyed with him? She folded her arms and looked Meilin in the eye. 'So, do you want to explain why you've been stalking us?'

Wu Meilin gulped. The damp had spiked her pixie hair up into little points so that she looked like a baby hedgehog. Her green tracksuit was splotched with dark patches from the wet leaves. She couldn't hold Cleo's stony glare.

'I knew it!' Cleo burst out. 'You didn't just *happen* to be visiting your grandfather at the orchard, did you?'

Meilin shook her head. 'No. I mean yes! I really *was* just visiting Grandfather. We had a half-day holiday from school so I went to help him with some housework. I wasn't following you then. I'm sorry I followed you today, but it wasn't for a bad reason, I promise.'

'Yeah, right!' Cleo snorted. 'So you've got a *good* reason? Like informing for the Tiger's Claw gang?'

Meilin's hands flew to her mouth. 'Of course not! I would never be involved with those criminals.'

Ryan reached up to Cleo and tried to pull her down to sit next to him. 'I think Meilin's telling the truth. Why don't we let her explain?'

Cleo backed away. She was sure it was all just an act. No doubt you got trained in deception techniques if you were working for a gang.

Meilin was kneeling as if about to make a confession. She placed her hands on her knees and paused for a long moment. 'My grandfather didn't tell you the truth at the pomegranate orchard.'

Cleo was so surprised that she sat down, although still a short distance from Ryan and Meilin.

'He told you that his father – that's my great-grandfather – didn't work with any foreign archaeologists in the old days.' Meilin looked to Ryan. Ryan smiled encouragement. 'But he did.'

'So Mrs Long was telling the truth at the museum?' Cleo asked.

Meilin nodded. 'Before Great-Grandfather died two years ago, he told me all about it.'

Cleo edged closer. 'What did he tell you?'

'About working with those two men you talked about.'

'Stubbs and Lymington?' Cleo prompted.

Meilin nodded again. 'Although he couldn't pronounce the name *Lymington*. He called him Pipe Man!'

'So the man on the film really *was* your grandfather's father,' Ryan laughed. 'I knew it! They share the family ears!'

Meilin looked puzzled. 'I don't know about a film, but you are right, Great-Grandfather Long Yi's ears did stick out. I loved listening to his stories about all the digs he went on with Lymington and Stubbs,' she went on. 'He called them his English Gentlemen Friends. That's why I was so interested when you two first came into Aunty Ting's restaurant and

189

I overheard you talking about archaeology and old tunnels. But I had no idea it would have anything to do with Great-Grandfather.'

'So you started following us?' Cleo asked. 'We both knew there was someone tailing us,' she added, just to make sure Meilin didn't think she'd fooled them. 'Like that time in the park . . .'

'No. I told you. Today is the first time.'

'But why did your grandfather lie to us?' Ryan asked. 'What's the big secret?'

Meilin sighed. 'Everyone in my family thinks Great-Grandfather brought bad luck by disrespecting the ancestors and guiding foreigners into the tombs. After he worked with Lymington and Stubbs everything went wrong for him. He gambled away all the family money. That's why nobody in the family ever talks about him – apart from Aunt Long Dao-Ming, of course! Grandfather was right about that. She loves to gossip! Everyone else thinks that Great-Grandfather was just an embarrassment. They say he had lost his mind, because he talked about strange things like dragons.'

'*Dragons?*' Cleo echoed, excitement clawing at her throat.

'Yes. I know it sounds crazy, but he said he'd seen men killed by fire-breathing dragons.'

'Did he say *where* this happened?' Cleo exchanged excited glances with Ryan.

But Meilin shook her head. 'No, he always got upset if I asked him too much about it. He just said it was underground and a place nobody should go.' She shrugged. 'I think he was afraid. When I saw that jade bracelet you took out of that bag just now, I almost fell out of the tree.'

Cleo realized that she was still hiding Pierre Segal's knapsack and jade ring behind her back.

'Because Great-Grandfather had one exactly the same!' Meilin went on. 'He would never tell me where it came from.'

Cleo stared from Meilin to Ryan and then back again. 'So that means *three* dragon rings were taken from the tunnel.'

'Three?' Meilin asked.

Ryan nodded. 'Cleo's grandmother had one too. She gave it to Cleo.'

Cleo shot Ryan a look. *So much for keeping their mission a secret!* But then she relented. She was sure that Meilin was telling the truth now and she felt bad about accusing her of working for the Tiger's Claw gang. Especially when Meilin's family was part of the Dragon Path story too. Cleo took Grandma's jade ring from her jeans pocket and held it out next to the one from Pierre Segal's bag.

Meilin's eyes widened. 'Yes. They are just the same as my great-grandfather's one.'

'Where is it now?' Ryan asked.

'At the old house at the orchard. I hid it under the floorboards. Grandfather wanted to get rid of it. He was terrified that our family would be accused of being involved in tomb robbing. And he was sure it was cursed.'

Ryan nodded. 'He might have been right. Pierre Segal met a sticky end falling down this mountain.' He looked at Cleo. 'Although nothing bad happened to your grandmother.'

'That's because *she* didn't take the ring from the dragon,' Cleo pointed out. 'I'm sure one of the men must have dropped it and she just picked it up. Not that there's anything in all that nonsense about curses anyway,' she added quickly.

Meilin's eyes widened. 'You mean Great-Grandfather was right? There really *were* dragons?'

Between them, Cleo and Ryan told Meilin the story of the Dragon Path, from Eveline Bell's request that they return the ring to the dragon, finding the missing film of Lymington and Stubbs entering the tunnel and setting off the dragon booby traps, through to the newspaper story about Pierre Segal, the cameraman, falling to his death on the mountain in 1953.

'We're sure Segal was trying to find the tunnel again,' Cleo said, holding up the jade ring. 'Ryan found his knapsack down in that cave behind the waterfall.'

'I wonder,' Ryan said. 'Was old Pierre planning to give the jade ring back to the dragons, or was he just going to search for more treasure?'

'Either way,' Cleo said, 'now we can return *both* rings to the dragons.'

'And mine too!' Meilin exclaimed. 'I mean my *great-grandfather's*. I will fetch it from Grandfather's house.' She smiled. 'Then the bad fortune will be lifted and my family will be lucky again. Maybe Aunty Ting will have enough money to stop working so hard at the restaurant.'

'And you'll win an Olympic gold medal in gymnastics!' Ryan laughed.

Meilin beamed at him. Then she turned to Cleo. '*Please* let me join you.'

Cleo had to admit it would make sense to return all three rings at the same time. 'OK. If we *do* find the tunnel today we'll come back tomorrow with all three rings.'

Meilin poked a finger at Segal's soggy canvas bag. 'Is there anything else in there?'

Cleo could have kicked herself. Meilin had dropped out of the trees at the exact moment she'd found the jade ring, and she'd forgotten to even look in the bag again. *It might be stuffed full of clues!* She tipped it up, but all that fell out was a rusty old tobacco tin. Ryan grabbed it just in time to stop it sliding over the rocks into the stream. Cleo felt a pang of disappointment; she'd been hoping for a map or a notebook. But when Ryan prised open the lid, she saw a look of surprise on his face. She and Meilin leaned in closer. Inside the tin lay a small book bound in maroon leather. The initials *P. S.* were embossed on the cover.

Cleo lifted the book out and peeled open the first page. The paper was fat and soft with damp but the tin had kept it dry enough that the ink was only a little fuzzy. The handwriting was a beautiful copperplate.

'It looks like a journal!' Cleo breathed. *We're getting closer by the second*, she thought.

Surely Segal would have written down detailed directions to the tunnel so he could find it again.

She turned the page . . .

26

CODE

CLEO'S FACE FELL as she turned over page after page.

'What's wrong?' Ryan asked. 'Don't tell me it's empty.'

Cleo shook her head and handed him Pierre Segal's journal. Now Ryan could see the problem for himself. The pages were full all right. They were full of line after line of numbers. 'Is this some sort of code?' he asked.

Cleo nodded.

'Trois, vingt-deux, dix-sept . . .' he read out in his best accent.

'Why,' Cleo snapped, 'are you reading the numbers in French?'

Ryan thought it was obvious. 'Because Pierre Segal was French, of course.'

194

'Well, it doesn't make any difference what language you read it in. It's still code. This could take *ages* to decipher.'

'Secret writing?' Meilin asked. 'How exciting. It must mean that this Mr Segal didn't want anyone else to find the tunnel.'

Cleo didn't exactly roll her eyes, but Ryan could tell she was *thinking* an eye-roll. Although she'd agreed to Meilin joining the search, she still didn't seem a hundred per cent happy about it.

The fog had almost disappeared and the sun was growing warm. Ryan stretched out on the rocks. In spite of the scare with the giant salamander, the mountain expedition had been a major success. They'd found the journal that belonged to the cameraman and solved the mystery of why Meilin's grandfather had lied to them. On top of that, they had two more jade rings to return to the dragons, *and* they had Meilin on the team!

The bubbling of the stream and swishing of the pine trees was lulling him into a doze. Until Cleo grabbed his hand and pulled him up, that is.

'Come on! Let's have a last look around for the tunnel. If we don't find anything we'll try to figure out this code tonight.'

Meilin looked worried. 'Won't that be very difficult?'

'Don't worry,' Ryan laughed. 'Cleo is a code-breaking genius. I know this from when we were in Egypt.' He snapped the journal closed. 'If there are directions to the tunnel in here, Cleo will soon winkle them out!'

Cleo didn't say anything but Ryan saw her smile at the vote of confidence.

The team of three walked up the steep slope. After a

time – during which the nearest they'd found to a tunnel was a rabbit hole – Meilin stopped beside the remains of a tumbledown bridge that had once spanned the stream.

'I know where we are now,' she said. 'I used to come and play here with my friends. We called this Rotten Tooth Bridge.'

Ryan poked at one of the blackened posts. It fell into the water with a splash and bobbed away downstream. 'I can see why!' Suddenly he remembered something and turned to Cleo. 'Didn't your grandmother mention passing an old bridge on the way to the tunnel?'

'That's right!' Cleo ran to his side. 'When I phoned her, she said they'd turned left at the rickety bridge.'

There was no discernible path but they set off to the left, pushing ever deeper into forest so dense and dark that Ryan felt like a character from a fairy tale. *Not a Disney one,* he thought. *One of the old-fashioned kind, where people get eaten by big bad wolves.* He was about to ask Meilin whether they *had* wolves in China when she stopped, looked at her watch and grimaced.

'I'm sorry, but I have to go back. Aunty Ting will need me.'

Cleo looked round from beating at the undergrowth with a stick, still doggedly searching for a tunnel.

Ryan took her arm. 'We should go too. The light will fade soon.'

As they trooped homewards, Ryan hoped that Cleo really would be able to crack Segal's code. It was a very big mountain. *Without further directions,* he thought, *we've got about as much chance of stumbling across the Dragon Path as we have of discovering the Isles of Immortality.*

Cleo sat cross-legged on her bed, surrounded by notes. The pages of Segal's journal had turned crusty and brittle as they dried so she'd copied them out to avoid further damage. Then she'd torn the pages from her notebook and arranged them in a row.

Gazing at line upon line of numbers, Cleo chewed the end of her pencil, remembering Ryan's words: *Cleo is a code-breaking genius*. She didn't *feel* much like a genius. She just felt a bit overwhelmed. *All it needs is a systematic and logical approach,* she told herself. *It's clearly a numeric substitution cipher*. She counted the number of different numbers: forty-two. That was obviously more than the letters in the alphabet, so it wasn't as simple as one number standing for one letter. Pierre Segal must have padded the message out with 'vacant codes' to make it more difficult to see how many letters there were in each word.

Cleo had spent a lot of time researching codes when she'd been trying to figure out the Phoenix Code in Egypt. She knew there was a long tradition of numeric substitution codes in France. Everyone from Louis XIV to Napoleon had used complex ciphers with hundreds of numbers standing for different syllables and letters to send secret messages. *Maybe that's what gave Segal the idea,* Cleo thought. She just hoped he hadn't gone for anything quite so complicated.

She found a large sheet of paper and a ruler and started to make a table. In the first column she listed the forty-two numbers that Segal had used. Then she counted how many times each number occurred and entered the total in the next column. Some numbers cropped up hundreds of times. Those almost certainly stood for letters that occurred in lots of words. Other numbers only came up a few times. Those would represent the more unusual letters . . .

But now Cleo hit a problem. If she were decoding into English she'd know which letters were the frequent ones – like E and S – and which were the rarely used ones – like Z and Q and X. But Pierre Segal was French! No doubt his coded message was in French too. Maybe E *wasn't* the most frequent letter in French. Maybe Q and Z and X were used all over the place. Cleo sighed and leaned back against the wall. French was one of the few languages she'd never studied.

Decoding in a language she barely knew made things a lot more difficult.

Cleo stared down at her empty number table. She could hear Mum and Dad talking to Professor Han and Joey Zhou in the kitchen. They were making plans for the visit of Mum's boss, Sir Charles Peacocke, Director of the Department of Museums and Culture, who was arriving tomorrow to look around the Kitchen of Eternal Life site. Cleo knew that time was running out.

We're only in China for seven more days. If only I could find a fluent French speaker somewhere . . .

There was a knock on her bedroom door. She could tell it was Ryan because he was tapping out the theme tune from *Friends*.

Of course, Ryan! Ryan had read the numbers in the journal out in French. His accent had been way over the top, but anything would help.

'How good is your French?' she asked as he entered the

198

room. 'Which letters can occur on their own? Is a Q always followed by a U like it is in English?'

For some reason Ryan began talking to himself. 'Hello Ryan, how are you?' he said. 'Not too bad, thank you for asking, apart from a few scrapes and a touch of post-traumatic stress after my close encounter with Frankenstein's Amphibian.'

Cleo suspected that Ryan was trying to make a point with this strange monologue but she had no idea what it was, so she ignored it. 'I'm doing a frequency analysis on Segal's code,' she explained. 'I need to know the pattern of letter distribution in French.'

Ryan pulled the chair from the desk to the side of the bed, flipped it round, and sat leaning on the back.

'How good is my French?' he repeated. 'Well, I'm doing it for GCSE. As long as Segal sticks to what he did on his holidays last summer and his favourite school subjects we'll be OK.'

Cleo groaned. This could be even more difficult than she'd thought. 'Let's start with letters that can be on their own. Like I or A in English.'

Ryan thought for a moment. 'Well, there's Y and A.'

It's a start, at least, Cleo thought. There were five different numbers in Segal's journal that occurred on their own, which meant they could all be a Y or an A. She pencilled the possibilities into her table. 'Now, what about Q and U?'

Cleo had been frowning, scribbling and chewing her pencil for ages.

Every now and then she would look up and fire a question at Ryan. It reminded him of a nightmare he'd had where he'd somehow volunteered as a team captain on *University Challenge*. He'd accidentally pressed his buzzer to a question on neuroendocrinology (whatever *that* was!) and the quizmaster was yelling at him, 'Come on now, Flint, your answer please!' It had been a relief when he'd woken to find it was just Mum shouting to get him up for school.

'What's the most frequent bigram in French?' Cleo demanded.

Ryan played for time, dragging his hands through his hair and narrowing his eyes as if mentally running through his vast French vocabulary. In fact, he wasn't entirely sure what a bigram was.

'It means two letters that occur together,' Cleo said.

'What about *le*?' Ryan suggested. 'That means *the*.' Then he remembered that one of the many annoying things about French was that there were different words for *the* depending on whether the noun was feminine or masculine. 'Or it could be *la*.'

Cleo smiled up at him. 'Excellent point!' She made some notes in her table. 'In that case, there's a good chance that number 21 stands for L.'

Ryan enjoyed his moment of being star pupil. But now Cleo had gone back to scowling and pencil-chewing and he was getting bored. He picked up Segal's journal from the desk and flipped through. The only page that wasn't covered with numbers contained a drawing of an animal. Ryan held it up to the light. It was a side view of a tiger or a leopard about to pounce: sleek body, long curling tail, small ears pressed to its head, teeth bared in a snarl. On the facing page Segal had drawn five straight lines of different lengths, each with a number above it. Ryan flapped the picture under Cleo's nose. 'Have you seen this?'

Cleo glanced at it. 'Yeah. Looks like Segal was a doodler. Like you!'

Ryan examined the drawing again. There were tiny crosshair marks in pencil at nose and tail where Segal must have carefully measured the length of the animal. This was no random doodle. And he'd written a word beneath it in his number code: 22-9-16-9. Presumably it was a label for the drawing. 'A four-letter word,' Ryan mused out loud. 'It can't be French for *tiger* or *leopard*. *Tigre* has five letters and *léopard* has seven. Maybe it's a dog? No, *chien* has five letters too . . .'

'What are you muttering about?' Cleo asked.

'I'm trying to figure out what this animal is supposed to be.'

Cleo glanced at the picture again. Then she sprang off her bed and ran out into the living room.

Ryan looked at the Cleo-sized space she'd left behind. 'Was it something I said?'

Cleo had left the door open and he could hear snatches of her parents' conversation from the kitchen. '*Guided tour of the Kitchen of Eternal Life for Sir Charles . . . banquet in his honour with local VIPs . . . press conference . . .*' Ryan crossed his fingers and made a wish that he'd be able to get out of all the official activities. They sounded about as exciting as a double-length school prize-giving assembly.

Cleo burst back in to the room and slammed the door shut behind her.

'*Hufu!*' she exclaimed.

27

TIGER

CLEO PICKED UP Segal's journal and waved it with a flourish. 'This animal is a *hufu*. I suddenly remembered I'd seen one like it before when I was looking in the kitchen drawer yesterday for a map of Mount Li.' She held up a glossy leaflet and joggled it up and down next to the old journal. 'Look! There's one just like it in the Shaanxi History Museum in Xi'an.'

Ryan looked from the leaflet to the journal. It was true. The photograph of the small bronze figurine in the museum brochure looked very similar to Segal's drawing. The only difference was the position of the tail and the angle of the head. 'Just one tiny question,' he said. 'What's a *hufu* when it's at home?'

Cleo did a flying leap to sit back on her bed. 'A *fu* was a kind of a passport or proof of identity. It was made in two halves that came apart. A person would be given one half. The other half would be held by an official at, say, a border crossing or the entrance to a high-security area of the palace. The inscriptions on the two pieces would have to match for the person to be allowed through. A *hufu* was a special kind of *fu* in the shape of a tiger. It's usually translated as a *tiger tally*.'

Ryan whistled in awe. 'I can't believe that there is actually room in your brain to store all this stuff. The only kind of *fu* I've ever heard of is kung fu!'

Cleo looked serious for a moment before breaking out into a big smile that showed off the gap in her front teeth. 'Actually, I only just found this out too. It's all in the leaflet.' She pointed to the information box next to the photograph.

'You've totally shattered my illusions!' Ryan pulled a devastated face, but really he was delighted. *First French and now hufus.* That made two things in one day that Cleo didn't know. That had to be a record! He took the leaflet and read the information box out loud. *'Qin Dynasty bronze hufu tally. The tiger emblem was mainly used by the military. A local governor would have to match his half of the tally to the emperor's half to prove that he had the authority to send troops into battle.'* He looked up at Cleo, suddenly realizing the significance of the little tiger figure. 'Qin Dynasty? That's the First Emperor's time.'

Cleo nodded slowly. 'If the *hufu* that Segal has drawn is from the same period – which is likely, as it's almost identical – it might just be some sort of entry permit for the Dragon Path tunnel. That would explain why he's copied it into his journal.' She grabbed her magnifying glass and pored over the drawing. She threw it down again. 'Segal has written some Chinese characters on the side of the tiger, but they're tiny and they've all blurred together on this damp paper. I can't make them out. If only we had the figurine itself.'

'It wasn't in Segal's knapsack,' Ryan said. 'And before you even think it, I am *not* going back down into the salamander's lair to see whether it fell out down there.'

'Cedric Lymington or Harold Stubbs probably kept it anyway.' Suddenly Cleo jumped up from the bed again and did a sort of bouncing dance around the room.

Ryan couldn't help noticing that Cleo's version of skipping about was a lot less elegant than Meilin's. He flinched as Cleo's elbow narrowly missed his ear. 'Is this a victory jig,' he asked, 'or have you decided to translate the code using interpretive dance?'

Cleo collapsed back onto the bed. 'I just realized – this *hufu* is the key!'

'The key?' Ryan repeated.

'Remember when Grandma first told us about following Lymington and Stubbs into the tunnel? She heard them saying something like *We hold the key to a discovery of immense historical significance*. This could be the key they were talking about.'

Of course! Ryan felt like doing a dance himself now. 'In the film, Lymington is holding something in his hands. He keeps looking down at it when they are searching around for the tunnel entrance. I bet that writing on the side gives instructions for how to find the right place.'

Cleo nodded. 'This *hufu* must be what Lymington found in the cave mouth of the Kitchen of Eternal Life. Remember how he was looking at something in his hand then as well. So we were right about them finding the clue in that cave.' She squinted through the magnifying glass again. 'Aggh! It's no good. I can't read it.'

'Never mind. I'm sure Segal has written the instructions out in his journal,' Ryan said. 'He's drawn the figurine so carefully, he's bound to have copied out the words on it too – in code, of course.'

Cleo grabbed her code table. 'You're right. Which means I have to crack this code if it kills me!'

While Cleo got back to work Ryan picked up the journal and examined the tiger again. Now he noticed five dots marked at points along the body, one at the nose, neck, front paw, hind paw and tail. Were they something to do with those five lines on the next page? He studied the coded word underneath it again: 22-9-16-9.

'Maybe it says *hufu*?' he suggested. 'That's four letters.'

'That's it!' Cleo leaned forward to snatch the journal from Ryan's hands. In her excitement she forgot she was sitting cross-legged. She toppled forward and fell off the bed with a resounding crash.

The door flew open and Cleo's dad's head appeared round it. 'Is everything all right?' The murmur of conversation from the kitchen had ebbed to a worried silence. 'Sounds like you've got a troupe of clog-dancing elephants in here!'

Cleo peeped round from the back of Ryan's chair, where she was lying in a heap. 'We were just, er . . .'

'Trying out some kung fu moves,' Ryan chimed in quickly. 'You know, getting into the Chinese culture!'

Pete McNeil's bushy red eyebrows twitched behind his glasses.

'Be careful!' Cleo's mum shouted from behind him. 'We need you in one piece for Sir Charles's visit tomorrow.'

Cleo clapped her hands over her mouth to stifle her laughter and sat on the floor leaning against her bed. 'You're right,' she whispered, as soon as the door was closed again. '22-9-16-9 says *hufu*. The 9 must be the letter U. It's repeated in second and fourth place.' She began filling in squares on her grid. 'That means the 22 at the beginning is H and the 16 is F. This is a breakthrough!' Then she was riffling through all the copied pages of the journal, underlining letters here and circling others there. 'There's a lot of words starting 13-9. If nine is U and it always follows Q, then it looks as if thirteen stands for Q . . . We're really getting somewhere now!'

Cleo could hardly keep her eyes open at breakfast the next morning.

It had been almost first light by the time she'd fallen asleep, with pages still scattered over her bed and her pencil still in her hand. But she'd filled out the entire table of numbers and deciphered every word. All she needed now was a bit of help from Ryan and a French dictionary and they should be able to translate the entire message into English. She was sure it would reveal directions to the Dragon Path tunnel. With any luck, they'd be on their way back up the mountain by lunchtime.

'Sir Charles is arriving at ten,' Mum was saying. 'We're taking him for a tour of the Kitchen of Eternal Life and the Tomb of a Thousand Poisons. Then Professor Han has hired a conference room in the university so we can show him some of the artefacts we've taken out of the cave already – including the silk scroll showing the Isles of Immortality. He'll be very impressed to see the work that you and Ryan have done on piecing together the map of the islands.'

Cleo lifted her chin from her hands and smiled vaguely.

'Then there'll be a big press conference so we can tell the media all about it,' Mum went on. 'And finally a banquet and show at the Grand Opera House in Xi'an with lots of local dignitaries . . . Cleopatra, have you heard a single word I've said?'

Cleo jerked awake. 'Yes, yes. It sounds like you've got a packed day ahead.'

Mum shook her head, hands on hips. 'Cleo. When I say *we*, I'm talking about you too!'

Cleo looked at Dad, who was reading a photocopied article about arsenic poisoning in ancient Chile and munching on leftover fried rice. 'Do I *have* to?'

Dad nodded. 'I'm afraid so. Sir Charles said he was particularly keen to talk to you and Ryan about how you found the Kitchen of Eternal Life. You're the stars of the show!'

Mum looked down at Cleo's torn jeans and T-shirt. 'You should probably wear something a bit smarter.'

Cleo glanced at the clock on the wall.

She ran into her room and swept her notes into her shoulder bag. 'Just going out for a few minutes,' she called back as she flew out of the apartment. She ran along the walkway and banged on Ryan's door. His mum answered in her dressing gown, a mug of coffee in her hand. 'He went out for a walk,' she said.

'A walk?' Cleo echoed. 'Ryan? On his own? That's the second time this week!'

Julie laughed. 'I know. That's what I thought. He said he wouldn't be long, but he had a present to deliver. Sounds like he might be a bit soft on someone.'

Cleo turned on her heel. The *someone* was obviously Meilin. What was Ryan thinking of, rushing off with soppy presents when there was important work to be done on translating Segal's journal? *Which I've been up all night decoding*, she fumed. She jumped on her bike and sped out into the morning rush-hour traffic so fast she was almost ploughed down by a speeding tuk-tuk.

28

TRANSLATION

CLEO MARCHED INTO Aunty Ting's restaurant. It was full of
workers wolfing down dumplings and omelettes, but there
was no sign of Meilin or Ryan. She remembered the back
yard and hurried down the alley at the side of the building.
Hearing voices coming from the shed, she marched straight
in.

Serves them right if they're kissing or something, she thought.

Ryan and Meilin weren't kissing. They were kneeling
next to the dog basket.

Ryan looked up and grinned. 'I brought Bao Bao the bones
from last night's spare ribs.'

Cleo watched as two of the pups played tug of war with a

bone, their tails wagging so hard their whole bodies shook. Cleo couldn't help smiling. Julie was right. Ryan was soft, but maybe it wasn't on Meilin!

Ryan gently scooped up one of the pups. 'We're giving them names,' he said. 'This one is Lucky.'

Meilin stroked the puppy. 'See how the white patch on its chest looks just like a bat? That's a lucky sign, because the Chinese word for bat is *fú*.'

'And *fú* also means *good fortune*,' Cleo cut in. 'Yes, I know that.'

'I've told Meilin all about the *hufu*, by the way,' Ryan said, handing Cleo the smallest of the puppies. 'What shall we call this one?'

Cleo shrugged. The puppy was cute, but she had more urgent things on her mind. And she wasn't sure she liked Ryan telling Meilin *everything* about their operations, even if she *was* meant to be part of the team.

'How did you get on with the code, Cleo?' Meilin asked. 'Ryan told me that you had almost solved it last night.'

'I've *completed* it, actually.' Cleo's words came out a little more sharply than she intended. She tried to make up for it by explaining in a more reasonable tone. 'That's why I'm here. We need to translate Segal's words from French.' She turned to Ryan. 'And we've got less than an hour before we have to *meet-and-greet* with Sir Charles Peacocke.'

A sudden barrage of shouting made them all jump. Cleo put her eye to a crack between the wooden boards of the shed and saw Aunty Ting on the kitchen step, brandishing a ladle and a plucked chicken.

Meilin began reversing at a stoop through the low door. 'I

have to clear the tables,' she said. 'Come and have breakfast and I'll join you when I can.'

Cleo stroked the puppy and set it back in the cardboard box with Bao Bao. It had faint stripes of amber through its black fur, she noticed. 'What about Tiger?' she said.

A few minutes later, Ryan and Cleo sat down at a corner table and ordered egg pancakes and bean juice.

Ryan glanced around, checking for spies as he doused his pancake in chilli sauce. But there was no chance they would be overheard in Aunty Ting's restaurant. The clatter of chopsticks, slurp of noodles and beat of a Chinese pop song from a speaker behind the small counter made it impossible to hear a thing.

Cleo took out her notebook and slid it across the table. 'We need to get this done by ten. We might not have another chance all day.'

'No pressure, then,' Ryan muttered. He looked down at pages of Cleo's neat writing – all in French – and felt panic writhe in his stomach like a knot of snakes. This was like being in an exam. He read the first line. '*Mardi, je suis arrivé en Chine . . .*' That wasn't too bad. 'I have arrived in China on Tuesday,' he muttered, as he wrote the translation on a blank sheet of paper.

Ryan scanned the page for more familiar words. His eyes homed in on *dragon*. Of course, *dragon* was the same in French. He'd watched enough *Dragon Ball* episodes dubbed into different languages on YouTube to know that. *Who says cartoons aren't educational?* He could feel Cleo's eyes searing into his brain. *Il faut que je redonne l'anneau de jade au dragon . . .* That was a stroke of luck! 'Il faut que' was one of the phrases Miss Percival made them use in every French essay. It meant 'it is necessary that' . . . And it looked as if 'jade' was the same word in French. But what was an *anneau*? He had a vague idea it meant a lamb, but a lamb of jade wouldn't make any sense at all. *No,* he decided, *it must mean a ring of jade.* He put the pieces together and wrote, *It is necessary that I return the ring of jade to the dragon.*

Cleo pushed her plate away and scooted closer on her chair. 'Does he say where the Dragon Path is?'

'Give me a chance,' Ryan grumbled. After a few moments he had the next sentence figured out too: *Ever since I took the jade ring from the dragons the bread has been upside down on my table.*

Cleo's eyebrows rocketed under her fringe. 'The bread has been upside down on my table? That can't be right!'

'It's a French superstition,' Ryan explained. 'It's bad luck to put a loaf upside down.'

He still hadn't forgotten putting his foot in it on the first day of his French exchange trip last year, when he'd plonked a baguette down on the breadboard the wrong way up. The family had all been very nice about it, but he might as well have turned up with thirteen broken mirrors and an albatross.

Cleo nodded. 'So Segal thought the jade ring was bringing him bad luck.' She tapped the notes with her chopstick. 'What's this part here about the *hufu*?'

Ryan read. *C. L. a trouvé l'hufu dans la caverne.* He was stumped for a moment. C. L. didn't look like a French word. The he realized: C. L. stood for Cedric Lymington, of course!

He was getting into his stride now and had soon puzzled out almost the whole paragraph.

'*Cedric Lymington found the hufu in the mouth of the cave near the foot of Mount Li,*' he read aloud to Cleo.

'I knew it! The *hufu* came from the Kitchen of Eternal Life, where the *fangshi* worked on their experiments. It's the key that led Lymington and Stubbs to the Dragon Path. Does Segal say . . .'

Cleo was so excited she couldn't finish the sentence. Ryan did it for her. 'Does Segal say what's written on the side?' He smoothed down the page and added a comma and dotted an i, spinning out the dramatic moment.

'Well, *does* he?' Cleo gripped his arm and shook it.

Ryan nodded.

'Now we get to the good part,' Cleo murmured. She'd inched in so close that she was practically sitting on Ryan's lap. Meilin had finished serving the last table of customers and had hotfooted it across the room to lean over the back of his chair.

Note to self, Ryan thought. *Do not drop French as soon as possible, as previously planned. I never realized translating would make me such a girl magnet!* He cleared his throat and began to read in a hushed tone. '*The carrier of this hufu is permitted to enter the Road of the Dragons.*'

'*The Road of the Dragons?*' Cleo breathed. 'That's the Dragon Path! This really is it!'

'What does it say next?' Meilin whispered. Ryan could feel her breath on his neck.

'*To find the hidden door, follow the little white dragon to the,* er, *demi-lune.* I think that means *half-moon.*'

'But that doesn't make any sense!' Cleo dropped her head

213

onto the table. 'You must have got the translation wrong.'

'No, wait!' Meilin squeezed Ryan's shoulder so hard her nails dug through his T-shirt. 'Little white dragon – *Xiaobailong* – is the old name for that stream we followed yesterday! I remember Great-Grandfather telling me it was called that because it looks so white and fierce as it rushes down the mountain.'

'But what about the half-moon?' Cleo asked.

Meilin bounced up and down on her toes. 'It could be the old Rotten Tooth Bridge. I know it is all broken now, but it would have been a curved shape once.' She gestured a graceful arch with her arms.

Cleo looked up at her, nodding thoughtfully. 'Good thinking! I've heard of a *moon bridge*. It's shaped to make a circle like a full moon when it's reflected in the water. So the bridge itself would be the half-moon.'

Ryan continued to read out his translation. *'Turn to the west and when you come to the saule pleureur take nine steps down. This hufu is the only key to finding the way.'*

'Saule pleureur?' Cleo and Meilin repeated in unison. 'What's that?'

Ryan squinted at the words, hoping that the meaning might come into focus if he looked at them hard enough. It didn't. He thought *pleureur* might have something to do with raining, but he had no idea what a *saule* might be.

'Er ... it's not on the GCSE vocabulary list.' He remembered that he'd brought his French dictionary to China with him to do some essays Miss Percival had set him. The dictionary was still waiting, unopened, under a pile of clothes in his room. 'I'll look it up as soon as I get the chance,' he promised.

Cleo jumped up so fast that her chair toppled over backwards. 'It's five to ten!' she gasped. 'Mum will kill us if we're late for Sir Charles.'

Ryan sprang to his feet too. He had no idea that they'd been there so long. The restaurant was empty, the door still swinging as the last customers left.

'When will we go back up the mountain to look for the Road of Dragons?' Meilin asked, as Cleo and Ryan scrambled for the door.

'Tomorrow, of course,' Cleo said. 'First thing.'

'Perfect!' Meilin did a twirl. 'It's the Mid-Autumn Festival. There's no school and Aunty Ting will let me have the day off from the restaurant too. I'll collect my great-grandfather's jade ring tonight. I can't wait!'

Cleo made it home with seconds to spare.

The morning seemed to drag on forever. First there was an official welcome for Sir Charles Peacocke in one of the function rooms in the university. It was hot and stuffy. There were long speeches about preserving national heritage and the importance of Anglo–Chinese friendship. Normally, Cleo would have been interested. Today she just fidgeted on her uncomfortable chair.

Sir Charles stood up and thanked everyone. He was a solid-looking man, smartly tailored in a pinstriped suit with a silk handkerchief carefully arranged in the pocket. With his sweep of white hair and smooth pink skin, he looked like an advert for luxury watches or single malt whisky. He'd been Mum's boss at the Department of Museums and Culture for a long time. He had a habit of droning on and on, but he was so important that nobody dared interrupt him. 'Pontificating', Mum called it in private. Cleo could hear the tappety-tap of Ryan's chair as he rocked on its back legs, and the click of fingernails as Alex Shawcross checked her text messages under cover of a pile of notes. The only person who didn't look bored was Sir Charles Peacocke's assistant, Melanie Moore. She gazed up at him adoringly through her eyelashes.

At last it was over. They all piled into a convoy of jeeps and headed to the Kitchen of Eternal Life and the Tomb of a Thousand Poisons. The tour of the caves all went to plan, apart from Melanie breaking a high heel, and having to stumble around clutching Sir Charles's arm. Then it was back to the university for the display of the fragments of the Isles of Immortality scroll, which were being stored in a safe in the Department of Archaeology. Sir Charles smiled and congratulated everyone on the unique and priceless find. Then came the press conference and more speeches . . .

It wasn't until the banquet, when they were seated at a huge round table in the hall of the Grand Opera building in downtown Xi'an, that Cleo had a chance to talk to Ryan again.

The place was teeming with important people, including local government officials and the chief of police. In spite of the opulent surroundings – chandeliers, red velvet curtains, Tang Dynasty-style wall-hangings of beautiful ladies and mountain scenes – Cleo wasn't in a good mood. Not only had Mum insisted she wear a *dress* for the occasion, she'd then had to endure the minibus journey with Melanie Moore complaining about the hairdryer in her hotel room. She had some kind of elaborately constructed coiffure that required 'ultra-volumizing with diffuse heat', whatever that meant. Cleo had almost got trapped sitting next to Melanie again for the meal, but she'd managed a quick switch with Joey Zhou.

Joey was more than happy with the deal. His quiff quivered with delight as he pulled out a chair for the glamorous Melanie and her volumized hair.

'How *you* doin?' he crooned.

'Weeping willow,' Ryan whispered in Cleo's ear as he sat down next to her.

29

BANQUET

'WEEPING WILLOW?' CLEO echoed.

'That's what *saule pleureur* means.' Ryan had looked it up in his French dictionary the moment he'd got back from breakfast at Aunty Ting's. *'Turn to the west and when you come to the weeping willow, take nine steps down.* Now we know how to find . . .' – he broke off, remembering they might be overheard – '. . . the you-know-what.'

Cleo toasted him with her glass of rice wine. 'Good work,' she whispered.

Ryan ducked as a waitress reached over his shoulder with a tureen of soup. They were coming in from all sides now, loading the table – which had one of those revolving middles – with platters and bowls and trays of food. The waitresses announced each dish in Chinese and English as they set it down: whole carp, special Xi'an mutton broth with wide noodles, braised white fungus, spicy pig kidney, stewed squid . . .

Ryan piled his plate high. Cleo had begun discussing Ming Dynasty tomb construction with one of Professor Han's students, so he turned to talk to Alex Shawcross on his other side. He soon regretted it. She looked stunning, in a red satin dress with low-cut top and full swishy skirt, but her idea of dinnertime conversation was a detailed discussion of some ancient disease featuring boils or pustules or phlegm, or preferably all three. This evening's choice was bubonic plague.

Alex paused to smile at a waiter as he set another bowl of food in front of her. 'Pig tripe with duck gizzard,' he announced.

"Yummy,' Alex said, taking a large helping. She dangled what looked like an old grey dishcloth from her chopsticks. 'I do love tripe. It's the lining of the stomach, you know.'

Ryan didn't even *want* to know. He took a bite of unidentified meat from his soup. It tasted good but had an odd spongy texture.

Alex waved her chopsticks at his bowl. 'Those are slices of congealed sheep's blood. They make it by—'

'Have you heard anything from Tian Min?' Ryan spluttered, gulping from his cup of sweet rice wine. Anything to steer the subject away from plague and offal!

Alex shook her head. 'No. I asked in the university office. I thought I'd get his address and send a card to say we were sorry to hear about his mother.' She frowned at her gizzards.

'It was rather peculiar. The lady in the office said they'd had a computer glitch and they'd lost all his records.' She leaned closer to Ryan. 'I'm starting to wonder whether Tian Min wasn't quite what he seemed.'

'What do you mean?' Ryan asked.

Alex tucked a curl of golden hair behind her ear. 'Could he have got in with this Tiger's Claw bunch?' she whispered. 'I can't help thinking it's all frightfully suspicious.'

Ryan saw her point. Tian Min had seemed such a genuine down-to-earth guy, but the way he'd disappeared just as the spate of tomb robberies had started didn't look good.

As if on cue, Ryan heard someone on the other side of the table say the words 'Tiger's Claw'. He looked up and tuned into the conversation. He wasn't surprised to see that it was his mum who was talking about the gang. She'd positioned herself between the police chief and a government official, no doubt so that she could quiz them both about the latest criminal activities.

'I hear there have been several more robberies in the north of Shaanxi,' she said. 'All with the Tiger's Claw calling card.'

The official blinked, his eyes owl-like behind thick black-rimmed glasses, and frowned as if he didn't know what she meant.

'You know,' Mum persisted. 'Their graffiti tag – five lines, like scratch marks.' She made a claw of her hand to demonstrate. She turned to the police chief. 'I heard that a valuable collection of Zhou Dynasty bronze vessels was stolen from the museum in Hanzhong. How are the police responding? Do you think the gang might be planning an even bigger heist during the Mid-Autumn Festival?'

Ryan cringed. Mum really didn't know when to stop.

Professor Han was glancing around nervously. Sir Charles glowered disapprovingly from under his seagull-wing sweep of white hair. There was an awkward silence. The police chief pushed his bowl away. He had a fleshy face and small eyes that reminded Ryan of the giant salamander, but his lips curled into a smile.

'No need to worry, Miss Flint,' he said. 'We will have double security. Triple security. There will be no more problems.' His eyes ranged around the table like searchlights, as if challenging anyone to disagree.

Melanie Moore giggled nervously. 'Well, that's good to know.'

Nobody else spoke. A long awkward silence parked itself across the entire table. Then, to Ryan's relief, the tension broke as velvet curtains at one end of the hall parted to reveal a stage, set as a magnificent palace scene. In the centre stood an announcer who introduced the show and explained that it would feature traditional music and dance from the golden age of the Tang Dynasty. Then musicians dressed in flame-red gowns, richly embroidered in sparkling gold, struck up a rousing performance on zithers, lutes, flutes and bells. Graceful girls floated in floor-length dresses with long flowing sleeves that swirled like streamers in the breeze as they fluttered their arms.

As Ryan watched the Lotus Flower Dance, the Feather Dress Dance and the Spring Rain Dance, an odd feeling kept nagging at him. He was sure something had been said around the table that was significant, but he couldn't pin it down. He replayed the conversation as the dancers twirled in a wash of jade-green stage lights. It was something to do with the Tiger's Claw gang ... Mum had been describing their graffiti tag ... *That was it – the five scratch marks!*

The phrase had reminded him of the five lines Pierre Segal had drawn so carefully next to the *hufu* tiger. Ryan had been trying to figure out what they meant ever since he'd first seen them in the journal. He sneaked his small sketchbook from his pocket and examined the copy he'd made. Could these lines be the symbol of the Tiger's Claw gang? Was the gang even operating back in 1936? *They don't look like scratch marks,* he thought. The lines ran horizontally across the page, for a start, rather than from top to bottom. And then there was the number Segal had written above each line, as if to label it. The shortest line was marked 21, which Ryan knew stood for L in Segal's code. But the others – including 45 and 52 – didn't appear in the code at all.

Ryan was still mulling over the mystery of the five lines when the music stopped for the interval. He'd set off down a corridor, looking for the bathroom, when he passed Melanie Moore coming out of the ladies' toilets, holding forth to Alex Shawcross on her favourite topic.

'Top tip,' she said. 'Travel adaptors! There's nothing worse than finding you can't plug your hairdryer into those funny foreign sockets. Absolute nightmare!'

Ryan stopped in his tracks. *Of course,* he thought. *That's the answer! The lines Segal drew are like pins on a plug. And the numbers aren't part of the code. They're measurements!* Suddenly he knew what he had to do. And he had to do it before tomorrow morning! He turned on his heel and sped back down the corridor.

'Sorry, sorry,' he mumbled to Sir Charles Peacocke and Joey Zhou as he barged past them in the middle of a conversation.

He slowed to a wobbly pace as he entered the hall. 'I've started feeling really sick,' he informed the company at the table in a weak-but-brave voice. 'I think I'll just get the bus straight home.'

Alex was sitting back down. 'Perhaps it was the congealed blood,' she said. 'I thought you looked a bit peaky.'

Professor Han looked round. 'Joey can give you a lift back on his motorbike. Where's he gone?'

'Last seen on the way to the toilets,' Melanie said. 'Perhaps he's been taken ill too.'

'No problem,' Ryan mumbled, pretending to sway a little. 'I'll be fine on the bus.'

Mum got up and grabbed her handbag. 'I'll come with you, love. A taxi will be quicker.'

'I'll explain later,' Ryan whispered to Cleo as he staggered out, clutching his guts.

Cleo pressed her forehead against the cool glass and gazed out of the minibus as they drove through the suburbs of Xi'an. The windows of the high-rise blocks of flats lined up in rows and rows of yellow squares against the black sky. Red lights on the booms of giant cranes winked as the machines worked through the night, building ever more skyscrapers. *What in the world,* she wondered, *is Ryan up to?* She was almost certain he was faking that sudden attack of gastroenteritis. Even the fastest-acting bacteria like *Staphylococcus aureus* would usually take at least an hour to produce food-poisoning symptoms. She'd texted him three times but he hadn't replied. It had been a long day. She nodded off and was still half-asleep when they reached the front door of their flat in the university guest block.

Dad fumbled with the key before standing back and peering over his glasses at the lock. 'It's been forced,' he muttered. 'We've been burgled.'

Mum pushed past him and threw open the door. Cleo followed, to see the furniture tipped over and papers strewn across the floor. She automatically felt for the two jade rings – the one from Grandma and the one from Pierre Segal's knapsack – safely stowed in the side pocket of her dress. She ran into her room. Her laptop was still on the desk. She yanked open the drawer and found Segal's journal still taped to the back where she'd hidden it. She flopped down on the bed, dizzy with relief.

'It doesn't look as if they've taken much,' Dad called from the kitchen. 'My credit card's still here . . .'

But he was interrupted by a wail from Mum in the living room. 'They've taken all our work on the Isles of Immortality scroll – the copied fragments that Cleo and Ryan pieced together, my translation notes, everything!'

Cleo was running to Mum's side when Dad's phone rang. His expression as he took the call filled her with a cold, creeping dread. It took a lot to erase the cheerful smile from Dad's freckled face. He hung up.

'That was Professor Han,' he said flatly. 'Someone's broken into the Department of Archaeology. They've taken the original silk scroll from the safe as well.'

30

KEY

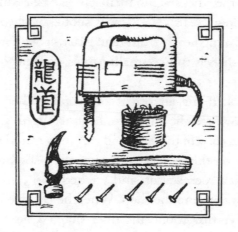

MEANWHILE, RYAN WAS in Gao Xin's grandfather's workshop at the back of the hardware store.

The moment they'd arrived home from the banquet he'd scooted out of the door before Mum had time to argue, claiming that he needed fresh air. He'd cycled at top speed, and had found Gao Xin – the friendly Xbox-playing rock god – outside the shop, working on the engine of a clapped-out motor scooter.

Gao Xin had smiled. 'Play *Crazy Mouse?*' he offered, throwing his spanner into a toolbox and wriggling out from under the scooter.

Ryan had shaken his head. 'Can I ask you a favour?' he'd

225

asked. 'I need to make something using wood . . .' It had taken a complicated pantomime of sawing and hammering to explain what he wanted, but Gao Xin seemed to understand; he'd given a thumbs-up and led Ryan through to the workshop.

Luckily Gao Xin's grandfather had already gone to bed, so they had the workshop to themselves. The cramped space, lit by a fluorescent tube light, was spotlessly clean and tidy. Equipment hung neatly from metal racks and the walls were lined with shelves full of smaller tools and tins of nuts and bolts.

Ryan looked for an offcut of wood. When he found something of the right thickness, he took out his sketchbook, turned to his copy of the *hufu* and carefully traced the outline of the tiger on the surface of the wood. Gao Xin tuned an old radio to a rock station and fetched two cans of Future Cola from a fridge in the shop. When he returned, Ryan did a mime of cutting round the tiger shape. Gao Xin handed him a small electric jigsaw from a rack. It was similar to one that Ryan had used before in Design and Technology lessons – although he'd never cut out anything more advanced than a toy banana. He took a gulp of cola, grabbed a pair of goggles off a hook, clamped the wood to the workbench and set to work, to the soundtrack of a Chinese rock anthem.

As Ryan concentrated on guiding the saw blade around the tiger's outline he thought through his brainwave again. It had been Melanie Moore going on about her travel adaptor plug that had given him the idea: the *hufu* could have been designed to fit into a socket in just the same way. If he was right, the five lines Segal had drawn next to the *hufu* represented five pins that stuck out from the back of the tiger's body. The number next to each line gave the length of the pin in millimetres, while the five dots he'd spotted on the nose, neck, paws and tail of the tiger showed the position of the pins.

He wasn't thinking of an *electrical* socket, of course! Ryan could almost hear Cleo's voice putting him right on that point. *They didn't* have *electricity in 200 BC!* It was more like a key fitting into a lock. After all, the final line of the inscription on the side of the tiger said, *this* hufu *is the only key to find the way.* They'd assumed that it meant the *hufu* was the key in the sense that it held the vital information – but what if it was also *literally* the key that would unlock the door to the Dragon Path tunnel?

Cleo would approve of that, he thought.

Ryan eased the blade through the wood around the tiger's fiddly curled tail. He cast his mind back to the Dragon Path film. It was so frustrating that the damaged section, when the film went black for a few seconds, had been at the critical point when Lymington and Stubbs were opening the tunnel – it had skipped straight from the men standing outside on the mountain to them being inside in the dark – so there was no way of knowing for *sure* that they'd inserted the *hufu* into a door as a key.

But, Ryan thought, *I'd be willing to bet my entire collection of* Dragon Ball *comics that they did . . .*

Which is why he was now in the workshop doing his best to fashion a copy of the *hufu.*

If I can just get it the right shape, with all the pins exactly to length and in the correct positions to slot into the keyhole, it might just work to unlock the door to the Dragon Path tunnel. That's assuming we can actually find the door when we go looking tomorrow, of course . . .

He was almost all the way round the outline when the jigsaw blade slipped and cut the tail off. Ryan cursed and found another piece of wood, traced the outline and started all over again. On the third attempt he managed to complete the job with the tail intact. He found an old milk powder tin containing long metal panel pins and hammered one through the tiger template in each of the five positions marked, so that they poked out of the back. Then he adjusted each pin by pushing it in or out until it matched the exact length that Segal had noted in his journal.

At last Ryan stood back to admire the finished item.

'Rock on!' Gao Xin held up both hands for a high five, even though he must have been totally mystified by the entire episode.

Perhaps, Ryan thought, Gao Xin just figured that crafting wooden tigers in the middle of the night was a bizarre English custom, like Morris dancing or cheese rolling!

What can be taking Ryan so long? Cleo wondered as she hammered on his front door the next morning.

She knocked again. Today was the day! They were going to return the jade rings to the Dragon Path and they needed to get moving. They'd agreed to meet Wu Meilin at the bottom of the mountain track at nine o'clock. Cleo double-checked she had everything she needed in her tool belt. In addition to her usual archaeologist's kit of trowel, brushes, magnifying glass, penknife, gloves, tweezers and torch, she'd packed binoculars to look out for suspicious followers. She'd also dressed especially for the mission, in zip-off hiking trousers, new all-terrain trainers, microfibre top and her favourite long white cotton scarf.

She pressed her ear to the door.

'But you're sick,' she heard Julie Flint shout. 'You should be resting, not gallivanting about with Cleo!'

Gallivanting? Cleo was sure she had never gallivanted in her life. She bumped her forehead against the door. This was a disaster! Had Ryan's ridiculous food-poisoning act ruined the whole mission? *I'll have to go alone,* she thought. *But it won't be the same without . . .*

At that moment the door swung open. Cleo, who was still leaning against it, stumbled into Ryan's arms as he came barrelling out. He bulldozed her along with him.

'Quick,' he muttered. 'Keep going. Before Mum changes her mind. I had to promise to go straight home if I feel the slightest bit queasy, to eat nothing but dry bread, and to rest for the next fifty years.'

They hustled along the walkway, which took them past Cleo's apartment. Ryan slowed to stare at the yellow crime tape across the door and the policemen standing outside. Mrs Long was there too, sweeping leaves that had blown in from outside. She looked up and smiled at Ryan before going back to glaring at the policemen for making the building look untidy.

'What's going on?' Ryan spluttered.

'We were burgled,' Cleo whispered. 'I called round to tell you last night but your mum said you'd gone out for fresh air.'

'What did they take?'

'Nothing except the scroll that we helped Mum work on. The one with the map of the missing Isles of Immortality. They took the original from the university safe too. Mum's in a real state about it . . .' Cleo paused, noticing that Ryan was frowning intently at the door of the flat.

'It's the Tiger's Claw gang,' he murmured.

'Quite possibly,' Cleo agreed. 'That's what the police think.'

'No, I mean it's *definitely* the Tiger's Claw. Look, they've left their mark!'

Cleo followed Ryan's eye line. She'd been in such a hurry to leave that she'd not noticed it before: five parallel lines gouged into the doorframe, one shorter and slightly below the others. It was proof that the Tiger's Claw gang were behind the theft. Not that it came as any surprise, Cleo thought. The Tiger's Claw obviously ran a major operation stealing ancient artefacts to sell on the black market. And the scroll would fetch a high price. Although it was in fragments, such ancient silk manuscripts and maps were incredibly rare. And collectors were always desperate for anything associated with the First Emperor or the search for immortality. No doubt the gang thought that it would fetch an even better price if they had all Mum's translations and notes and the copies of the pieces showing how to put them together, to sell as part of the package.

'You weren't really ill, were you?' Cleo asked, as they jogged down the steps.

Ryan shook his head. 'No. Although listening to Alex talk about plague and gizzards was enough to make anyone lose their lunch. It was just a cover story to get away quickly because I'd suddenly figured something out . . .'

As they unlocked their bikes Cleo listened in astonishment to Ryan's account of how Melanie Moore's hairdryer troubles had sparked his brainwave about the *hufu* being a key that could slot into the door to open the Dragon Path tunnel.

'I had to pretend to be ill,' Ryan explained, 'so I could get back and make a replica of the *hufu* in time for this morning.'

Cleo stared at him as they wheeled their bikes towards the gate. 'You just went off and *made* a bronze tiger figurine?'

Ryan laughed. 'Of course not. I cut the shape out of wood and hammered in panel pins.'

'In the middle of the night?' It suddenly occurred to Cleo that this might be one of Ryan's inexplicable jokes. 'Where, exactly?' she asked suspiciously.

'Gao Xin's grandfather's workshop.'

Now Cleo was *sure* Ryan was teasing her. She'd never heard of Gao Xin, let alone his grandfather. She decided to call Ryan's bluff. 'Oh, yes? Show me this wooden *hufu* you made, then!'

Ryan stopped, unzipped his backpack, pulled out a small biscuit tin, opened the lid and handed it to Cleo. Inside was a block of wood in the exact shape of the tiger in Pierre Segal's journal. Five metal pins of different lengths protruded from the back.

Cleo shot Ryan a sideways glance. Maybe he hadn't been joking after all. She put the tin back in Ryan's backpack. 'I still don't know who Gao Xin is,' she said, as they walked their bikes out into the busy street.

'He's a rock god. He lives above the hardware store on Meilin's street.'

I should have known, Cleo thought as she got on her bike. *Another of Ryan's friends! If we landed on a planet in the outer reaches of a distant galaxy he'd be having afternoon tea with the microbial life forms within half an hour. Not that extra-solar microbes would drink tea, of course,* she corrected herself. *They'd synthesize methane and sulphur compounds into energy.*

Just then, as if to prove the point, a little boy shot out from the traffic and thrust a carrier bag into Ryan's hands. He did a mime of bouncing a ball and leaping up towards an invisible net and then darted back off down the street.

Cleo couldn't help laughing. 'Yet another of your buddies?'

Ryan grinned. 'He's one of Meilin's cousins. He came to see the puppies when I was there the other morning. We played a bit of basketball.'

He balanced the bag on his handlebars and slid out a beribboned white cardboard box containing four small round pastries.

'Mooncakes!' Cleo said. 'They're traditional for Mid-Autumn Festival. A special *romantic* present for you from Meilin, I expect.'

Ryan opened the card tucked under the ribbon. '*Happy Mid-Autumn Festival to my friends Cleo and Ryan,*' he read out. '*Make sure you eat these all yourselves. From Wu Meilin.*'

Cleo smiled. She didn't even like mooncakes very much, but she was glad that the gift wasn't just for Ryan.

Ryan propped his bike against a bus shelter and opened the box. 'Great, I'm starving! Mum only let me have toast and water this morning.' He sat down on the bench next to a queue of ladies with shopping bags, offered Cleo a mooncake and then bit into one himself.

'Not bad,' he mumbled with his mouth full. 'A bit like Eccles cakes.'

'The filling is red bean paste,' Cleo told him, sitting

down and nibbling at the pastry. Suddenly she spat it out. There was something poking out from inside the cake! Something white. It looked as if a label or a scrap of a receipt had fallen into the mixture. She picked out the little roll of paper and unfurled it. Someone had written the single word 'everywhere' in the centre.

'Wait!' Cleo cried, snatching the half-eaten mooncake out of Ryan's hand. 'Don't eat that!'

31

MESSAGE

RYAN ALMOST CHOKED as Cleo swiped the mooncake right out of his mouth. 'What are you *doing*?' he coughed. 'If you're that hungry, we can get some more!'

Cleo didn't reply. She was too busy poking at a lump of red bean filling. Ryan saw something small and white and round in the goo. *Oh, no, was there a maggot in there? Or, even worse, half a maggot?*

But Cleo was waving a little slip of paper at him. 'I knew it! This is just like the Ming revolutionaries in the Yuan Dynasty. They used mooncakes to send secret messages!'

Ryan was totally lost. 'Why are Ming revolutionaries sending *us* messages?'

Cleo shook her head. 'I didn't say it *was* them. That was the thirteenth century! This message is from Meilin. Look, it's her writing.'

Ryan took the sticky bit of paper from Cleo and inspected it. '*Ten!*' he read out. 'What's that supposed to mean?' Cleo handed him another piece of paper. '*Everywhere?*' he read. 'No, not helping.'

Cleo had started pulling the last two cakes apart. She extracted another roll of paper. '*Eyes,*' she read. And then the last one. '*Meet!*'

'*Everywhere ten eyes meet?*' Ryan asked. 'What kind of message is that?'

'Try a different order.' Cleo shuffled the papers. '*Ten eyes meet everywhere.* No, that's not it. What about this? *Eyes everywhere. Meet ten.*'

Ryan nodded. At last it was making some sense. They'd planned to meet Meilin at nine. She was going to be an hour late for some reason. *Eyes everywhere?* Ryan glanced up and down the street. It was true. There were police and security guards patrolling all over the place. *Double security,* the police chief had told Mum at the banquet. *Triple security.* They must be on the lookout for the Tiger's Claw gang.

'Can I eat the mooncakes now?' he asked.

Cleo handed him the whole box. 'Eat the message too. It's rice paper.'

龍
道

The meeting place was a small paved square shaded by maple trees. From one corner, steps led up to the well-trodden paths on the north side of the mountain, where tourists strolled, stopping off at temples and cafés on the way to the summit. But tucked away behind the trees was the unmarked trail that snaked its way up to the remote southern slopes. The sun was shining and the square was bustling with traders setting up food and knick-knack stands for the Mid-Autumn Festival. The smoky fragrance of roast sweet potatoes and grilled kebabs filled the air. One man was attaching hundreds of kites to flutter above his stall, while another was hanging up wind chimes.

While they waited for Meilin, Ryan stocked up on picnic supplies. He packed hard-boiled 'tea eggs', pork buns, watermelon slices and more mooncakes into his backpack.

Cleo kept glancing nervously around. 'I've been thinking,' she said, shading her eyes to look back down the hill. 'What if that message was a trap?'

'A trap?' Ryan asked.

'Meilin could have told the police what we are doing. Maybe they're waiting to arrest us as soon as we find the tunnel. Or she's working for the Tiger's Claw after all. That message could have been a ploy to delay us while *they* go and find the Dragon Path. She knows all the directions from the *hufu* now.'

'You're getting paranoid,' Ryan told her. 'Meilin will be here soon. It's only ten past ten.' But they'd already been asked to show their proof of identity three times by the police and security guards. There was only so long they could pretend to be photographing each other in front of the gnarled old gingko tree smothered in red ribbons that people had draped there to request good fortune. Ryan noticed an old lady nearby selling the red ribbons. He bought one and snagged it on a low branch. He wasn't sure whether you were meant to make a wish too, but he did anyway.

I wish Meilin would hurry up! Then, because that didn't seem serious enough somehow, he added another. *And that our mission to return the jade rings to the dragons goes without a hitch.*

'Nice work, tree,' he murmured as he turned round and saw that it had granted his first wish already. Meilin was on her way into the square at last. To Ryan's surprise, she was riding a small black pony, and was leading two more by the reins. She waved to a policeman as she passed and shouted something in Mandarin.

'She told him we're going pony trekking!' Cleo whispered to Ryan.

Meilin trotted up to the wishing tree and hopped down. 'Did you get my message?' she asked.

Cleo nodded.

Meilin spoke quietly, pretending to be adjusting the bridle, so that Ryan and Cleo had to lean close to catch her words. 'I heard on the radio this morning that the police would be all over Mount Li. They think that the Tiger's Claw gang might be hiding out up here somewhere. I realized we'd never be able to stray away from the main tourist trails without a good . . .' she paused, searching for the English word.

'Cover story,' Ryan offered.

'Yes, that's it. So I borrowed these three from my grandfather's orchard.' Meilin handed him the reins of a scrawny grey pony. 'You can take Starlight. You *can* ride, can't you?'

'Sure!' Ryan said. He'd had a couple of lessons when he

was six and had watched the show-jumping finals in the Olympics.

Cleo looked terrified as she swung herself up onto the third of the ponies. 'Come on,' she said in the *let's-get-it-over-with* tone of someone about to dive off the high board for the first time.

Riding is all about confidence, Ryan remembered hearing somewhere. Confidently, he snapped the reins. The pony bolted up the path so fast he was almost catapulted backwards. He grabbed the mane and clung on. It wasn't exactly the ice-cool cowboy swagger he'd been aiming for, but at least they were on the move.

The ponies ambled along the path through the pine forest. They seemed to know where they were going and Ryan soon relaxed and settled in to the swaying gait. They made good time and before long passed Sunrise Pavilion and came to the Little White Dragon stream. The surefooted mountain ponies picked their way up the steep slope, following the course of the tumbling water. When they came to the rickety bridge, the three dismounted and looped the ponies' reins over an old post. Without the fog that had blindfolded them on their last visit, Ryan realized just how high up they were. He could see for miles across the plain, patchwork fields, that gave way to a winding river glittering in the sunshine, and villages and towns beyond.

Cleo seemed to have forgiven Meilin for being late. 'It was a good idea to bring the ponies,' she said, smiling. 'It was much quicker than walking.' She pulled her notes from her tool belt. 'So this is Half-Moon Bridge, according to Segal's journal.' She consulted Ryan's translation of the inscription on the *hufu* for a moment. 'We have to turn west here.'

Ryan pointed to the right. 'West is that way.'

Meilin looked puzzled and pointed in the opposite direction. 'But last time you said it was that way.' She turned to Cleo. 'You said your grandmother told you to go *left* at the bridge.'

'That's right!' Cleo agreed. 'I mean, that's *correct*. Grandma said left.'

Ryan couldn't help laughing. He remembered sitting in Eveline Bell's room in London. Cleo and her grandmother were so alike, perhaps their sense of direction – or rather lack of it – was something else they had in common. 'Do you think she might have got her left and right muddled up?' he asked. 'She *was* only eight at the time.'

Cleo frowned. 'I can't imagine Grandma would make such an elementary mistake. Are you sure you translated the word properly?'

'Certain,' Ryan said. 'It's definitely west.'

They took the path to the right and set off on foot, leaving the ponies to graze. Meilin skipped across the stream, balancing effortlessly on the slippery rocks. Ryan and Cleo picked their way across and caught her up on the other side.

'According to the *hufu*, we're looking for a weeping willow,' Cleo said, as they trekked through the undergrowth. '*Salix babylonica*, to give it its proper name, is native to northern China but it would be pretty unusual at this altitude . . .'

Ryan caught Meilin's eye and she grinned back. *More of Cleo's fascinating facts!*

'But how would it have survived for two thousand years since the time of the First Emperor?' Cleo went on. 'A willow has a life span of seventy years at most.'

Ryan didn't reply. He'd stopped to climb over an enormous

twisted tree stump when he was reminded of a scene in the old film. Lymington and Stubbs had stood posing with one foot up on a stump just like this. He called Cleo and Meilin to look.

Cleo knelt and examined the bark and some shoots that were sprouting from beneath the stump. 'Yes, it's willow!'

Ryan felt his pulse race.

They were getting so close he could almost smell those dragons!

32

ENTRANCE

MEILIN CROUCHED DOWN next to the willow stump and began clearing dry leaves and soil with her hands. 'There's something hard under here. I just stepped on it.'

Ryan and Cleo knelt on either side of Meilin. Between them they'd soon uncovered a round bronze plaque about the size of a dinner plate. A weeping willow design had been engraved in the centre.

'That's small seal script,' Cleo breathed, pointing out the characters around the rim. 'It's Qin Dynasty.' She looked up. 'It must have been a marker to show where the weeping willow was first planted over two thousand years ago. This old stump and these shoots could be descendants of the original tree.'

Ryan punched the air. 'We're nearly there! According to the *hufu* inscription we just have to take nine paces down the hill.'

Ryan, Cleo and Meilin exchanged glances of nervous excitement and set off down the steep bank, counting each stride in chorus. When they reached nine, they each faced in a different direction and began to search.

Just as in the old film, the slope was matted with a sprawling jungle of rhododendron bushes. Ryan soon gave up tearing at the branches and crawled right in under the canopy of tough, waxy leaves. It was hot, dusty, scratchy work. After a while, he stopped for a drink of water. But as he twisted round, feeling for the bottle in the pocket of his backpack, he slipped. He skidded down through the tangle of stems and roots until he crumpled to a halt against something solid.

Shaking out the loose grit and dry leaves that had collected up the legs of his jeans, Ryan sat up and saw that the 'something solid' was a huge outcrop of rock that looked as if it had been split down the middle by a giant's axe to form an enormous V shape. He looked around to see that he was in a small clearing enclosed by shaggy mounds of rhododendron that completely hid the rock from view from outside.

He stood up and stepped between the two walls of the V.

'I've found something!' he yelled. 'Over here!'

The girls came crashing through the wall of foliage. The bushes towered high above their heads.

'What is it?' Meilin cried.

Cleo hurtled into the V, stepping on Ryan's toe in her haste. 'Is it the Dragon Path?' She fell silent as Ryan pointed out a hollow in the surface of the rock. If you didn't know what

242

you were looking for, you could mistake it for a random dent. But within the hollow was a hole. Cleo took her torch from her tool belt and shone it inside. Ryan reached in and pulled away a little clump of yellow lichen.

'What have you found?' Meilin bounced up and down to see over their shoulders. Ryan stood aside and showed her. The hole in the rock was in the shape of a tiger.

'See if it fits!' Cleo urged.

Ryan was already removing his wooden replica of the *hufu* from its box. Meilin – who hadn't seen it before – watched in amazement as he positioned it over the socket and tried to insert it. He frowned. 'The pins won't go in.'

'The little holes must be all clogged up with dirt,' Cleo pointed out.

'Here, use this.' Meilin unpinned her Third Place gymnastics medal from the collar of her tracksuit.

Ryan scraped at each of the holes with the little pin until they were clear of dirt and tried again. The pins of the *hufu* still didn't fit properly. Some of them were too long. He pushed harder. He'd been so sure this would work . . .

Cleo pulled his hand away. 'It'll break if you force it!' She took the replica, turned it over and frowned. 'How did you know which length pin to put in which position?' she asked.

Ryan leaned his forehead on the rock. 'I assumed Segal drew the five lines in the right order,' he said flatly.

'The *right* order?' Cleo queried.

Ryan peeled his forehead away from the rock. 'Yeah, the first one should obviously be the nose, then the neck and so on to the tail.'

Cleo shook her head. 'Theoretically, Segal could have drawn the pins in *any* order. That's five pins in any of five positions. There are one hundred and twenty possible permutations.'

Ryan stared down at the wooden tiger. *Theoretically* he felt like hurling it down the mountain – closely followed by Cleo and her permutations. It had taken him long enough to fit the pins in *this* order! It would take days to work through one hundred and twenty possibilities.

There was a long, frustrated silence.

'Perhaps Segal just ordered the lines the other way round?' Meilin ventured at last. 'Going from tail to nose instead of nose to tail?'

Ryan could have hugged her. *A simple, sensible suggestion at last!* It was definitely worth a try. He pulled out the pins and put them back in reverse order, using the heel of the trowel from Cleo's tool belt as a hammer, and her tape measure to check that each pin was sticking out to the right length. At last the delicate operation was complete.

'Let's hope it works this time,' he muttered as he inserted the tiger into the hollow in the rock. 'I'm not doing that another hundred and eighteen times.'

All five pins of the *hufu* slotted perfectly into place.

Ryan held his breath. There was a clicking sound inside the rock. From deep underground came a rumbling like the snores of a hibernating grizzly bear.

One half of the rock V twitched and began to move. It stopped and juddered as if stuck, the noise growing louder, grating like huge gears grinding together. Ryan gave the rock a push and it continued to slide very slowly back to reveal a large round hole in the ground beneath. Cleo and Meilin clutched each other by the elbows.

'It's the tunnel!' Meilin breathed.

Cleo took her torch from her tool belt and shone it down into the space. There was a short drop down to what looked like a wide ramp.

'This is it,' Ryan said. 'Now, let's give those rings back to the dragons and get out of here before anyone sees us and thinks we're trying to break into the forbidden tomb.'

Cleo looked round. 'No one's going to see us here!'

Ryan knew she was right. They were in the middle of nowhere, hidden by mutant vegetation. The only sound was of sparrows twittering overhead. But he still felt uncomfortable about opening the ancient tunnel. He turned to Meilin. 'Have you got the ring from your great-grandfather?'

Meilin opened the gym bag she wore over her shoulder, pulled out a jade ring and handed it to him. 'I brought these too,' she said, fishing in her bag again. She took out three objects that looked like tin cans attached to shower caps made out of foil. 'They're gas masks to protect us from smoke. Just in case there really are any fire-breathing dragons down there. I got them from my cousin who works at a big hotel in Xi'an. They have them in all the rooms in case of fire.'

'Good thinking,' Cleo said as they all hung the masks round their necks.

Ryan gave what he hoped looked like a brave grin. 'And I'm wearing my lucky Manchester United pants too, so we should be fine.'

Cleo shook her head. 'What possible connection could there be between your choice of underwear and anything whatsoever?'

Meilin giggled. 'Wait, that reminds me,' she said. 'I almost forgot.' She held out her hand. 'Lucky charms. One for each of you. I made them myself.'

245

Cleo took one of the charms and stuffed it in her trouser pocket. Ryan thanked Meilin and took the other one – a tiny silver coin attached to red thread knotted into a flower design. He was just threading it onto the lace around his neck, next to his St Christopher medal and his scarab amulet, when someone grabbed him from behind.

33

TUNNEL

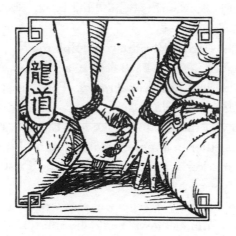

CLEO KICKED AND lashed out with every gram of strength in her body, but it was no good. The man who had her arms pinioned to her sides just tightened his grip.

'Keep still!' A garlic-laden Chinese voice spat in her ear. 'You vicious little eel!'

She twisted her head and sank her teeth into the muscly forearm clamped across her chest. The man screeched, grabbed hold of her plait and yanked her head back so hard her teeth clattered together.

Still with her head pulled back, Cleo swivelled her eyes to look around. Ryan was on the ground. The man holding him down suddenly swung into view. Cleo's insides shrivelled in horror as she saw the handsome face and the smile with its perfect white teeth. His trademark quiff was hidden beneath a black wool beanie hat pulled low over his forehead, but it was definitely Joey Zhou. And he seemed to be in charge.

'Tie them up!' he barked.

A third man – skinny, bearded and covered in tattoos – began to bind Cleo's wrists behind her back. The nylon cord pinched her skin.

'Joey!' Cleo cried. 'Why are you doing this?'

Joey laughed a cold hard laugh a million miles from anything Cleo had heard on *Friends*. The cheesy wink and '*How you doin'?*' were long gone.

'Why do you think?' Joey asked in English, rubbing his fingertips together in a money-making sign. 'I think there'll be quite a market for treasures from the First Emperor's tomb, don't you?'

Cleo stared in horror at Joey as the terrible truth hit her like a sledgehammer blow. 'You!' she spluttered. 'You're in the Tiger's Claw gang!'

Joey smiled. 'Smart girl, aren't you?'

Cleo felt the air being crushed from her lungs. This was her worst fear! *We've led the tomb robbers to the First Emperor's tomb.* 'No,' she squeaked. 'There's nothing here.'

'That's right!' Ryan pitched in. 'It's just a big rock.'

Joey sneered and shoved his knee in Ryan's back. 'Save your breath! I know all about the Dragon Path.'

Cleo closed her eyes. Joey must have been spying on them all along. *He was in the computer room when we played the Lymington and Stubbs film, he was listening at the living-room door when we were talking while we were watching the* Friends *DVD . . .* Suddenly she realized she'd seen the other two

248

men before too. *They were in Aunty Ting's restaurant when we were translating Segal's journal. They were the last customers to leave . . .*

The tattooed man had finished tying both of them up at the wrists and ankles. 'What are we waiting for?' he asked, moving towards the tunnel. 'Let's check it out.'

Joey ordered him back. 'The boss said to wait until he gets here. He had to take a detour because of the police sniffing all over the place.'

The other guy nodded. 'Yeah, and he's got the breathing equipment.'

'The boss can decide what to do with these kids as well.' Joey grinned at his accomplices. 'I'm pretty sure it won't be a day at the park.' He drew his finger slowly across his throat.

A jolt of panic gave Cleo the strength to pull away from the man holding her plait and butt him on the nose with the back of her head. She lost her balance and fell to the ground. The man clapped his hands over his bleeding nose. 'You'll pay for that!' he spluttered.

'That's enough!' Joey roared. 'Shut them inside that tunnel until the boss comes. They're not going anywhere tied up like that! Maybe a bit of time in the dark will teach them not to try any more stupid stunts.'

Ryan looked up at the slice of light above his head. It narrowed and then disappeared as the rocks crunched together. They'd been thrown through the trapdoor like sacks of potatoes and were now lying on the ramp in total darkness.

'Cleo!' he called.

'I'm over here!'

'Meilin!' Ryan yelled.

The only reply was the dull echo of his own voice.

'Meilin!' he shouted again. 'Where are you?'

There was still no reply. Ryan did a sort of crab-like shimmy down the slope towards Cleo. 'I'm worried that Meilin's been knocked unconscious,' he said. 'She's not answering.'

Cleo was silent for a long moment. 'When did you last see her?' she asked finally in an odd, brittle voice.

'Just before those thugs ambushed us, of course.'

'Exactly!' Cleo said. '*Just before*. Did you actually see Meilin get caught?'

Ryan thought back to the moment of attack. 'No. But Joey walloped me off my feet. I had my face in the dirt.'

'Our friend Wu Meilin,' Cleo said, 'seems to have conveniently disappeared at the crucial moment.'

'But she was right there,' Ryan protested.

'Well, she's not here now, is she?'

'You think she . . .' Ryan couldn't finish the sentence. He let his head fall back and bang against the rock. The truth was staring him in the face. It had been all along; he'd just been too blind to see it. Meilin was working for the Tiger's Claw gang. *She tricked us into letting her come along so she could lead the tomb robbers straight into the First Emperor's tomb*. It had all been a set-up. It was just as Cleo had suspected.

'That whole story about her great-grandfather working with Lymington and Stubbs was a pack of lies after all,' he said bitterly. But then he thought of something. 'No, it can't have been! She had the jade ring. She gave it to me just before the attack.'

Cleo snorted. 'No doubt it's just a cheap bangle from a

250

gift shop. She didn't exactly give us much time to examine it, did she? And that whole routine with the message in the mooncakes and being late must have been to delay us so that Joey and his men could get into position to follow us.'

Ryan felt as if he were sinking right through the solid rock. Cleo was right, of course. 'It's all my fault.'

Cleo didn't reply.

Ryan squirmed onto his side to face her – even though he couldn't see her in the dark. 'Go on, say it! *I told you so.*'

Cleo sighed. 'No. I won't. I fell for Meilin's act as well. She seemed so helpful – bringing the ponies and the gas masks, and even the stupid lucky charms! She's thorough, I'll give her that.'

And Joey Zhou too? Ryan thought miserably. He'd seemed like such a great guy, but it was all so obvious now. *It explains why he wasn't around at the banquet last night when Professor Han suggested he could give me a lift home. He must have sneaked off early to steal the Isles of Immortality scroll from the university, and all of the notes from the McNeils' apartment too. Only someone on the inside would have known where to look.*

'How come *everyone* I like turns out to be a total psychopath?'

'Not *everyone*!' Cleo's shoulder bumped his ear. 'Sorry,' she said. 'I was trying to pat you on the arm. I forgot my hands were tied.'

Ryan tried to cheer himself up with a feeble attempt at a joke. 'On top of everything else, Joey Zhou has totally spoiled *Friends* for me. I'm never going to be able to watch it again without having nightmares.'

Cleo made a sound that was almost a laugh. 'Ow,' she winced. 'My head hurts where I butted that guy on the nose.'

'I recognized him,' Ryan said. 'He was the creepy guard watching us at the Terracotta Army Museum. Obviously he was only posing as a guard so he could follow us and see what we found out.'

Cleo suddenly snapped into all-action mode. 'We've got to get out of here before their boss arrives and gives the order to finish us off.'

Ryan swallowed hard, remembering how Joey Zhou had sliced a finger across his throat. He hadn't understood the Chinese words, but the message had been clear enough. And it wasn't just talk. All three men had been packing knives. *Is that what happened to poor old Tian Min?* Ryan wondered. Had Joey bumped him off and then phoned Professor Han with the story about Tian Min visiting his sick mother so Joey could take his place as a guide and get access to the archaeological sites?

'First we need to see what we're doing,' Cleo said. 'Try to get my torch out of my tool belt.'

That was no easy feat in the pitch dark with their hands tied. They both wriggled around until they were lying back to back, bracing themselves with their feet to avoid rolling down the ramp. At last Ryan found the leather belt around Cleo's waist and pulled the torch from the pocket. There was more fumbling behind his back as he located the switch and turned it on.

'Wow, this tunnel's huge,' Cleo whistled. She took the torch and shone it around so that Ryan could see. He spotted the trapdoor near the top of the ramp: a circle of smooth rock surrounded by a deep groove. He struggled to his feet and made out a small hole in the shape of a tiger. There was no other handle or catch.

'That must be how you open it from the inside,' he murmured. 'You just slot the *hufu* in there . . .' He sank to his knees. 'Except we *can't* because the *hufu*'s still on the outside.'

Cleo's face was carved with deep shadows in the torchlight. 'Not to mention that there are three armed gangsters guarding the other side.'

Ryan sat down next to her. 'So what do we do? Wait here for them to fish us out when their boss turns up and fancies a spot of throat-slitting?'

'There's only one logical answer. If we can't go up, we'll have to go down.'

Ryan shook his head. 'But the tunnel goes straight to the ancestor temple. We saw it on the film. It's a dead end.'

'Not if we go through that door behind the throne statue.'

Ryan stared at Cleo. Was she really suggesting that they enter the tomb of the First Emperor?

'We – we can't . . .' he stammered. 'We said we wouldn't go anywhere near it.'

'That's before we were cornered and threatened with death,' Cleo pointed out. 'We'll just have to go through the tomb and find another exit. Obviously, we won't touch a thing.'

'But what about the booby traps?'

Cleo chewed her lip. 'Have you got any better ideas?'

Ryan had to admit he didn't. 'OK,' he said. 'Let's do it. We need to cut these ropes off. I guess that means it's Eveline Bell's trusty trowel to the rescue again. Sorry,' he added as he tried to open the pocket of Cleo's tool belt and accidentally prodded her in the side. 'Next time we go anywhere together, remind me to bring my own trowel.'

'If we get out of this alive,' Cleo said, managing a small, brave smile. 'I'll insist upon it!'

By the time they'd hacked through each other's ropes with the side of the trowel blade they were both drenched with sweat. But there was no time to rest. Cleo patted the two jade rings in her pockets. 'At least we can do what we came to do and return these to the dragons on the way.' She swept the torch round for a last look back towards the sealed entrance. 'Let's get going.'

'What's that?' Ryan gasped, recoiling in horror. A dark squat *thing* was hunkered in the shadows at the top of the ramp. An image of the giant salamander's leering grin flashed across his mind. 'Careful!' he blurted, as Cleo stepped closer to it.

'Careful?' Cleo asked. 'It's just your backpack!' She picked it up and threw it to him. 'It must have fallen in when they shoved us down here.'

Ryan laughed with relief. 'Yeah, I just meant *careful you don't trip over it!*'

He hugged his trusty Manchester United backpack to his chest. He'd never been so happy to see anything in his life. Not only was it *not* a gargantuan mutant amphibian, it was also full of supplies: food and water, an extra torch, sketchbook and pencils . . . Ryan suddenly remembered the wish he'd made on the gingko tree: *that our mission to return the jade rings to the dragons runs without a hitch.* As hitches went, being ambushed in the rhododendrons by knife-toting gangsters was a pretty major one. *I'm definitely going to ask that lady selling the red ribbons for my money back,* he thought as he took out the torch, shrugged the backpack onto his shoulders and set off down the tunnel with Cleo.

254

The walls were painted with friezes showing dragons with long serpentine bodies soaring over mountains, writhing in swirls of mist and riding on billowing clouds.

'Have you noticed,' Cleo asked, 'that each panel shows nine dragons?'

Ryan hadn't. He had more pressing things on his mind – like not having his throat cut, for example.

'The number nine was always associated with the emperor and with dragons,' Cleo explained as they hurried along. 'Several writings from the Ming Dynasty describe the myth of the nine sons of the dragon.' She frowned. 'But that's fifteenth century, of course. These paintings suggest the legend could date back much earlier – to the Qin Dynasty.'

Ryan didn't comment. He *definitely* had more pressing things on his mind than discussing the finer details of Chinese legends. Especially as the first pair of real dragons – or rather, real statues of dragons – was looming out of the shadows ahead.

He stopped and stared. He'd seen the dragons on the old black-and-white film, of course. They reared up on either side of the tunnel, one front leg raised, the other reaching forward, fearsome claws outstretched. But nothing could have prepared him for the real thing. They looked poised to pounce at any moment. And the colour! Bright, glistening, blood red.

'Red jade,' Cleo murmured, sweeping her torch across scales and spikes and fangs. 'Of course, the emperor's symbol was the *red* dragon.'

Ryan was puzzled. 'I thought jade had to be green.'

Cleo shook her head. '"Jade" actually refers to two

255

different gemstones – nephrite and jadeite – and they can be many colours. Green is the most highly prized . . .'

Ryan let Cleo's geology lecture wash over him as they continued past more dragons. A few of them, he noticed, still had a green jade ring hanging from their noses. He figured that they must be the ones that failed to go off when Lymington and Stubbs triggered the booby trap. But most of the dragons had an empty slot between their flared nostrils, where the jade rings had shot out. They were still lying where they'd fallen on the floor of the tunnel.

Ryan began to gather the rings up as he went. He was wondering which dragons the jade rings from Cleo's grandmother and Pierre Segal belonged to, when he picked up a ring that felt different to the rest. He shone the torch on it. It wasn't a jade ring at all. It was a chunk of bone – bone scored with tiny teeth marks. *Rats!* he thought, dropping it in horror. It landed among a scattering of other bones. Ryan tried not to look, but he could tell they were human. He remembered the fate of the two Chinese diggers in the film. The poor men must have slipped from the dragon claws and provided a meal for the local wildlife.

Ryan backed away, and scooted to the next pair of dragons. Trying to block the image from his mind, he held up the handful of rings he'd collected to show Cleo. 'Do you think it matters,' he asked, 'which ring goes with which dragon?' Before Cleo had a chance to answer, he picked a ring at random, reached up and hooked it into the slot between the nostrils of the nearest dragon.

Ryan saw Cleo's mouth open in a scream.

At the same moment he heard the whip crack of an

explosion behind him, and then another and another.

As he dived to the side, he looked back to see five razor-sharp claws coming at him through the eruption of fire.

NINE

CLEO THREW HERSELF on Ryan, thrashing at him to beat out the flames. She continued long after the final spark had been extinguished.

Ryan held up his hands to shield himself from the blows. 'OK! OK!' he spluttered. 'I think you've got it now!'

Cleo didn't stop. On top of being utterly petrified, she was furious with Ryan. Her anger burned hotter than the gunpowder breath of the dragon. He'd got them into this disaster by trusting that traitor, Meilin, and now he'd nearly got himself killed. If he thought he could just die and leave her to find her way out of the tunnel by herself, he could think again! She kept on hitting him.

'Yes,' she yelled. 'It obviously *does* matter!'

'What?' Ryan shouted over her. 'What matters?'

Cleo dropped her arms to her sides. All of a sudden she'd run out of steam. 'You asked if it matters which ring goes with which dragon.' She blinked back tears. 'I think you got your answer.'

Ryan sat up and brushed a smouldering cinder from his T-shirt. The white material was singed in shades of brown and black. He looked up at the dragon, still veiled in a cloud of blue smoke. 'Yeah, sorry. I should have realized. That dragon behind me had its ring in its nose. It was still *armed*.'

Cleo nodded. 'Until you tried to insert the wrong ring into the dragon opposite. That must have triggered the mechanism.'

Ryan gave her a sheepish grin. 'That was a close one.'

Cleo shuddered. She'd seen the dragon's claws graze Ryan's shoulder with barely a millimetre to spare. It had been closer than he knew. 'Are you OK?' she asked.

Ryan stretched out his arms. His fair skin was streaked pink where the flames had licked at it. 'Just lightly toasted,' he said. 'My backpack took the brunt of the fire and I managed to pull it off my shoulders. And you put the rest of the flames out.' He squeezed her hand. "Thanks, by the way.'

Cleo was relieved the burns weren't more severe. The fire must have looked worse than it was. She stamped on the backpack to put out the last sparks, and handed it to him.

'Come on,' she called, starting to jog along the tunnel. 'But don't touch any more of the jade rings,' she warned as Ryan caught her up. 'It's too dangerous. We'll just leave the ones we've brought with us next to one of the dragons. That will

259

have to do— Aagghhh!' Cleo's words turned into a startled scream as Ryan bundled her to the ground.

Just in time! Another dragon was shooting towards them in a blaze of flames. Moments later, they heard a second one go off farther down the tunnel, and then another just behind them.

'Half these dragons are still armed and dangerous,' Ryan said with a grimace when the fireworks finally ceased. 'If they keep firing at random we could go up in flames at any moment. There are hundreds of them to get past.'

Cleo looked down the tunnel. Ryan was right. There were pairs of dragons as far as she could see in her torch beam, many of them still waiting to be triggered. 'It started happening when you tried to put the ring in the wrong dragon. Maybe the way to stop them going off is to put the rings back in the *right* dragons. That might reset the system somehow.'

'But the problem is, how?' Ryan sighed. 'All the rings look exactly the same.'

'Not *exactly*,' Cleo reminded him. 'There are the little symbols.' She pulled the two jade rings from her pocket. 'There's the six crossed lines on Grandma's and the curled shape on Segal's.' She suddenly remembered the ring that Meilin had fetched from her grandfather's house. She was sure it was a fake. 'I don't suppose Meilin's one has a symbol, does it?'

Ryan held the ring up and turned it slowly in the torch beam. To Cleo's amazement there was a little gold fan shape on the inside. Did that mean it was genuine after all?

'They've *all* got symbols,' Ryan said, examining the rings he'd picked up from the ground. 'There're two swords, another curly shape like the one that we found in Segal's knapsack, and this one could be a box or a bell.'

As Cleo looked at the rings, she slowly realized that she'd seen all of the symbols before. It wasn't only the crossed-line pattern that had appeared on the Isles of Immortality scroll from the Kitchen of Eternal Life. The curled line, the fan shape, the bell – all had been painted around the border. The *fangshi* had written those symbols on the scroll. And Cleo was sure the *fangshi* had produced the gunpowder for the dragons. They'd probably designed the triggering mechanisms too. All the more reason why the symbols had to mean *something*! *The logical solution*, she thought, *would be for the symbols on the rings to pair up with matching marks engraved on the dragons.* But she'd already checked. There was nothing. 'The dragons *are* all the same,' she murmured.

'Apart from the stands,' Ryan said.

'Stands?' Cleo echoed.

'Every pair of dragons is mounted on a different stand.' Ryan pointed at the closest dragons. 'These two look like they're perched on the roof of a building. Some stands are in the shape of a drum or a bell or . . .'

Cleo couldn't believe she hadn't noticed. *A roof, a drum, a bell* . . . suddenly the pieces were starting to fall into place. Forgetting all about the danger, she jumped to her feet and ran along the tunnel, checking the stands of the dragons and counting. *One, two, three . . . roof, drum, bell . . .* She got to the ninth pair — with a stand that curved like a wave – and then the sequence began to repeat. *Roof, drum, bell . . .*

'Nine!' she shouted to Ryan, who was running along behind her, a bemused look on his face. 'There are nine types of dragon in each group . . . like the wall paintings . . . they're the nine sons of the dragon.'

Ryan still looked confused.

'There are various versions of the legend,' Cleo explained, 'but each of the nine dragon sons has a different character. One likes standing on roofs, one likes music, one is ferocious, one looks like a clam . . .'

'A dragon that looks like a clam?' Ryan cut in. 'Are you making this up?' But suddenly his face lit up. 'Hang on! The symbol on Meilin's jade ring. We thought it was a fan – but it could be a clamshell.' He juggled through the jade rings. 'So, we've got the sword, and this round shape could be a drum.' He held up another ring. 'What about the curled line? Is it a snake or something?'

Cleo thought for a moment. There was no snake dragon. Then she got it! 'That line represents the upturned eaves at the corners of a pagoda-style roof. So it belongs to the dragon that stands on roofs.' She took out the ring that her grandmother had given her. 'And I've finally figured out what this crossed-line symbol means too,' she said. 'One of the dragons likes justice. It keeps guard over prisons. These lines represent prison bars.'

'So we have to slot the right kind of ring into the nose of each dragon,' Ryan said.

Cleo held up Grandma's jade ring. 'I think we should start with this one.'

Ryan nodded. 'But be ready to dive clear if it doesn't work.'

Cleo stood on tiptoes and, with trembling hands, inserted the jade ring – Grandma's closely guarded, heart-troubling secret for almost eighty years – into the nostrils of one of the dragons that stood on a stand carved in the shape of a prison gate. As it clicked into place she held her breath and waited, poised to run. Had she triggered more dragons into fire-breathing action? But nothing happened. Then, slowly, the prison-gate dragon slid back against the wall.

'It worked!' Ryan cried. He inserted Segal's jade ring into the nose of a dragon on a roof stand. It slid back. Then he took Meilin's great-grandfather's jade ring. He thought of the frightened young man with the sticking-out ears from the film as he slotted it into a clamshell dragon. There was a grating sound as the dragon moved back.

Cleo looked down at the pile of jade rings on the ground. It was going to take hours to put them all back. Hours they didn't have. *Joey and his gang could come down the tunnel after us at any moment!*

'Let's leave the rest,' Ryan said, as if reading her thoughts. 'The explosions have stopped. We must have done enough to disarm the system for now.'

Cleo listened. The tunnel was dark and silent again. Nothing moved. The acrid smell of gunpowder filled the air. It was a risk, but one they were going to have to take.

The tunnel is much longer than it looked on the film, Cleo thought. By the time it began to climb steeply again, she had estimated they had gone three miles and she had counted nine sets of nine dragons. To her relief, they all stayed in place.

The tunnel ended in a pair of huge double doors made of deep-red lacquered wood inlaid with gold and ivory. A figure stood in the middle of three panels – the lower one an underworld full of monstrous creatures, the middle one showing figures carrying out rituals and the top one full of swirling clouds, the sun and the moon. *The path to the immortal heavens,* Cleo thought. But there was no time to study it. Ryan pushed open the doors and they found themselves in the underground ancestor temple.

Everything was as in Pierre Segal's film. The colossal bronze statue of the First Emperor gazed down on them from his high-backed throne, his right hand firmly grasping the hilt of a mighty sword. The carving was so detailed that in the wavering torchlight Emperor Qin Shi Huangdi's face seemed alive, the thin lips twitching, the arched eyebrows puckering in contempt for the lowly mortals who dared approach him.

The *banliang* coins still lay on the low offering table where Harold Stubbs had spilled them from the three-legged jar. The statues of tomb guards still stood to attention. Now Cleo could see the wall paintings too, their colours vibrant beneath millennia of dust. Most were battle scenes: warriors fighting to the death, swords, halberds and axes flashing; horse-drawn chariots charging; flights of arrows soaring overhead. Other panels showed the First Emperor wielding his sword over the heads of the defeated kings of warring states.

I wish Mum could see this, Cleo thought. *She'd be in heaven* ... She turned to point out the details to Ryan. He was standing motionless behind the First Emperor's throne, an appalled look on his face.

'I've found Cedric Lymington,' he murmured.

Cleo went to his side. Lymington's skeleton was lying across the threshold of an open door. The bones were a pale ochre colour. The skull had tilted to one side so that she could see the empty-eyed, fleshless grimace of death.

Ryan pointed to the short bronze arrow shaft protruding from between the ribs. 'It's the bolt from the crossbow.'

As she crouched for a closer look, Cleo's foot scuffed against a small black object. She watched Lymington's beloved pipe skitter across the stone floor, remembering the moment in the film when Lymington had thrown it aside and dived to save Harold Stubbs. He'd paid for his heroic action with his life.

'What's that in his hand?' Ryan asked.

Cleo looked. Curled within the finger bones was something small and made of metal. She reached out, but then drew her hand back. She wasn't usually squeamish about skeletons. She'd taken part in hundreds of tomb excavations, and having a paleopathologist for a father meant that death was more or less a family friend. But somehow, having seen Lymington alive, if only on film, made it all different. She looked at Ryan. His face was pale. He was *never* good around death. A deceased beetle was enough to give him the vapours!

Cleo steeled herself and gently nudged Lymington's finger bones. The object that fell into her palm was cold and heavy and smooth – and it was shaped like a tiger. She held it out to show Ryan.

Ryan pushed his hair off his forehead. 'Wow!' he murmured. 'The original *hufu*.' He took it from her and turned it over. 'Both halves of it.' He dug his thumbnails into the join along the spine and prised the two pieces apart. One side had pins sticking out from the back – just like the wooden replica he'd made. The other side was punched with the matching holes into which the pins slotted – presumably to keep them from snapping off when not in use.

Cleo looked back down at Lymington. The hand in which he'd held the *hufu* was outstretched as if he'd been reaching for something. She felt the fizz of neurons firing in her brain. A theory was forming. *What if he'd been trying to . . .* She jumped up and began to examine the wall around the door.

'Yes!' she cried. 'I knew it! There's another socket here for the *hufu*.'

Ryan was by her side in an instant. He held the little figure next to the slot in the stone. 'You're right. It's just like the one at the entrance.' He frowned. 'But Stubbs clearly managed to open this door without it.'

'Exactly!' Cleo said. 'You don't need the *hufu* to *unlock* this door, but you have to insert it into the socket to disarm the booby traps. That's what Lymington was trying to do, but he was too late. I've figured it out,' she went on. 'I think the *fangshi* used the *hufu* so that they could come down here and work on the booby traps without being caught in them themselves. They probably gave out copies to the First Emperor's trusted relatives as well, so that they could come and give offerings without setting off the booby traps. Remember what it said on the inscription: *the carrier of this* hufu *is permitted to enter the road of the dragons*.'

'Just like swiping a security pass to stop the alarms going off in a building.' Ryan closed his hand round the little bronze tiger. Then he looked at the door into the tomb. 'We can use it so we don't get the crossbow treatment.'

Cleo felt a pulse of fear. Finding Lymington had transported her back to the events of eighty years ago. She'd almost forgotten their own predicament. She glanced over her shoulder to the tunnel. *How long*, she wondered, *before Joey and his men come looking for us?*

Ryan, meanwhile, had perched on the low table, unzipped his scorched backpack and started pulling out the picnic supplies. 'A bit of a smoky barbecue flavour,' he said, holding up a slice of watermelon, 'but not too bad.'

Cleo gaped at him in astonishment. 'How can you even think about eating?'

'You should have something too. We need to keep our strength up if we're going to find a way through the tomb.'

Cleo supposed Ryan was right. If she didn't take on calories, she would become weak and lose concentration. Reluctantly she took a tea egg. 'I feel like a condemned criminal having my last meal.'

Ryan made a face at Cleo's egg. 'At least on Death Row they get to choose their favourite food. I think I'd go for steak and chips and a massive ice-cream sundae.' He brandished a kebab. 'And this skewer full of chargrilled chicken,' he added, 'is just a bit too close for comfort. This is how I nearly ended up when that dragon went off!'

Cleo couldn't help laughing. But the laughter suddenly froze in her mouth.

She'd heard something. Voices were coming from the tunnel! She sprang up, pulling Ryan towards the door.

'Put on your mask,' Ryan said, fumbling with the straps. 'There could be mercury fumes inside.'

Cleo wasn't sure how effective the smoke filter would be against mercury fumes, but she pulled on the foil hood and positioned the filter canister over her nose and mouth. It was better than nothing.

Ryan slotted the *hufu* into the socket.

Then they ran through the door and into the tomb of the First Emperor.

35

TOMB

AS HE FOLLOWED Cleo up the steep flight of steps from the ancestor temple, Ryan couldn't remember ever feeling so uncomfortable in so many different ways at the same time.

The dragon burns were much worse than he'd let on to Cleo. It was true that his backpack had protected his back, but he'd caught a blast of flame right across his chest. It was smarting as if he'd been wandering in the Sahara Desert for days without sunscreen. Every time his T-shirt brushed his skin it was like being tattooed by thousands of tiny needles. He couldn't tell whether it was delayed shock or the effect of mercury fumes, but his legs didn't feel wholly up to the job of keeping him upright. They had that folding feeling they got when he stepped off the bottom of an escalator. That's why he'd insisted they stop to eat – it was just an excuse to rest for a moment.

He hardly had energy left over to worry that they might just be the first people to set foot inside the tomb of the First Emperor of China in over two thousand years.

As he plodded, zombie-like, through a maze of small rooms and passageways, Ryan could see the tips of crossbows poking out from the walls. He felt like a bank robber looking out for security cameras. Except these 'cameras' could fire a bolt into your back at any moment. But so far the *hufu* seemed to be doing its job. Nothing had fired.

Must be my lucky pants at work, Ryan thought grimly. He felt for his St Christopher medal and his scarab amulet. The charm Meilin had given him was there too. *Will the luck still work,* he wondered, *even though it was given by a traitor under false pretences?*

They came at last to a vast hall. The walls were lined with panels of gold engraved with intricate designs that glittered in the torchlight. Pillars of marble and jade gleamed pink and mauve and green. For a heart-stopping moment Ryan thought the room was crowded with people. But they were, of course, only life-sized terracotta statues, like the warriors they'd seen at the museum.

'These look like government officials and army generals waiting for an audience with the emperor.' Cleo's voice was robot-like through the gas mask. 'We must be right inside the inner walls in the heart of the underground palace.' She looked up. 'We're directly under the tomb mound.'

Ryan remembered sitting with Tian Min outside the Tomb of a Thousand Poisons, gazing down at the tomb

mound rising from the plain like a tree-cloaked pyramid –
vast, mysterious and *totally* forbidden. If anyone had told him
then that he'd end up wandering around inside that mound a
few days later, he'd have laughed at them.

But right now, he felt more like crying than laughing.

Cleo pulled him by the arm. They passed a set of enormous
bronze bells inlaid with designs of silver and gold and entered
another large room. Although blanketed in rubble and dust,
the ancient splendour shone through: wall-hangings painted
with scenes of magical gardens and strange beasts; lacquered
screens encrusted with jade, turquoise and garnet; rolls of silk
cloth tumbling from their stacks; pots and jars of cosmetics
and polished bronze mirrors laid out on gold tables.

In the centre a group of statues of beautiful ladies reclined
on couches, drinking from small gold cups and playing zithers
and drums. They were dressed in flowing wide-sleeved silk
gowns and their elaborate wigs – once shiny black but now
grey with dust – bristled with jewelled pins and combs.
Glancing back as he passed. Ryan's heart suddenly ballooned
with fear. His breathing, amplified by the gas mask, roared
in his ears.

Beneath their robes and wigs, the ladies weren't statues
sculpted from clay or cast in bronze.

They were all skeletons.

Cleo looked back and saw what had caught his attention.
'So it was true,' she said. 'The Grand Historian wrote that
hundreds of courtesans were locked in the tomb along with
the emperor.'

Ryan gulped. After his encounter with the entombed
servants in the Royal Tomb in Egypt, he'd hoped never to
see such a ghoulish sight again. Now he was sure that the

skeleton ladies – like a macabre display of mannequins in a shop window – would be joining the Egyptian workers in his nightmares.

He hurried to catch Cleo up at the far end of the great hall and up a flight of wide steps between imposing gold statues of a dragon and a phoenix. The stairs ended on a wide landing in front of a large round opening in the wall. They rushed through it and came out onto a balcony, stopping just in time to avoid plunging headlong over the edge. Only a few stubs of gold posts remained of what had once been a railing. Ryan looked down. Even though he knew they were now deep underground beneath the tomb mound, his eyes were telling him that he was looking out over a surreal landscape of gardens, forests, mountains, rivers and seas. Giddy with vertigo and confusion, he reeled back.

'It's the model of the universe,' Cleo sighed. 'I was sure it was just a legend, but it's *real*!'

Ryan gazed in wonder as their torch beams swept across the scene far below. The model was bigger than he'd ever imagined. It had to be half a mile across at least. Rivers of bright silver liquid mercury flowed through fields of gold and valleys of jade. Mountain peaks were snow-capped with pale mother-of-pearl. Whole towns and cities were laid out with miniature towers and palaces of gold and silver. Roads of beaten copper radiated out across the First Emperor's domain. A stone wall, complete with an army of soldiers marching from one watchtower to the next, snaked along its northern border. And above it all, a high domed ceiling of deepest blue was studded with constellations of pearl-encrusted stars, a golden sun and a full silver moon.

Although it wasn't completely accurate, Ryan soon figured

271

out that the model was a 3D map of China, bordered by the sea to the south and east, and the Gobi Desert and Tibetan mountains to the north and west. The mighty Yellow River flowed across the north and the Yangtze to the south. He could even identify landmarks closer to home: the city of Xi'an, Mount Li and – in the very centre of the entire universe – the tomb mound itself, a flat-topped pyramid surrounded by a miniature version of the Terracotta Army. On top of the mound stood a golden pavilion, bigger and more magnificent than any other structure on the map. Ryan was sure that the First Emperor's coffin would be centre-stage inside those glittering walls.

'It's beautiful. But how on earth do we get out of here?' he murmured.

Cleo didn't seem to hear. 'So if that's the East China Sea,' she said, teetering on the edge of the balcony in her excitement, 'those islands could be the Isles of Immortality.' She pointed with her torch beam at the craggy jade islands rising out of the gleaming expanse of mercury. She produced a pair of binoculars from her tool belt and held them to her eyes over the mask.

'Look! That's the way out!' she said, pointing to the wall beyond the islands. Ryan took the binoculars and saw that the wall was decorated with a mountain scene, teeming with the symbols of immortality that Cleo had told him about: cranes, tigers, rabbits, bamboo and pine trees. In the middle, flanked by two beautifully painted peach trees, was an enormous gate. *Or false gate,* Ryan corrected himself. Behind the ornamental metalwork was solid stone.

'But that's no good. It's just an imaginary "way out" for the emperor's soul to travel to the afterlife.' Ryan had visited enough ancient tombs since he'd met Cleo to know how these things went. False doors and gates were often added as symbolic entrances to the next world.

'No, it's the *literal* way out,' Cleo said. 'There's a much smaller *real* door set into the big false gate.'

Ryan squinted and tried to focus. He could just about see the bolts and hinges of a door hidden among all the decorative metalwork.

'It's an exit that lies *beyond* the Isles of Immortality!' Cleo's voice came in fast, breathless bursts. 'I think the First Emperor . . . believed that he could still become immortal . . . even after he was dead and buried. He had that door built . . . so that when he came to life . . . he could escape from the tomb . . . body *and* soul.'

'*Body and soul,*' Ryan repeated. He turned to Cleo, just as she turned to him. They were standing so close that the snouts of their masks clashed. He could see from the spark in her eyes behind the visor that she was thinking the same thing. It was as if they had both heard an echo. 'Isn't that the phrase in that riddle on the Isles of Immortality scroll that we found in the Kitchen of Eternal Life?' he asked.

Cleo nodded slowly. '*For the one you seek you must find the two. The way to the two lies in one that brings death but is not tarnished by it,*' she recited from memory. '*Drink the two before sands run through, for body and soul to flee from this world.*'

'To flee from this world,' Ryan murmured. '*This world* could mean this tomb with its model of the world, not just life in general.'

'Exactly,' Cleo said. 'I knew that scroll was important from when we first saw the symbol of the crossed lines on it. I just didn't know *how* important. It's a set of instructions for how to get out of here! The map is of this model sea and the islands in it. The *fangshi* must have designed all this too. The scroll we found in their cave was their own copy. The First Emperor probably has another copy in his coffin so he can find his way to that door – and the afterlife – which for him, meant coming back to real life as an immortal!'

'But why does it all have to be in riddles?' Ryan groaned. 'I *hate* riddles.'

'It's *obvious*,' Cleo told him. 'It's so that if the information fell into the hands of tomb robbers or enemy forces they wouldn't be able to discover the emperor's secret exit and use it to get in and out of the tomb.' She glanced over her shoulder. 'We've got to solve the riddle and escape through that door before Joey and his gang catch up with us.' She tightened her gas mask. 'It's a simple matter of logical deduction . . . *For the one you seek you must find the two*. We worked out that *the one* means the fungus of immortality and that *the two* means the two missing islands that drifted away from the other three when the giant stole the turtles they rested on.'

Ryan looked out across the shining sea. It was the size of a small lake, and there were definitely *five* islands floating in the mercury. It seemed the missing two were no longer missing. 'I don't suppose we can just wade out there and check which islands have the secret mushroom we need to get out through that gate?'

'It's not *that* simple!'

Why am I not surprised? Ryan thought. He'd learned that, when it came to tombs, nothing was ever simple.

'We can't touch the mercury, for a start. It's highly corrosive and toxic. And it's bound to be booby-trapped if we don't do it the right way,' Cleo said. 'So we need to work out the next part of the riddle. *The way to the two lies in one that brings death but is not tarnished by it.* You had the brilliant idea that the thing that *brings death but is not tarnished by it* could refer to a sword. So let's start by looking for something engraved on a sword. It's probably another part of the map.' Cleo paused and threw out her arms. 'But *which* sword? There are hundreds down here. All the terracotta soldiers and guards have them.'

'Surely it'll be some *special* sword,' Ryan suggested. 'Something big and shiny and impressive – like that monster the First Emperor in the ancestor temple was brandishing.' His heart sank. 'But we can't go back up there to find it.'

'That's not even a real sword, anyway,' Cleo pointed out. 'It's just part of the bronze statue. It's probably a replica of . . .' She broke off and slapped her forehead, rustling the foil hood. 'Of course! If that's a copy of the emperor's favourite sword, the real thing is probably buried with him in his coffin.'

'Which means,' Ryan said, 'we've got to get down there.' He pointed to the golden pavilion on the model of the tomb mound.

Getting down was easier said than done. What must once have been a grand staircase leading from the viewing gallery had collapsed and was now a steep crumbling bank of rubble. Blocks of marble and clay tiles were jumbled with chunks of stonework. They had clambered down about halfway when Ryan lost his footing, landed flat on his face and took the rest of the slope in a high-speed belly slide, the burned skin across his chest bumping and scraping on the jagged stone. By the time Cleo caught up with him he was biting back tears of pain.

275

'What is it?' Cleo started. Then she caught sight of the mess where his T-shirt had ridden up. She took the hem and gently lifted it further. 'You complete *idiot*!' she snapped. 'Why didn't you tell me it was this bad? We should have cooled it with cold water for at least twenty minutes.'

'Exactly!' Ryan said through gritted teeth. 'Like we *had* a spare twenty minutes to hang around!'

'Keep still!' Cleo unwound the scarf from her neck, soaked it in water from her bottle and bound it tightly round his chest, tying it at the back. The first moment of contact was agony but then the soothing cold and pressure of the makeshift bandage kicked in.

Cleo peered at his eyes through the mask. 'You look terrible.'

Ryan pulled a tragic face, which he forgot Cleo couldn't see. 'You mean the whole gas mask and bandage-bikini-top look isn't working for me?'

'Definitely not,' Cleo scrambled to her feet. 'Come on! The quicker we get out, the quicker we can get some proper treatment for those burns.'

They crossed a narrow bridge and entered the model universe, striking out northwards from the shore of southern China along a copper road bordered by cedars and poplars fashioned from jade. They climbed over shoulder-high foothills of sparkling quartz, squeezed through valleys between gilded mountain peaks that towered above their heads, and jumped over glistening rivers of mercury. Up close, the details were exquisite: cat-sized tigers and rabbit-sized bears roamed the mountainsides, geese and ducks swam on lakes, farmers worked in the fields . . .

But there was no time to stop and admire the craftsmanship.

They kept running until they came to the army of brightly painted child-sized terracotta warriors. The silent surveillance of rank after rank of lifeless eyes was one of the creepiest things Ryan had ever seen – and he'd seen a few by now. *Even a coffin would be a relief after that lot*, he thought, as he scurried past and scrambled up the slope of the model tomb mound.

He barrelled right into Cleo, who had stopped in the entrance to the grand pavilion, and for the second time that day they came face to face with the First Emperor of China.

36

SWORD

AT FIRST CLEO thought she was looking at another statue. The First Emperor was standing on a war chariot pulled by four life-sized galloping bronze horses. Then, as she peered through the misted-up visor of her mask, the truth slowly dawned on her.

Encased within a suit of armour made up of thousands of small squares of jade linked with fine gold wire was the mummified body of the First Emperor himself. His head was concealed within a magnificent jade helmet. One hand was covered by a long gauntlet of gold chain mail, but the other glove had slipped off to reveal leathery brown fingers, hooked like talons around reins that had long since fallen away. The gloved hand was raised. And it was gripping the hilt of a mighty double-edged sword.

'First Emperor ... jade armour ... big sword ...' Ryan spoke as if he'd forgotten how to put words together to make a sentence.

Without letting herself think about what she was doing, Cleo climbed up onto the wheel of the chariot and stood on tiptoes, searching for any trace of a map engraved on the sword. The bronze blade was thick with dust. She reached up and gave it the gentlest of wipes.

To her horror, the sword – with the golden glove still attached – wobbled and then fell. It clattered to the ground with a clang that rang round the huge vault.

Ryan jumped back. 'Are you trying to kill me?' he yelled.

'Sorry!' Cleo called down. *How did it come to this?* she wondered. *We said we weren't going to go near the tomb. Then we vowed not to touch anything. Now I'm knocking bits of the First Emperor's armour off!* She felt her breathing begin to race, fast and shallow. *Slow down,* she told herself. Hyperventilating inside the gas mask was not a good idea. 'Sorry!' she whispered to the emperor.

She clambered down from the chariot. Ryan was already kneeling over the sword and easing the gauntlet away from the hilt for a better look.

The sword was an impressive sight. Almost a metre long, the bronze blade still glimmered. It was shot through with a diamond pattern. The metal was darker at the centre and paler at the sides. Cleo knew that different proportions of copper and tin had been blended to make the core flexible and the edges bite sharp and true. The hilt was fashioned from gold and set with an exquisite design of garnet and turquoise.

The blade was embellished with a column of small seal script near the hilt. 'I've seen that before,' Ryan said, pointing to one of the characters. 'It was all over the Isles of Immortality scroll.'

Cleo had seen it too. 'I think it means *life*.'

'The Sword of Life,' Ryan said. 'That sounds right.'

But there was no map. Cleo stared blindly at the blade. She'd been so sure the sword was the answer, she didn't know what to do next.

'Let's check the other side again.' Ryan closed both hands round the hilt of the sword and hoisted it up. His arms trembled. 'Wow, it's heavy!' he muttered as the sword dropped from his grasp. As it hit the ground, the jewelled hilt snapped into two pieces.

'What have you done?' Cleo gasped.

'You dropped it first!' Ryan pointed up at the First Emperor. 'From much higher.'

Cleo was about to object that at least she hadn't smashed it to pieces when she noticed something that whisked her words away. The hilt was hollow. And poking out from one of the broken halves was a roll of silk no bigger than a pencil.

Ryan leaned in closer. 'Is it a map?' he asked, his air filter almost in her ear. 'Odd place to hide it.'

'No, I've just realized; it makes sense.' Cleo could hardly get her words out fast enough to explain as she handed Ryan her torch while she looked for the tweezers in her tool belt. 'There's a famous story about a plot to assassinate the First Emperor. His enemy sent a man with a sword hidden inside a rolled-up map so that he could smuggle it into the palace.'

She closed the tweezers gently around the edge of the scroll and began to ease it out. 'It didn't work. But it looks as if the emperor took the idea and turned it around. Instead of a sword hidden in a map, it's a map inside a sword!'

The scroll was out. Cleo unfurled the tissue-thin silk.

Tears of disappointment misted her eyes.

It wasn't a map! Instead, a single line of black ink wandered from one edge to the other, looping and weaving as if dodging invisible obstacles. 'This can't be it,' she groaned.

But Ryan began turning the tiny silk scroll one way and then the other. 'It *is* it!' he said at last. 'It's the route. You position this page over the map on the Isles of Immortality scroll and it guides you round the islands to the other side – to that door in the wall.'

Cleo slumped over, hitting her air filter on her knees. 'But we don't *have* that map. The Tiger's Claw gang stole it.'

'That's where you're wrong!' Ryan pulled his sketchbook from his backpack. 'Ta-da! I made a copy, remember?' He flattened the page out on the ground. 'It's more or less to scale. I even put in all the turtles.'

Cleo was so relieved, she almost threw her arms round him. But she remembered his burns at the last minute. *It's a good thing we're both wearing gas masks*, she thought, *or I might even have kissed him. And there's no time for that kind of complication.* She placed the finely woven silk carefully over the sketchbook. It was as transparent as tracing paper; Ryan's map showed through perfectly – right down to the cartoon faces on the turtles. The meandering black line on the top page plotted a course around the first three islands, landing at the fourth and fifth and then continuing on to a spot marked on the map as an archway formed by two peach trees.

Cleo looked up at Ryan. 'That must be the gate in the wall.'

'This is our ticket out of here!' Ryan jumped up. 'Let's go. I saw some little boats on the eastern shore when we were looking down from the balcony. We can use one of those to get across the mercury to the islands.' He hesitated and picked up the sword and carefully propped it on the chariot against the First Emperor's leg. 'There, he can reach it if he needs it.'

Cleo placed the golden glove next to the blade. She apologized to the emperor once more and, as she backed away, she felt herself bowing.

Then they sprinted back through the model valleys and over the model hills until they came out on the shore, where sparkling minerals had been ground up and sprinkled to create a rainbow-coloured beach. Five small boats were lined up along a narrow golden jetty. Cleo looked out across the sea. Her torch beam picked out the pink and green glittering peaks of the closest island, only about a hundred metres away. The beam of light made a path across the flat silver mercury. It looked as if you could just run across the shining surface, but Cleo knew that the touch of the beautiful liquid could be lethal. She turned back to the boats. The curved bow of each small skiff had been carved into the shape of an animal's head: fish, dragon, phoenix, tiger, cow.

Ryan began to tug the nearest one away from the jetty.

'No, wait!' Cleo cried. 'I'm sure it matters which one we pick.'

'Yeah, that's why I've picked the fish,' Ryan said. 'They live in the sea. They're good swimmers!'

But Cleo had a better idea. That fifth animal wasn't a cow at all, she realized. 'It's this one,' she said. 'The deer.'

Ryan didn't budge from the fish. 'The deer? Of course, they're well known for their superior swimming skills!' he said sarcastically.

'Actually, deer are surprisingly accomplished swimmers,' Cleo said. 'But that's not the point. In the legend of the Isles of Immortality, deer are the only animals that know how to find the *lingzhi,* the fungus of immortality.'

Ryan gave up. 'Who are we to argue with legend?' He began to untie the deer boat from its mooring.

Cleo felt around in the pouch of her tool belt. 'We should wear these,' she said, pulling out two pairs of the disposable plastic gloves that were used for handling the ancient remains in the Tomb of a Thousand Poisons. 'Just in case we touch the mercury. They might offer a little bit of protection.'

Ryan pulled the gloves on. 'Now we just need some paddles.' He looked around. 'Typical!' he grumbled. 'There aren't any. Don't tell me! The *legend* says we have to catch a dragon and craft our own oars out of its toenails!'

Cleo ignored Ryan's grumbling and kept searching. She peered into the bottom of the boat. There was nothing there. The hull was very flat, she noticed, more like a punt than a rowing boat. Perhaps they needed a pole to propel themselves along, rather than paddles. It would make sense. The mercury was probably only a shallow layer.

She cast around for something suitable. To her surprise she spotted it straight away: a long bronze pole propped against an oddly shaped stand on a platform that looked a bit like a lifeguard's tower.

'Have you ever been punting?' she called to Ryan as she ran to the stand, climbed up onto the platform and grabbed the pole. She sprang away, dropping the pole as she felt something falling on her head, rattling on the foil hood of her gas mask like rain. She looked up and saw that it was not water but fine white sand, trickling out through the base of a huge square jar attached to the top of the stand. The end of the pole must have been plugging the hole . . .

'Don't just stand there!' Ryan yelled. 'That's the sands of time!'

Of course, Cleo thought. *Ryan's right. It's part of the riddle: drink the two before sands run through, for body and soul to flee from this place.* She had no idea what would happen to their bodies and souls if they *didn't* make it to that door on the other side of the sea in time, but she had no intention of finding out. She ran with the pole to the boat, climbed aboard and began pushing off from the jetty.

'It seems very unfair,' she complained. 'We don't even know how long we've got before the timer runs out.'

'You think that's the only part about all this that's unfair?' Ryan muttered, as he tried to take the pole from her hands. 'Let me do the punting,' he said. 'I'm stronger.'

But Cleo pulled back. She could see that Ryan was flinching with every move. The burns on his chest must be agony. 'Not at the moment, you're not.'

Ryan wouldn't take no for an answer. He grappled for the pole again. The boat lurched from side to side.

'Stop it!' Cleo yelled, looking down as the thick silver liquid churned into glossy bubbles beneath them. 'You'll tip us both in.'

Still Ryan wrestled for the pole.

'OK,' Cleo snapped in frustration. 'If it means you'll let go, I'll admit it – I have no sense of direction. *You* need to navigate – which means I have to punt.'

284

Ryan backed down at last. 'Can I get that on record?'

'I, Cleopatra Calliope McNeil, hereby admit to having no sense of direction,' Cleo mumbled as fast as she could. 'Now *let go!*'

That's when she heard a voice high above. At first she thought it was only an echo. Then torch beams began to sweep across the sea like helicopter searchlights.

Four men were looking down from the viewing balcony.

ELIXIR

RYAN'S HEART THUNDERED as if a herd of buffalo were stampeding around his ribcage.

He'd seen people punting on TV in scenic places like Cambridge and Oxford. They were always swanning along on sunlit rivers in blazers and straw hats, sipping champagne and scoffing strawberries. But those guys weren't trapped on an underground sea of liquid mercury, racing against the sands of time and a gang of throat-slitting maniacs.

And steering a punt wasn't as easy as it looked either – especially not by remote control. He had to shout and wave his arms to relay directions to Cleo, who was balancing on the back of the boat, pushing them along with the pole. Ryan held both torches, pointing one ahead and one behind, so that Cleo could see what she was doing. At least they didn't have to go far. They were already close to the first island.

'Steady,' he yelled. 'We're getting close!' But it was too late. There was a gut-curdling crunch as the hull ground over something solid. 'I said *steady*!' he shouted.

'I *was* being steady!' Cleo fired back. 'And I didn't hit the island!'

Ryan looked over the bow and saw that she was right. They were still several metres away. But they'd definitely hit *something*. He checked the bottom of the boat. If a hole had been punched in the hull, the mercury would start pouring in, but to his relief it looked intact. He studied the route map. What else could they have run into? The only other possible obstacles on the Isles of Immortality scroll were the three turtles holding up each island on their backs. He couldn't see any turtles in the mercury, but that didn't mean that they weren't there, of course, lurking beneath the gunmetal-grey surface.

'I think we have to dodge the hidden turtles as well,' he called to Cleo. 'We'd better give them a wide berth.'

Cleo didn't say a word. She just nodded and plunged the pole back into the mercury.

Ryan glanced back to the sands of time. They were still running steadily from the hole in the jar where Cleo had removed the pole. Then he scanned the steep rubble bank that led down from the viewing balcony. Joey and his three sidekicks were already halfway down. They'd obviously come well prepared for the tomb's legendary killer mercury fumes; they looked like scuba divers in their high-tech breathing equipment.

287

Ryan did his best to focus on guiding Cleo around the second island. They were almost past the northernmost point when the boat suddenly pitched backwards. Dropping the torches, Ryan reached out to hold on to Cleo. He could only grasp a handful of trouser leg, but it was enough. She fell back against him as the boat swung violently, pivoting on the pole, which was being sucked down into a swirl of mercury.

'It's a whirlpool!' Cleo cried. 'It's dragging us in!'

Ryan scrambled up and grabbed hold of the pole. Together they pulled, leaning back, battling against the force of the vortex. Suddenly the pole wrenched free and they both sat down hard. The deer-head prow reared up at the front. Ryan threw himself into the bottom of the boat just in time to stop it doing a back-flip.

I get it, Ryan thought, as he picked himself up. *That's what happens if you steer too wide a course to avoid the turtles. You have to stick exactly to the route on the silk scroll to stay in a narrow channel of safety.* He felt around and retrieved the torches. *Those* fangshi *guys the First Emperor had in to design his tomb defences had a very nasty streak,* he thought. *If they were alive right now, they could get a top job writing computer games. Well, I've played enough of those in my time. They're not going to beat me!*

'Did any of the mercury splash on you?' Cleo asked in a panicky voice.

Ryan looked down. There were some silver globules on the prow of the boat, but none had hit him. 'No. How about you?'

Cleo shook her head. 'No, I'm OK.' She stood up and grasped the dry end of the pole again. Ryan couldn't help noticing that her hands were shaking.

They navigated around the third island without further catastrophes, and approached the fourth. This, Ryan knew, was the first of the two *missing* isles. According to the riddle, they had to land here and drink something. Sticking closely to the route shown on the silk scroll, Ryan shouted instructions to Cleo to head straight for a small inlet on the eastern coast where they wedged the boat into a narrow cleft cut into the jade. It was exactly the right size and shape to hold the boat fast.

Cleo clearly made the right call picking the deer boat, Ryan thought as they stepped out onto the island.

It was spectacularly beautiful. The craggy rocks of jade were dusted with gold and laced with waterfalls of white crystal. Silver trees with golden fruit clung to the steep cliffs with jewelled bronze animals and birds grazing and perching among them. By the time they'd climbed a steep staircase to the summit, Ryan was out of breath. 'Now for our next impossible challenge . . .' he puffed.

Cleo was already rooting round the bottom of every artificial tree like an over-excited terrier.

Ryan joined the search. 'Even if we find these fungi magically growing on solid jade,' he muttered, 'I don't see how we can drink them. How do you drink a mushroom?'

Cleo looked up at him. 'OK, I agree, it doesn't make sense. But our only chance of getting out is to try to follow the riddle.' She scrambled further up the rocks. 'The fungus of immortality, or *lingzhi*, was probably a species of *ganoderma*, a bracket fungus that grows at the base of tree trunks. It looks like a—'

'. . . big, flappy, copper-coloured ear?' Ryan cut in.

Cleo spun round. 'Yes, how did you know?'

'Because I think I'm looking at one.' Ryan stooped down to peer at the tree of gold. It had maple-shaped leaves but also fruit that looked like peaches. He reached out to touch the fungus growing from the bottom of the twisted trunk. Although it looked organic, it was made of metal. 'It's not just copper-coloured, it *is* copper,' he told Cleo as she knelt next to him. 'With a solid gold centre.'

'I'm sure this is it,' she said. 'But how do we drink it?'

'Perhaps we have to drink *from* it,' Ryan suggested. In the shallow hollow at the base of the fungus a tiny puddle of palest pink liquid, with an opal-like sheen, had collected.

Cleo nodded. 'Maybe . . .'

Ryan placed both hands round the fungus and gently tugged. Nothing happened. He tried sliding it up and then down. Suddenly it came free from the trunk. At the same moment, he heard a loud creaking noise from the wall beyond the sea.

Cleo jumped up. 'It's the door in the gate under the peach trees,' she cried. 'One bolt has drawn back!'

Ryan held the fungus up to his face.

'What are you doing?' Cleo demanded in horror. 'We don't actually need to *drink* it. Just detaching the fungus from the tree trunk has triggered the door to start opening. Let's get to the other island and do the same. That must be how we open the second bolt.'

'The riddle says we drink it,' Ryan said grimly. 'If we don't do this right, it might not work. I'm not taking any risks.'

'But what about your mask?'

Ryan had thought of that. 'I'll just lift it up for a second.'

Cleo sighed. 'That's totally irrational. You say you're not taking any risks, but you're about to breathe in toxic vapours and drink a two-thousand-year-old unidentified liquid!'

'Yeah,' Ryan said. 'Wish me luck.' He touched his St Christopher medal and his scarab amulet. He crossed his fingers and, then, before he could change his mind, pulled up his mask, held the fungus to his lips and took a tiny sip.

It didn't taste as bad as he'd expected. It had a metallic tang, then it fizzed on his tongue with a fruity taste that reminded him of the Three Whites pomegranate at Mr Long's orchard. 'Delicious,' he said. 'Well, don't blame me when I live forever and you don't.' He was about to slot the copper fungus back on to the tree trunk when Cleo took it from his hand, pushed up her mask and touched the tip of her tongue to the liquid. She grimaced, pushed the fungus back onto the tree, turned on her heel and hurried back down the steps to the boat without another word.

When Ryan caught her up Cleo handed him the binoculars. The sands were still running, the white cone beneath the stand heaping taller and taller. Joey and the other three men were now gathered around the row of boats. It looked as if they were arguing.

We should have set the rest of the boats adrift so they couldn't chase us, Ryan realized. 'Onwards,' he urged, as Cleo pushed them out to sea again. He was starting to believe that they might just make it out of the tomb alive.

The fifth island was even smaller and steeper than the last. The fungus of immortality was hard to find and even harder to reach – clinging to the base of a small tree smothered in flamingo-pink crystal blossom, growing from an almost vertical cliff of lilac jade. But somehow they scrambled up and pulled the bracket of fungus from the tree trunk. A dull thud boomed out. The second bolt on the peach tree door had opened. This time there was no argument about drinking the elixir. They both took a sip.

'Yuk!' Ryan croaked. This mysterious liquid was much worse than the first: thick and yellow, it tasted like the grey bits in fish, raw pastry and dust.

Ryan was still gagging as he replaced his mask and helped Cleo down over the rocks. They looked back across the sea. The sands of time had slowed to a trickle. One of the Tiger's Claw men had climbed into the boat with the fish-shaped prow and was paddling after them across the mercury with what looked like a strip of copper pulled from the model universe. Without the route map, how long would he last before he ran aground on a submerged turtle or was sucked into a whirlpool?

Ryan knew it was crazy to worry about someone who wanted to cut his throat, but he couldn't just watch the man paddle to his death. . .

'Stop!' he yelled. 'It's dangerous!'

The man looked up. He didn't stop.

'Come on!' Cleo cried, pulling Ryan into the boat. Ahead of them the little door in the wall was opening wider and wider. Cleo pushed with the pole and they raced towards it. Ryan heard a yell and looked back to see the fish-head boat tip up and sink beneath the mercury. There was a gurgling noise – like water being sucked down a drain – and then it was gone.

There was no time to dwell on the man's fate. They were already bumping up onto the narrow spit of land near the door.

'We did it!' Ryan cheered. He had one leg out of the boat and was turning to help Cleo out when he glanced back across the sea and saw that the sands of time had stopped running. 'Quick!' he yelled. 'We're out of time.' He looked over his shoulder and saw that the door in the wall was already slowly creaking closed again. He turned back to Cleo, holding out his hand, ready to pull her from the boat and through the door to freedom, ready to jump up and down together in celebration . . .

Then everything began to happen very fast and all at once.

The boat was rocking. Cleo was toppling backwards. The mercury sea was quivering and shaking as if coming to life. Something was erupting from the silvery surface. Some kind of creature – some kind of *enormous* creature – was thrusting up from the depths. It had a wide smooth head. *Is it a whale?* Its jaws gaped wide. *Or the giant salamander again?* But then Ryan saw the eyes, the nose, the ears. It was a *human* head. A human head made of metal with huge golden teeth. *A giant! The giant from the legend of the Isles of Immortality. The giant that stole the turtles . . .*

Cleo had dropped the pole. Her arms were windmilling. She was flying through the air. Ryan threw himself across the boat to try to catch her.

She screamed his name. His fingers closed round her trainer but her foot slipped out of it and she kept on falling. She fell between the rows of teeth. The giant's mouth snapped shut.

The mechanical giant sank as quickly as it had appeared. The mercury closed seamlessly over it.

Cleo was gone.

38

GONE

RYAN LAY FACE-DOWN in the punt, the gas mask pressing into his nose.

He struggled to his knees. The mercury sea glimmered as flat and still as ever. *Please,* he implored, *please let me have imagined it.*

But he knew it was real. Cleo had disappeared into the jaws of a metal giant.

He could still hear her screaming his name as she fell.

He still had her trainer in his hand.

We were too slow. We didn't make it before the sands of time ran out and we triggered the final – and biggest – booby trap of all.

It was *game over*. But it wasn't a game.

Ryan didn't know what to do. Stay and look for Cleo? Or get out and fetch help? He turned and saw that the door in the wall was almost closed. *How can I find her on my own? I'd need special equipment to drain the mercury.* He leaped out of the boat, ran for the door and shoved a foot in the gap just in time. He squeezed through sideways, the door pushing hard against his bandaged chest.

As the door clanged shut behind him, Ryan ripped the gas mask from his face and leaned against it, gulping air into his lungs.

This should have been their moment of victory. Instead, it was the worst moment of his life. It was right up there with the moment Mum had told him that Dad had disappeared in South America and might not be coming back. *In fact, it's worse,* he thought, *because this time it's all my fault. I should have been the one at the back of the boat with the pole. I'm taller and stronger and older than Cleo. It should have been me.*

Ryan ground bitter tears from his eyes with the heels of his hands and stumbled along, hardly noticing that he'd emerged into a deep crevasse between two walls of packed earth. He came to a long staircase and staggered up and up for what felt like hours. He had to keep stopping, doubled over, head spinning, legs buckling, stomach heaving. At last he came to a solid wall of rock. He flung himself at it with all the superhuman strength of fear and desperation. A small hole opened up near the base of the rock and he shot out into the open.

Blinking in the dazzling sunlight, Ryan half-ran, half-fell down a thickly wooded slope. *I have to find someone who can help. The fire service? The police?*

He stopped to catch his breath, leaning his forehead against the rough, dry trunk of a pine tree. He could hear voices far below and looked up to get his bearings. He had come out about halfway down the western slope of the tomb mound. The voices came from mothers chatting and laughing as they pushed children in buggies through the park at the foot of the mound. Older children were playing chase among the trees. In the distance, birds were flying over the jagged peaks of the Qinling mountains. Ryan could even see the cable car slowly climbing to the summit of Mount Li. Somehow, the world was going on as if nothing had happened.

I promised Cleo's grandmother I'd keep her safe, he thought, torturing himself with the memory. *I've failed. I've as good as killed her myself.* He was sure she had died in the jaws of the giant. There was no way that the First Emperor's final booby trap was going to spare anyone. Ryan was sinking into a black hole of misery. *If Cleo were here,* he thought, *she'd be telling me the precise astronomical properties of a black hole and why it's physically impossible to sink into one. I never thought I'd miss her lectures.*

How, he thought, with a wave of despair that made him groan with pain, *am I going to tell her mum and dad?*

He heard a noise and spun round. The hairs stood up all along his arms. Terror squeezed the breath out of his lungs. It was Cleo's voice! It was coming from somewhere further down the slope. *That's impossible. I must be hallucinating.*

Or it's her ghost.

It would serve me right if she came back to haunt me forever.

Now he could hear the crunch of horses' hooves on pine needles. Through the trees he saw the lime-green tracksuit of

Wu Meilin. She was trotting up the hill towards him on the little black pony.

Meilin!

It's all Meilin's fault!

It was Meilin who betrayed us to the Tiger's Claw gang. Meilin who got us trapped in the Dragon Path tunnel . . .

The blood boiled, black and bitter, in Ryan's veins. His vision blurred, closing in to nothing but the lime-green tracksuit and the smiling face.

How could she be smiling?

With a primal roar of rage and pain, he charged down the slope and hurled himself at Cleo's killer.

39

DUNGEON

CLEO OPENED HER eyes.

She closed them again. It was so dark it didn't make any difference. *There's a distinct possibility that I'm dead and have just arrived in the afterlife*, she thought. But she immediately ruled out that theory. *One, I'm not sure I believe in the afterlife. Two, I'm lying on top of a pile of stones. Three, my ankle is extremely painful. On the other hand, they could have stones and sprained ankles in the afterlife, so the evidence isn't entirely conclusive. It's the same ankle I sprained in Egypt. I'm really going to have to look into some physiotherapy to strengthen the ligaments...*

Stop rambling! Cleo scolded herself. *You're not in the*

afterlife. You're in a dark, damp hole. You need to focus. How did you get here? Jumbled images started to gather. *I was punting. With Ryan. In the First Emperor's tomb.*

Now the memories were all tumbling back at once. *We were escaping from the tomb across the sea of mercury. That's why I've got this thing on my face.* She pulled off the gas mask and took a deep shuddering breath. *That's better. Now, where was I? We'd made it to the door. The sea erupted, the boat rolled, I was falling backwards. I saw giant metal teeth. I heard Ryan call my name and felt him grab my foot and then it was all a chaotic hurtling tailspin down a dark chute until I landed here . . .*

Cleo wiggled her toes. *That's why I've only got one shoe. The other one came off in Ryan's hand. I hope he's hung on to it. Those were my new all-terrain trekking trainers . . .*

All at once, panic flooded every cell in Cleo's body. *Ryan! What happened to Ryan? Is he still in the tomb? He'd better have acted rationally and got out while he could. If he's wandering around looking for me and missed his chance to escape I'll never speak to him again.* She felt hot tears prickling her eyes. *This is all my fault. He would never have gone near the tomb if he hadn't been helping me return the jade ring for Grandma. I can't let anything happen to him . . .*

Focus, Cleo told herself again. *I have to get out and find Ryan.*

She sniffed back her tears, shifted her weight until she could reach into her tool belt, pulled out her phone and switched it on. In the faint light of the screen she saw that the pile of stones on which she'd landed was, in fact, an enormous heap of human bones.

She was staring straight into the eye sockets of a skull.

The phone's eerie blue light glinted on metal objects among the bones. She picked one up: a jewelled gold hairpin. She found another: a bronze jar inlaid with silver. Then a jade figure of a lion, a bag of gold coins, a jewelled brooch . . . *I must be lying on the remains of looters who've tried to make off with treasures from the First Emperor's tomb.*

Cleo sat up and looked around. She appeared to be in some kind of dungeon. The hole through which she'd dropped was high above her head. It would be impossible to climb out that way. *The booby trap may have been designed to imprison its victims rather than kill them*, she thought, although, from the evidence of the bones, many had been left to die here.

Cleo didn't plan on joining them. She slid down from the pile of bones and felt her way along the walls until she came to a small opening. On either side of it two small seal characters had been engraved into the stone. Even by the light of her phone she recognized them. She'd seen them in Mum's notes when she was translating the Isles of Immortality Scrolls: *fangshi.*

Now it all makes sense, Cleo thought, as she began to pull loose stones away from the opening. This was all the work of the emperor's recipe gentlemen. These failed tomb robbers – ensnared by the booby traps – would have provided a steady supply of guinea pigs on whom the *fangshi* could test their potions and elixirs. They were like spiders waiting for flies to wander into their web. Each time the booby traps were triggered, the recipe gentlemen must have gone back and reset them all – lining the boats up by the shore, refilling the sands of time, priming the mechanism on the metal giant's head – so that they were ready and waiting to catch their next victim. But the last time the traps were set, Cleo realized with a shudder, the wait had been much longer than usual. *The next victim didn't come along for two thousand years – and it was me!*

Cleo peered back down at the opening. She'd managed to clear enough rubble to reveal that it was the entrance to a narrow tunnel. *Of course,* she thought. *This was the final stage of their plan! The recipe gentlemen must have come down this tunnel to retrieve the looters and take them back to their 'laboratory'.* She climbed over a jumble of boulders and limped into the entrance. It seemed the way was clear of rock falls now. Her spirits soared. *All I have to do is follow this tunnel and I'll come out in the Kitchen of Eternal Life.*

Cleo was so sure she'd found her escape route that, when she came up against a wall of rocks only a few moments later, she simply stared in bewilderment. The roof of the tunnel had caved in. It was completely blocked. She forced herself to think logically. *Maybe I can burrow through!* She pushed against one of the smaller boulders with all her force but could barely budge it. This was never going to work. Suddenly she noticed a stripe of golden light across the rock. Light was slanting in from above! She looked up and saw a narrow band of sky through a crack in the rock. *Maybe I can climb up by wedging myself between the sides.* She leaned back against one wall of rock and pushed her feet against the other. A spasm of pain shot through her sprained ankle.

Cleo threw back her head and screamed. 'Help! I'm stuck down here! Someone help me, *please!*' Gulping for breath, she looked up. Through her tears the sky was clear and blue and so very far away.

And then a face appeared.

A small face with a pixie haircut above a lime-green tracksuit top.

Cleo was engulfed by a wave of white-hot fury. She thumped the rock with her bare hands and yelled. 'Meilin! You traitor! How could you? You *used* us to get the Tiger's Claw gang into the tomb!'

'No, Cleo! Don't say that! It's not true!'

There was a swishing sound on the rock above Cleo's head and small stones pattered onto her face.

'I'm lowering a rope down to you,' Meilin shouted. 'Hold on and I will pull you up!'

'No way!' Cleo shouted. 'I'm not stupid. Why would you want to help me?'

'Because I am your friend!' Meilin sounded close to tears, but Cleo already knew what a good actress she was. 'I didn't know those men were following us, I promise.'

'So how come *you* managed to get away?' Cleo shouted.

'When I heard footsteps, I didn't stop to think. I leaped into the branches of the bushes to hide. I thought you and Ryan would do the same, but when I peeped out the men had caught you. I was so frightened. I didn't know what to do.'

The end of a plaited rope was dangling within Cleo's reach. It looked like the one that Meilin had used to lead the ponies.

'How do I know you won't drop me?' Cleo shouted.

'I'm holding on to the pony. She will pull too.'

Cleo wasn't convinced, but it was her only chance. There was no other way out. She grabbed the rope and wrapped it round her wrist. 'Ready!' she yelled.

There was a moment of slack, and then the rope jerked, burning her skin and almost wrenching her arm from its

302

socket. She braced herself against the rocks with her other arm and her feet, and began to scramble upwards with each heave of the rope. Every second of the climb, Cleo expected Meilin to let go and let her plunge to her death on the rocks below. But the rope kept on drawing her upwards and at last she rolled out onto flat ground. She lay shaking with exhaustion and panting for air.

Suddenly Cleo remembered where she was and sat bolt upright, all set to run for her life from the Tiger's Claw gang.

'It's OK.' Meilin offered her a bottle of water. 'I'm on my own.'

Cleo eyed the bottle suspiciously.

Meilin sighed. She sat down and put the bottle down between them. 'I waited in the bushes for ages after the men threw you in the tunnel,' she said. 'They were drinking beer. I thought they might fall asleep and I would be able to take the *hufu* from them and rescue you. But they stayed awake, guarding the entrance.'

Cleo forgot that she didn't trust Meilin and picked up the water. She was so thirsty she drained it in one go.

'Then their boss arrived with more men and some of them entered the tunnel,' Meilin went on. 'They all began shouting and swearing at each other. You and Ryan had disappeared! One of the men even said you must have been taken by ghosts! The boss was furious. He sent some of the men down into the tunnel to look for you.' Meilin shuddered. 'He told them not to make any more mistakes and to *finish you off properly* when they found you! I knew I had to do *something*.' Meilin plucked at a handful of dry leaves. 'I ran back to the ponies and rode down the mountain as fast as I could. I was on my way to the police station to fetch help when I figured out what must have happened. I remembered what you told me about the old film – that the Dragon Path led down to the ancestor temple and into the First Emperor's tomb. I knew that you and Ryan would be brave and clever and not just wait for the Tiger's Claw men to come after you. You must have escaped from the ropes and run down the tunnel into the tomb to look for another way out.'

Cleo nodded. 'That's right. We cut the ropes off with my trowel.'

Meilin smiled. 'My great-grandfather used to say that there were secret ways in and out of the tomb mound in ancient times, although I always thought those were just fairy stories. But if there *was* a way out from the tomb, up through the tomb mound, I was sure that you two would find it. So I galloped straight here instead of going to the police. I thought I might be able to help. All the time I was hoping . . .' Meilin's voice faltered. 'I was *praying* that you would find a way out.' She smiled. 'And I was right. The good-luck charm I gave you must have protected you.'

Cleo was about to point out that the gas mask had been a lot more useful than the charm, but decided against it. 'Thank you,' she murmured. She closed her eyes and flopped back down, her head resting on the soft blanket of pine needles. She was so tired that her bones felt as if they were melting into the ground . . .

'Has Ryan gone for help?' Meilin asked.

Cleo sat up so fast she almost passed out. 'You mean you haven't seen him?'

'I'd just got here when I heard you calling for help.'

Cleo stared at Meilin as the terrible reality sank in. 'He must still be inside the tomb!'

Meilin jumped to her feet and held her hand out for Cleo. 'Quick, get on the back of the pony with me. We'll look for him.'

They had only taken a few steps when the pony stopped, snorted and laid its ears back in fright. Something was coming straight at them, howling and snarling as it thrashed through the trees.

Meilin pulled the pony round hard. 'Hold tight,' she warned Cleo. 'It sounds like an injured animal.'

But when Cleo looked up, it was Ryan she saw hurtling down the path. He was waving her trainer in one hand and Meilin's good-luck charm in the other.

'You murderer!' he screamed. 'You've killed Cleo!'

Ryan threw himself at Meilin.

The little black pony whinnied and tossed its head in fright, knocking Ryan off his feet. He staggered backwards, landing hard on his tailbone on the steep bank. He couldn't make sense of what he was seeing. There was someone else sitting on the back of the pony. She was covered in dust, her zip-off trousers were torn and her hair was full of pine needles, but it was definitely Cleo. And she wasn't dead!

Ryan sprang back up. *Meilin must have taken Cleo prisoner* . . . He flew at her again, this time trying to grab hold of the pony's reins. 'Let Cleo go or I'll . . . I'll . . .'

'Ryan, it's OK!' Cleo was *smiling*. She reached out to him, almost falling off the pony. 'Can I have my trainer back? On second thoughts, could you hang on to it for me? I've managed to sprain my ankle again and it's too swollen to get in a shoe anyway.'

Ryan gaped at Cleo. Then he looked back to Meilin. Meilin was smiling too. It didn't *look* like the triumphant sneer of a ruthless traitor who had lured her victims into the trap of her evil gang-masters. It was just an ordinary happy grin. He looked back at Cleo. She was still smiling. Even the pony seemed to be smiling.

'But how?' he sputtered. 'But what? But when?'

'Long story,' Cleo said. 'But Meilin didn't betray us. She's on our side.'

Meilin patted the pony's neck. 'I pulled Cleo out of a hole.'

'A hole?' Ryan echoed.

Cleo slid down from the pony and hopped to Ryan's side. 'I'm so happy you made it out of the tomb alive, I won't even mind if you say it.'

'Say what?'

'Go on,' Cleo said. 'You know you want to.'

Suddenly Ryan got it. 'OK. You're right,' he laughed. 'I can't resist.' He pushed a strand of her hair out of her eyes. 'Cleopatra McNeil, you are the undisputed world champion at falling down holes, but nose-diving into the mouth of that booby-trap giant was a spectacular performance, even by your standards.' Relief welled in his throat, choking his words. He threw his arms around her and held her tight. 'I really thought you were dead,' he mumbled into her hair.

Cleo hugged him back. 'How could I be dead?' she asked, crying and laughing at the same time. 'You made me drink the elixir of life, remember?'

'Good point,' Ryan said. 'I forgot we're both immortal now.' He felt Cleo flinch as she put weight on her ankle. Her head pressed to his chest was making his burns blaze as if they were on fire again. 'Even we immortals could do with some medical assistance right now, though.' He smiled up at Meilin, who was looking a little embarrassed by all the hugging. 'Thank you,' he said. 'For everything.' He realized he was still clutching the silver coin on its red thread. 'Your good-luck charm really did the trick.'

'Or maybe it was your lucky pants!' Meilin laughed. 'Did you return the rings to the dragons?'

'All of them,' Ryan told her, 'including the one that your great-grandfather took.'

Meilin leaped down from the pony and did a cartwheel. 'Now we will all have good fortune!' She high fived with Ryan. Then she knelt and made a step of her hands to help Cleo back onto the pony. 'Next stop, hospital – for both of you,' she said.

40

SAFE

THE WEDDING WAS two months later.

It had come as something of a surprise to everyone when Eveline Bell had announced that she would be marrying Hector Pink, her neighbour at the Gracemont Home for Retired Archaeologists – not least because they hadn't been on speaking terms since 1967.

Didn't your grandmother refer to Hector Pink as 'a snooping little weasel' when we went to see her? Ryan had texted Cleo when he'd received his invitation.

Haven't you heard of love–hate relationships? Cleo had texted back.

Now they were at the reception, toasting the bride and

groom with glasses of champagne. The bride was resplendent in an orange silk trouser suit and a long chunky necklace Ryan suspected might actually be made of genuine oracle bones. Beside her, Hector Pink looked dapper in a blue blazer and orange cravat. He smiled mildly from beneath a walrus moustache and bulbous nose. Ryan looked round at the tastefully lit gallery, with its stripped oak floors and displays of sepia photographs, faded dig journals and old-fashioned tools. The History of Archaeology Museum made the perfect venue; Hector Pink and Eveline Bell must have notched up almost a hundred and fifty years of archaeology between them.

It was a small gathering. Cleo and her mum and dad were there, of course, as well as a few of Hector's nieces and nephews, and some friends and nurses from the retirement home. There was also a noisy Uyghur family from Khotan, descendants of a couple Eveline had befriended in the 1950s while travelling alone along the Silk Road.

Ryan had been a little wary about coming back to the History of Archaeology Museum at first. Last time he and Cleo were here, they'd been chased out of the archives by the guard. And Cleo was probably banned for life for assaulting Anthony Chetwynd, senior archivist. But, to Ryan's relief, Chetwynd was nowhere to be seen. It turned out that he'd received so many complaints about being rude to customers that he'd been transferred to an office job. Louisa Gupta had been promoted to senior archivist instead. She had welcomed Ryan and Cleo warmly. 'Did that old film that I sent you turn out to be useful?' she'd asked.

Cleo and Ryan had looked at each other.

309

'*Useful?*' Ryan had repeated slowly. 'Well, that's one way of putting it!'

The speeches were over. Ryan drained the last of the champagne he'd been allowed for the toasts, and headed to the buffet. This was the life! Especially as only two months earlier he'd nearly had his throat slit by the Tiger's Claw gang, been burned to a crisp by a dragon, skewered by a Qin Dynasty crossbow and drowned in a sea of mercury.

There had been a lot of trouble over the Dragon Path incident, of course.

By the time they'd left the Accident and Emergency department, with Ryan's burns dressed and Cleo's ankle strapped up, they had agreed they had no choice but to confess the whole story to their parents. It was the only way to stop Joey Zhou and his gang emptying the First Emperor's tomb: now that the gang knew the location of the Dragon Path tunnel, they'd be able to use it to get in and out of the tomb whenever they liked, looting its magnificent treasures and selling them on the black market. They'd be safe from the dragons as long as they didn't remove any of the jade rings, and they could disarm the crossbow booby traps by inserting Ryan's model of the *hufu* into the socket by the door in the ancestor temple.

'And, unlike us,' Cleo had pointed out, 'they don't have to cross the perilous mercury sea to get out; they can simply leave the way they came in, via the Dragon Path.'

There had been a lot of angry shouting around the kitchen table in the McNeils' apartment when the parents had first heard the tale. But once they'd realized that Cleo and Ryan were safe, and that they hadn't deliberately broken into the tomb of the First Emperor, they began to calm down. Cleo's mum had called Professor Han and the chief of police and Sir Charles Peacocke to explain the situation to them all. Security guards had been put in place at the entrance to the Dragon Path, and the very next night, they'd arrested four members of the Tiger's Claw gang attempting to make off with the Sword of Life, the elixir of immortality and assorted other treasures. They were all now facing long jail sentences for tomb robbing.

They could have been in much worse trouble, Ryan knew. The authorities seemed to have turned a blind eye to the fact that he and Cleo had set foot inside the forbidden tomb. Perhaps it was just because they were so pleased to have caught several members of the notorious Tiger's Claw gang red-handed. But Ryan's mum had heard from her journalist contacts in China a few weeks ago that it might have had something to do with a certain very important politician putting in a good word for them and persuading the police not to pursue the case.

'I wonder why he got involved?' Mum had mused.

'An act of random kindness?' Ryan had suggested with a shrug. Or maybe not so random, he'd realized when Cleo had informed him that the politician just happened to be the father of Chan Xiao-Ping, the missing boy they'd freed from the broom cupboard at the Terracotta Army Museum.

Ryan was loading his plate with sausage rolls, crisps, ham sandwiches, mini pavlovas and profiteroles when Cleo joined him and helped herself to couscous salad.

'Call this a buffet?' Ryan said. 'Where are the duck gizzards and the congealed blood soup?'

Cleo looked worried for a moment, and then realized he was joking. 'I don't think you'll starve,' she laughed, looking at his precariously heaped plate. 'This dress is so uncomfortable,' she grumbled. 'I can hardly eat anything.'

'It looks OK,' Ryan said. It looked more than OK, of course. Cleo looked more than OK in a baggy bumblebee jumper and zip-off trousers; in a fitted orange silk dress she looked outrageously stunning.

Cleo tucked her hair behind her ears. 'And as for these stupid flowers ...'

Her hair was piled up and studded with beautiful orange tiger lilies. Eveline had insisted everyone wear her favourite colour. Ryan had drawn the line at an orange outfit, but had reluctantly agreed to wear an orange tie with his new dark grey suit.

Ryan found a seat at an empty table.

Cleo sat down next to him. 'I've been dying to tell you,' she said. 'Mum's just had an update from the police in China. It's about Joey Zhou. You're not going to believe this.'

Ryan didn't reply, as he'd just stuffed a whole sausage roll in his mouth, but he gestured enthusiastically for Cleo to go on. Joey Zhou had turned out to be a man of mystery. He hadn't been with the other Tiger's Claw members when the police had arrested them leaving the First Emperor's tomb. There'd been a full-scale search, but it seemed that Joey had disappeared without a trace.

'What is it?' Ryan spluttered at last. 'Have the police tracked him down?'

Cleo shook her head. 'No, but it's really weird. Apparently, he's got an alibi for the day we entered the Dragon Path.'

'That's impossible!' Ryan spluttered a spray of pastry crumbs.

'I know, but several people have come forward and said

that he was at the Asian Archaeology Conference in Hong Kong.'

'Yeah, right! They must have been paid to say that by the Tiger's Claw gang.'

Cleo frowned into her salad. 'I don't think so. Two of the witnesses are Sir Charles Peacocke and that assistant of his, Melanie. Sir Charles was the guest of honour at the conference that day and he's confirmed that Joey was working there as a translator.' She sighed and speared a cherry tomato with her fork. 'The police chief says we must have been mistaken. I can tell Mum and Dad are starting to think so too.'

'No way! I'd recognize Quiff Features anywhere.' Ryan banged down his plate. 'He jumped out of the bushes, wrestled me to the ground, tied us up and threw us into the tunnel. I had plenty of time to be sure it was his cheesy grin I was looking at!'

'That's what I said.' Cleo smiled. 'Well, not exactly in those words. But I'm *certain* it was Joey who was in charge of that gang that ambushed us. There just has to be a logical explanation.'

'Let's see. Joey has cloned himself?' Ryan suggested. 'Or he's invented a time machine? Or maybe Charles Peacocke really needs glasses?'

Cleo laughed. 'Whatever the explanation, nobody's seen Joey since that day. He obviously didn't go back to Xi'an.'

Ryan nodded thoughtfully. 'At least Tian Min is safe.' Tian Min – the friendly young guide who'd originally been assigned to the McNeils' group – had been found wandering in a forest in the middle of nowhere just a few days ago. As Cleo and Ryan had suspected, the Tiger's Claw gang had taken him prisoner so that Joey could step into his place. Tian Min had been bundled into a van and delivered to another branch of the gang in Southern China. They'd beaten him up pretty badly, but somehow he'd managed to escape before they could finish him off.

Alex Shawcross had volunteered to go back to China to look after Tian Min, since he had no family of his own. *No doubt Tian Min was delighted to have the girl of his dreams at his bedside*, Ryan thought. But he couldn't help feeling sorry for him too; who'd want to be nursed back to health by someone as obsessed with death and disease as Alex?

The thought of death reminded Ryan of something. 'It's a good thing we both drank the elixir of immortality in the First Emperor's tomb,' he told Cleo. 'It means that, however long it takes the police to get to the bottom of the Joey Zhou mystery, we'll still be around to find out about it.' He leaned back in his chair and stretched his legs. 'After all, we're both going to live forever.'

'I'm not sure I can wait that long to find out the truth,' Cleo sighed.

Ryan clinked her glass with his. 'Here's to eternal life!' He didn't *really* believe that the tiny drops of revolting liquid they'd drunk from the ear-shaped copper fungi would make them immortal, but he didn't quite *not* believe it either. *It'll add a certain excitement when I'm an old age pensioner*, he thought. *It'll be like watching the lottery results when you've bought one single ticket. There's always that tiny outside chance* . . . And, of course, if the potion *did* work, Cleo would be there to keep him company. He watched her poking grumpily at the beautiful flowers in her beautiful hair. Maybe that wasn't such a bad prospect. *Although I'm not sure I can face being lectured on the nature of infinity and the precise probability of winning the lottery until the end of time . . .*

Ryan's ponderings were interrupted by a buzz from his phone.

'It's Meilin,' he told Cleo as he read the message. 'She says she can't wait to see us at the gymnastics competition tomorrow.' He grinned. 'Returning her great-grandfather's jade ring to the dragons has definitely brought her good luck.'

Cleo snorted into her Coke. 'It's nothing to do with luck! Meilin has worked really hard to be selected for the Junior Championships at Wembley tomorrow, and to win that scholarship to the gymnastics academy in Xi'an.'

'It's not just Meilin,' Ryan pointed out. The whole family had been showered with good fortune. Aunty Ting had won an award for her noodles and had expanded the restaurant and taken on lots of staff to help her. She'd even hired Gao Xin – the rock god – to set up an online takeaway business, and it seemed that he and Meilin had bonded over the noodle menus; Ryan was sure that romance was in the air.

'And don't forget,' he said. 'Grandfather Long Jian won Best in Show at the Pomegranate Festival. Come on! It doesn't get much luckier than that!'

'Maybe,' Cleo conceded. 'Even Bao Bao and the puppies have a new home.'

'I rest my case,' Ryan said. 'They'll have a lovely time being guard dogs at the pomegranate orchard.' He jumped as a frantic drumbeat struck up. The Uyghur group had pushed back the tables and were starting to perform a dance in the middle of the gallery.

'This dance is called a *senem*,' Cleo shouted over the music. 'It's traditional at weddings.'

Everyone was clapping. The drumbeat quickened. The dancers whirled and stomped.

'Let's get out of here,' Cleo whispered.

Ryan was surprised. 'I thought you liked this kind of cultural activity.'

'It's not the music,' Cleo said. 'My parents are getting up to dance.'

Ryan glanced across the room. True enough, Pete McNeil – sporting an orange shirt that clashed spectacularly with his red hair and freckles – was cavorting about in some kind of highland jig while Lydia swirled around him.

Cleo grimaced. 'They'll want us to join in.'

Ryan didn't need any further prompting. He was halfway across the gallery before Cleo caught up with him. They slipped through a door and entered the sanctuary of the Index Room, with its shelves of old books and wooden card cabinets. Hundreds of black and white photographs were scattered on one of the tables. Looking over Cleo's shoulder, Ryan recognized two men, one with fair hair and a moustache and one with a pipe.

'Louisa told me that she's preparing an exhibition all about Cedric Lymington and Harold Stubbs,' Cleo said. 'Apparently they carried out some important excavations, but they've largely been forgotten.'

Not by me, Ryan thought. The image of Lymington's skeleton with the crossbow bolt between his ribs was etched deep into his brain. It was time for an emergency change of subject. 'I never did get to see a giant panda in China.'

'You saw a giant salamander.'

'Not quite as cute!' Ryan sank into a leather chair.

They both turned at the sound of the door opening and the

tapping of a walking stick on the wooden floor. Ryan leaped up so that Eveline Bell could take his chair.

'I wanted to thank you both properly for returning the jade ring for me,' she said as she sat down. 'I know it can't have been easy.' The old lady patted her chest, rattling the necklace. 'It has been a weight off my heart.' She smiled. 'I feel as if I've had a new lease of life. That's why I've been making amends with all the people I've fallen out with over the years.'

'Like Hector?' Cleo asked.

Ryan almost burst out laughing. *Marrying* your arch enemy seemed a rather extreme form of making amends.

Eveline Bell seemed to read his thoughts. 'Oh, Hector and I always had a soft spot for each other. We just didn't like to show it.' She reached into her large orange handbag. 'This is to thank you for keeping my granddaughter safe,' she said, thrusting a small parcel at Ryan. 'Well, don't just look at it. Open it!'

Ryan pulled off the string. Inside the brown paper was an old, rather battered archaeologist's trowel. The initials *H. O. P.* were engraved on the handle.

'Remember when we were tied up in the dark in the Dragon Path tunnel?' Cleo explained. 'You said to remind you to bring your own trowel next time we went anywhere. I told Grandma that story.'

'This was Hector's trowel,' Eveline cut in. 'Hector Octavius Pink. It's not quite as high-quality as mine, but it'll do you. I have something for you too, dear,' she said, turning to Cleo before Ryan could even say thank you. She took a flat box from her bag. 'I've kept this a secret for too long.'

'Uh-oh!' Ryan groaned under his breath. 'Don't open it.

317

That's how all this started. I haven't recovered from your gran's last mysterious secret yet.'

'It's some photographs of your grandfather,' Eveline told Cleo. 'He was killed when your mother was about your age.'

Cleo was staring at her grandmother, hanging on her every word.

'We were living in San Francisco then. Lydia was a bit of a tearaway. She'd gone out late at night and got stranded in the wrong part of town. Your grandfather was out searching for her when he was set upon by a gang of thugs and stabbed.'

'So that's why you and Mum fell out?' Cleo asked.

Her grandmother nodded. 'I shouldn't have blamed Lydia. She was only young. But we've made up now.'

Cleo smiled and held the box to her chest. 'I always thought my grandfather must have been a spy or something, because Mum would never talk about him. But now it all makes sense. And it explains why she's always so worried about me getting into danger.'

Ryan grinned. *Luckily, she doesn't know about most of it!* he thought.

'Well, I have a husband to get back to,' Eveline said, pushing herself up from the chair and tapping her way back to the gallery.

Ryan turned the trowel over in his hands. 'Does this mean I have to get a bum bag to put this in now?'

'It's a tool belt, not a bum bag,' Cleo laughed.

They sat in comfortable silence listening to the beat of Uyghur drums from the gallery. Outside, the London November afternoon was already growing dark. Ryan noticed a fluttering at the window and looked up to see a snowflake land softly on the glass. Then another, and another.

Cleo followed his gaze. 'We're going to Mexico for the winter,' she said. 'There've been some amazing new finds at a Maya site there that Mum and Dad want to work on.'

Ryan snapped round to look at her. 'Mexico? Mum was only talking about Mexico the other day.' He'd overheard her on the phone talking to a colleague in China. It seemed that one of the Tiger's Claw men had given the police some information about an international crime ring based in Mexico that was involved in smuggling antiquities all over the world – and he had hinted that they might know something about the people who had kidnapped Dad.

It shouldn't be too hard to persuade Mum that she wants to go to Mexico for the Christmas holidays to follow up on the new lead! Ryan thought. 'Maybe we could be there at the same time,' he murmured.

Cleo's eyes sparkled greener than jade. 'We could explore the Maya dig together.'

'It would be a shame not to,' Ryan said, 'now that I have my own trowel.'

Author's Note

The Dragon Path is an entirely fictional story, although it unfolds against the backdrop of some real places and real historical events. To try to avoid confusion, this note outlines the main distinctions between fact and fiction.

All the modern-day characters exist only in my imagination. Most importantly, Joey Zhou and the Tiger's Claw gang are entirely my invention and are not based on any real person or group. Cleo's grandmother, Eveline May Bell, is a fictional character, but her name is inspired by the genuine pioneering female archaeologist, Gertrude Bell (1868–1926). The 1930s characters – Cedric Lymington, Harold Stubbs, Pierre Segal and Long Yi – are all fictional too.

There is no such place in London as the Gracemont Home for Retired Archaeologists or the History of Archaeology Museum. However, many of the key locations in China are real. Mount Li is a majestic mountain in the Qinling range, which runs across central China. The mausoleum of the First Emperor lies to the north in the shadow of the mountain, about twenty miles east of Xi'an – the historic capital of Shaanxi Province. (As Cleo explains, *Xi'an* was formerly spelled as *Hsian* in the older Wade–Giles system for writing Chinese characters in the Roman alphabet.) The Shaanxi Grand Opera House, where Cleo and Ryan attend the banquet, is also a real place. You can watch beautiful Tang Dynasty (618–907 AD) dances while feasting on local delicacies. (All the dishes Ryan eats at the banquet are genuine specialities – as are the *biang biang* noodles served in Aunty Ting's restaurant.)

The world-famous Terracotta Army Museum is, of course, real; here you can see the thousands of clay soldiers, horses, chariots and weapons that were buried in the First Emperor's tomb complex. The site was only discovered forty years ago, in 1974, by farmers digging for a well.

The district of Lintong (where the tomb is located) really is famed for its pomegranates (including the Three Whites) and the Pomegranate Festival takes place in September each year. The Mid-Autumn Festival is held all over China; mooncakes are traditionally served at this time, and Cleo's story about revolutionaries hiding secret messages inside them during the Yuan Dynasty (1271–1368 AD) is a genuine folk legend.

But not *all* of the places I describe in China are real. The university where Cleo and Ryan stay is fictional (although there are several important universities in the area). And I'm afraid you won't be able to find Aunty Ting's noodle restaurant or Gao Xin's hardware store either (although you can see similar establishments on any small street in China). As far as I know there is no Sunrise Pavilion on Mount Li (but there is a Sunset Pavilion on the western slope). There are many caves in the Qinling mountain range, but the ones in the story – the Tomb of a Thousand Poisons and the Kitchen of Eternal Life – are entirely imaginary.

Now for the real historical characters: Qin Shi Huang, the First Emperor of China (259–210 BC), conquered many of the warring states that existed at the time and combined them into a single empire for the first time. Qin (pronounced *Chin*) is where the name *China* came from. Over the years the First

Emperor has often been viewed as a cruel and ruthless ruler who crushed any opposition. Other historians emphasize the progress that he made in setting up a legal system, building roads and canals, and ending fighting between the different states. Either way, the First Emperor began work on his magnificent tomb complex shortly after he came to the throne, and it remains a monument to his great power. The complex covers an area of over fifty square kilometres.

The central tomb mound – which rises from the plain like an enormous tree-covered pyramid – has not been entered in modern times. Just as Tian Min and Cleo explain in *The Dragon Path*, there are no plans to excavate it, for fear of damage to the contents. Archaeologists wish to wait until technology has advanced further, to avoid many of the problems that occurred with excavations in the past (for example, the paint that covered the terracotta warriors was destroyed when exposed to the air).

Almost everything we know about the layout and contents of the tomb comes from Sima Qian, the Grand Historian, who was writing over a hundred years after the First Emperor's death. He described how the vast underground complex contained replica palaces and towers, priceless treasures and a jewelled model of the universe, with the rivers and seas filled with flowing mercury, the constellations above and the land below. Sima Qian also wrote of the crossbow booby traps that protected the tomb, and the many concubines and craftsmen who were buried inside.

We can't be sure whether Sima Qian's descriptions are accurate, but – judging from the amazing discoveries in the area surrounding the tomb (including the thousands of terracotta soldiers) – it seems likely that the contents of the tomb itself must have been truly spectacular. In addition, when archaeologists have carried out scans and probes of the mound from outside, their findings have supported Sima Qian's claims about the structures beneath. They have even detected unusually high levels of mercury.

The Dragon Path tunnel, on the other hand, is entirely my own invention. As far as I know, there is no such secret tunnel through the mountain to an underground ancestor temple. However, Chinese tombs *did* have ancestor temples attached, where descendants could carry out rituals (including offering ghost money for the dead to use in the afterlife, as mentioned in the story). It is also true that there would be a special road leading to the tomb, called the Spirit Path or Sacred Way. This was usually flanked by stone statues of real or mythical beasts. I thought that huge, red jade dragon statues would be just the sort of thing that the First Emperor might have wanted for his spirit path. The red dragon was the symbol of the First Emperor, and jade was much revered in China. And although I made up the jade rings and the dragon-nostril booby traps, the part about the nine sons of the dragon comes from traditional Ming Dynasty stories (1368–1644 AD).

All the details of the inside of the tomb are imaginary, but I tried to base them on materials, technology and styles that would have been available at the time. For example, Sima Qian tells how the First Emperor had the weapons of vanquished enemy states melted down to make twelve giant bronze statues of himself; this inspired the statue of the First Emperor sitting on his throne in the ancestor temple. The *banliang* coins, which were offered as ghost money, were the currency of the Qin Dynasty. The bronze chariot and horses are based on those displayed in the Terracotta Army Museum. The jade suit of armour the mummy wears is just like real ones that have been found in tombs from the Han Dynasty (206 BC–220 AD).

The Sword of Life that the emperor's mummy carries is fictional, but Qin Dynasty swordsmiths really did develop sophisticated metalworking techniques to stop their bronze swords from tarnishing. We know this from the many weapons found with the terracotta soldiers. Magnificent swords – both real and legendary – hold a special place in traditional Chinese stories, so it seemed only fitting that the First Emperor would be carrying one. The story Cleo tells of the attempt to assassinate the First Emperor by smuggling a sword into the palace hidden inside a rolled-up map is also a real one. The would-be assassin was called Jing Ke, and you can see a version of the story in the famous Chinese film *The Emperor and the Assassin*.

You might also be wondering whether the First Emperor really employed *fangshi*, or *recipe gentlemen*, to try to come up with the elixir of immortality. The answer is yes: that part of the story is completely true. We know that the First Emperor was obsessed with trying to live forever. Unfortunately, as Alex Shawcross points out in *The Dragon Path,* many of the substances the *fangshi* thought might help, such as arsenic and mercury, were highly toxic. The First Emperor died when he was forty years old; his death may well have been hastened by the potions and pills that they brewed for him. All of the ingredients that are mentioned in the story have genuinely been thought to have magical or life-giving powers in the past. It is also true that the number five was held to be special. Historians believe that several important inventions, including gunpowder, could have been discovered by accident during the *fangshi*'s experiments.

But as far as we know, the *fangshi* didn't have a laboratory in a cave called the Kitchen of Eternal Life (although they must have carried out their experiments *somewhere*). Also, there is no evidence that they used failed tomb robbers as their guinea pigs, or that they then carted them along a secret tunnel and buried them in a cave called the Tomb of a Thousand Poisons (although it's possible; you never know!).

The Scroll of Immortality that Cleo and Ryan find in the coffer in the Kitchen of Eternal Life was also invented for this story. However, the story of the Isles of Immortality is genuine. Just as Cleo tells Ryan, legend holds that there were five enchanted islands in the East China Sea, inhabited by immortals. Each island was secured by three giant turtles, but a giant captured six of the turtles and two of the islands drifted away. It was believed that *lingzhi,* the herb or fungi of immortality, grew on these mythical islands. The First Emperor sent out several (unsuccessful) missions to try to retrieve it.

Although the scroll is fictional, Chinese scholars did write on silk at this time (and also on the bamboo slips that are mentioned; paper was not yet in use). The riddles, map and the model of the sea and the islands in the tomb (with all their devious booby traps) are completely my own invention. However, the symbols of immortality on the coffer and the map – such as the deer, the crane and the peach tree – are all genuine, and small seal script was indeed the official system of writing developed during the Qin Dynasty.

The little bronze tiger *hufu* that provided the key to finding and opening the Dragon Path tunnel is based on real objects, called tallies, that were used in the Qin Dynasty (and beyond). Tiger tallies were especially important for military orders. One half would be kept by the emperor and the other half would be given to a general or other military official. If the two halves matched when placed together, it proved that an order was genuine when a messenger was sent out to move troops. The idea for the *hufu* in this story came from a real tiger tally that I saw in the Shaanxi Museum in Xi'an. Of course, the *hufu* in the museum is not the one that Lymington and Stubbs found in the Kitchen of Eternal Life (all of that is fictional), but it occurred to me that a device like this would make a perfect key and security pass to disarm the booby traps in the tomb (although there is no evidence that they were really used in this way).

The codes that Cleo mentions when she is deciphering Segal's journal are genuine. Louis XIV used complex numerical ciphers to send secret messages (as did other European courts, from as early as the fifteenth century). Napoleon and his generals encrypted their top-secret communications in a similar way, using the Great Paris Code. A British general called George Scovell finally cracked the code.

To answer some other questions you may have: the Chinese giant salamander Ryan encounters behind the waterfall is a real endangered animal that lives in shallow mountain streams and grows up to one and a half metres long. The many different lucky and unlucky numbers and objects that crop up in the story are all real. As Tian Min explains to Ryan, *Dragon Ball* was indeed inspired by the Chinese Ming Dynasty story, *Monkey King: Journey to the West*. The TV series *Friends,* from which Joey Zhou has picked his English name, is, of course, real, and is very popular in China. *Crazy Mouse*, which Ryan plays with Gao Xin, is a real computer game and was developed in China.

On a final note, when they become trapped in the First Emperor's tomb, Cleo and Ryan must make their way across a sea of mercury. In reality, the hotel gas masks they wear may not have protected them for long enough from the effects of inhaling the highly toxic mercury vapour. But, as this is a work of fiction, I have given my heroes a little bit of poetic licence here, and they survive without any long-term ill-effects.